Cause For Murder

Cause For Murder

Betty Sullivan La Pierre

Cover by Paul Musgrove

Copyright @ 2005 by Betty Sullivan La Pierre

ISBN : 1-4196-0706-5

To order additional copies, please contact us.
BookSurge, LLC
www.booksurge.com
1-866-308-6235
orders@booksurge.com

Cause For Murder

CHAPTER ONE

Hawkman sat in the living room in one of the swivel chairs overlooking Copco Lake. His legs were stretched out on the ottoman as he tried to read the paper, but Jennifer kept running the vacuum around him, making him move. "Honey, for crying out loud, it's only Sam, not the president coming home. Like most kids, he won't hang around long enough to notice whether the place is clean or not."

She shut off the noise maker and put a hand on her hip. "Hawkman, if it weren't for women, men would live in pigsties. And not only that, there wouldn't be any birthday celebrations, no Easter bunny, no tooth fairies and probably no Christmas if it were left up to the male population."

He looked at her with furrowed brows. "What brought that on? I didn't say anything about holidays. I just wanted to read the morning paper in peace."

She waved her hand and flipped on the vacuum. Hawkman finally exited to the deck. He'd no more gotten comfortable on a lounge chair than Pretty Girl let out several loud squawks from the aviary.

Hawkman glanced at the falcon. "Good Lord, what's with you females today? Can't a man have a little peace and quiet?"

The bird finally fluffed her wings and settled on the perch. Hawkman continued to read the local news, and spotted an article about a Mr. Burke Parker from Yreka found dead in a motel room. An autopsy would be performed.

The name rang a bell and Hawkman rubbed his chin. Reading down a few paragraphs, he spotted the list of survivors and it brought the name into focus. Parker's daughter, Maryann, was one of Sam's high school classmates and they now attended the same university. He raised his gaze to the lake and speculated on why Parker would be in a motel room. If he remembered correctly, they had a home in Yreka and he'd not heard mention of the Parkers separating. He scratched his sideburn. Have to ask Jennifer about that one. She knew more about Sam's friends than he did and might have heard some scuttlebutt.

When Hawkman didn't hear the vacuum for several minutes, he took a chance, ventured inside and sat down in his chair. Jennifer marched from the back of the house, rearranging strands of hair that had slipped out of her pony tail.

He smiled. "You sure look cute when you're frustrated."

She shot him a grim stare. "Hawkman, don't mess with me right now. I'm not in the mood to fool with your remarks. I'm worried about Sam. He should have called by now."

He put up his hands in defense. "Okay. I'll be good. Did he say he'd call?"

Her shoulders slumped. "Well, no, but he should."

"Come on, honey. He's a grown man. Men don't call their moms every time they head home."

"That's why I bought him the cell phone, so he'd keep in touch."

"Maybe he's got a buddy with him. But if it bothers you, call him."

"I tried. But I can't seem to get through. I keep reaching his voice mail."

"Maybe he lost it, or packed it away."

She threw up her hands in disgust. "You're probably right. Kids drive you nuts."

"Now, getting off that subject, can I ask you a question?"
She nodded.

"I read in the paper where a Burke Parker from Yreka died. The survivors listed are Lillian Parker and his daughter, Maryann. Do you know his wife and didn't Sam go to school with the girl?"

Jennifer flopped down on the couch and wrinkled her forehead. "That's sad. I don't think I ever met Burke and Lilly personally, but I do remember seeing Maryann at the high school on a few occasions. A beautiful girl, but very quiet and reserved. I believe Sam took her out a couple of times. I recall a big stink arose about Lilly and Burke last summer."

"Oh yeah, what about?"

"I gathered he drank a lot and they fought constantly. I heard he came home one night roaring drunk, staggered into Maryann's room and tried to rape her. When she let out a terrifying scream, her mother came running with a gun in her hand. Lilly chased Burke outside and shot at him, wounding him in the leg." She shrugged. "Of course, it's all gossip, so who knows the truth."

Hawkman flipped open the paper to the article and handed it to her. "Well, there might be some veracity to it. Your story certainly explains why they found his body in a motel and not at home."

Jennifer read the article and shook her head. "Poor Maryann. That's all she needs to have happen now. At least school is out for the summer. It will give her time to recover from the loss of her father."

❧

Sam packed what he needed and said goodbye to Dan, the fellow who'd sublet his apartment for the next three months. Sam decided he didn't want to go to summer school this year. After three years of college and constant studying, he needed a rest. Jennifer and Hawkman agreed. A few months at home sounded great. His last chance to relax before he conquered the world.

He loaded his stuff into the Toyota pickup his parents had given him as a reward for making the Dean's Honor Roll last year. The thought of fishing and riding his motorcycle in the hills around Copco Lake, with the wind whipping through his hair, made him feel good all over.

He'd contacted Richard, his close friend, at his university to find out when he'd be home. Even though they were the same age, Richard had just finished his sophomore year. Being deaf made it difficult for him to carry a full load. And his Uncle Joe didn't want him to get burned out on school, so he wouldn't allow him to attend the summer sessions. Even though Richard had a scholarship, he insisted on working for his spending money while he had this time off. Sam admired the guy's stamina and liked him a lot. He hoped they'd be able to get together and do some bike riding.

As he covered and tied down his belongings in the pickup bed, he spotted a figure approaching out of the corner of his eye. He recognized the female before she got close enough to speak. Her tall frame, skin tight Levi's, and cowboy boots with little conchos tied to the pull tabs gave her away. She lived in the next door apartment complex. How he wished he'd left fifteen minutes earlier. This woman had a big attitude problem.

She strolled up beside him and placed a hand on his shoulder. "Hi, Sam, when are you leaving?"

"In just a few minutes."

"Can I hitch a ride? I'll pay for half the gas."

"Sure, Maryann. But there's no charge. I don't think an extra person will make much difference in the mileage."

"Thanks. Let me grab my bag and I'll be right out."

When she got out of ear shot, Sam sighed. Maryann was quite pretty, sported a great figure and must have American Indian blood in her veins, as she had high cheek bones, olive skin and long black hair accenting dark brown eyes. But she had a negative approach about life and never appeared happy. He just didn't care to be around her.

They'd gone through high school together and dated a couple of times. He felt sorry for the girl as her family didn't have much money; only meager funds her grandmother had left for college expenses. Maryann worked at the university cafeteria and took any extra jobs she could find to supplement the school cost. He had to admire her. At least, she didn't have a lazy bone in her body. And to top it off, she had brains and made excellent grades. He resigned himself to the fact it might be nice to have company on the long ride home, and since she lived in Yreka, it wouldn't be out of his way to drop her off.

CHAPTER TWO

Sam tucked Maryann's suitcase under the tarp in the pickup bed and strapped it down. She climbed into the truck without so much as a nod. He jumped into the driver's side, put the key in the ignition and buckled his seat belt. Then he sat there without starting the engine. Finally, Maryann glanced at him.

"What are we waiting for?" she asked.

"You haven't fastened your seat belt."

She rolled her eyes and buckled up. "You're one of those."

"I guess so," Sam said, turning the key.

He pulled into a gas station and filled the tank, then headed for US-101 toward the Redwood Hwy. Maryann hadn't said a word. Sam shot a look her way, but her long black hair hung over her shoulder to her waist, and concealed most of her face as she stared out the side window.

"How'd school go this year?" he asked.

"Okay."

He exhaled loudly. "I hoped you'd be some company on this trip home. But appears you're going to remain silent the whole two hundred miles."

She ducked her head. "Sorry, I received some bad news, so I guess I'm not in the mood for chatter."

"You want to talk about it?" he asked.

"My dad died."

Sam gulped and glanced at her. "Oh my God. That's horrible."

Maryann shrugged. "Don't worry. You don't have to comfort me. We weren't close. In fact, I didn't even like the man."

He felt lost for words and fixed his gaze on the road ahead. "I see."

"My so-called father was an alcoholic. Whenever he came home drunk, he found some reason to beat my Mom. I could hardly wait to get out of there. Many times I begged her to divorce him, but she didn't believe in it, and tolerated his behavior. On several occasions she ran him out of the house, threatened to kill him if he ever laid another hand on me. The only thing that kept her from moving away was the support money he gave her every month so we'd have food on the table."

Sam cleared his throat. "Uh, had he always been mean?"

"No, not until I got old enough for him to see that I wasn't his daughter. He had red hair, freckles and blue eyes. Mom has pale blue eyes and used to have blond hair before she dyed it." She held out a long strand of her black hair, then let it drop to her chest. "As you can see, I definitely came from a different blood line. I'm half American Indian."

Sam's mouth felt parched, so he picked up the bottle of water from the tray between the seats and took a big swig. "There could have been Indian blood in your folks' genes."

She shook her head. "Nope. Both their ancestors migrated to this country. But my Mom told me about her Indian boyfriend, and how she'd fallen in love with him years ago. She knew her folks would never accept a man from another race, and I think it scared her to imagine living in a culture she knew nothing about. Even after she married Burke, she'd sneak off and meet her lover at the river. Thus, here I am."

Sam thought back on his life, and remembered at ten years old, the pain he felt when his folks were killed. But once Jennifer and Hawkman adopted him, things couldn't have been better. Losing his parents seemed like only a bad dream now. The other tragic event in his life had been losing Herman, his faithful dog, who died of old age. He couldn't imagine the horror Maryann described. "Sounds like you've had an interesting life."

She let out a disgusted laugh. "Yeah, really exciting if that's what you call getting raped by your so called "father" at twelve and being scared to death most of the nights. I used to lie in bed and cringe at the thought of Burke coming home from a drinking binge."

Sam noticed her eyes glistened with moisture, but no tears fell. He couldn't tell from her expression whether she felt rage or wanted to cry. "I'm sorry, sounds like you've had a rough go."

"Yeah, but I'll survive." She snickered. "Maybe one day I'll be rich and famous."

"I hope for your sake, those dreams come true."

"Thanks."

༄

Maryann turned her gaze toward the side window. Sam's blue eyes caused butterflies to flit about in her stomach. And the way his ash-blond hair casually fell over his forehead gave her goose bumps. More than one girl had vied for his attention as he strolled through the campus grounds at Humboldt. So far no one had succeeded in capturing it.

She'd fallen for Sam Casey in high school and even though he'd been intrigued with her at first, it only lasted a couple of dates. But she'd vowed then and there, no one else could have him. Unfortunately, she hadn't made much headway on this trip. Her short life history didn't appear to sit well in his mind. He gave her the impression of being very naive about what went on in true life. Well, she'd have to change his way of thinking this summer. School could wait until fall. She had better things to do with her time than study.

When Sam's voice brought her out of the deep fog, she jerked her head around. "I didn't catch what you said. Guess I drifted into another world."

Sam chuckled. "You hungry? I could use a bite to eat."

"Sure."

"Hope you like hamburgers. There's a little place up the road that makes great ones. I always stop on my way home."

"I'll eat anything."

They pulled into the small parking lot and went inside. As they carried their food to a corner table, three fire trucks sped by with their sirens wailing. A few minutes later, several patrons came in speaking loudly about the fire a mile up the road and how they'd all been turned back.

Sam got the attention of a young man. "Excuse me. Did you say there's a fire up the way?"

"Yeah. It's not bad yet, but the smoke is so thick you can't see the road ahead, so they're turning everyone around and not letting them through."

"Oh, great," Sam said. "Did they give you any idea when they might open it to traffic?"

The fellow shook his head. "No, but I think, unless the wind comes up, they'll have it out within an hour or so."

Sam nodded. "Thanks."

They finished their hamburgers and tossed the debris into the trash container. Back outside, they stood by the truck and watched the sun being blotted out by the smoke darkening the sky.

"Sure doesn't look good," Sam said, looking skyward. "Wonder if we should wait it out, or take the long way around, which would mean going back toward school and picking up 299 to Interstate 5. It will add a few hours to the drive."

"It's up to you. You're the driver."

"Your Mom expecting you at any certain time?"

Maryann shook her head. "She doesn't even know I'm coming."

"Oh." Sam opened the driver's side door and reached under the seat for his cell phone. "Well, I better give Jennifer a call. She'll be worried if I don't show up before dark." He glanced at the screen. "Uh oh, I've already missed two calls. Hell, I've got a 'low battery' message. I've got to charge this thing. Then let's hope I can get a signal in these hills. If not, would you search around and see if you can spot a pay phone." He hopped inside the cab, removed the charger from the glove compartment, and plugged it into the lighter. He had to start the truck and hated to burn the high priced octane, but decided it'd be worth it.

Maryann smiled to herself as she walked toward the side of the building in search of a telephone booth. At least she'd have Sam to herself a while longer.

CHAPTER THREE

Hawkman needed to get out of Jennifer's way since she appeared edgy over not hearing from Sam, so he decided to go mow the lawn. He felt concern, but realized with Sam coming over Highway 96, he might not be able to get a good signal for his cell.

After he finished, he stored the mower in the garage and brushed off the loose grass from his boots. When he entered the house, he noticed Jennifer had moved to the computer and sat staring at the screen with a frown.

"Something wrong?" he asked.

"No. I'm just having trouble focusing because I can't get Sam off my mind. He should be home any moment."

"Now, honey, you know kids. Time means nothing to them. Remember his last trip? He should have headed back to school early afternoon, but hung around here until dark. A long drive at night doesn't seem to bother young people. Who knows, he might not have even left yet. He could be saying goodbye to all his buddies for the summer and they're jawing the hours away."

She let out a sigh. "You're right. But I can't reach him on the cell and that bothers me."

"If he's driving on that mountainous road, there's a possibility he can't get a good signal. Give him time."

Hawkman crossed the room and turned on the television. A bevy of flames leaped across the screen. The newscaster reported a forest fire in their local area and because of low visibility due to the smoke covering State Highway 96, traffic had been turned back in both directions. The fire had been contained and the road would probably reopen in the next two hours.

"Ah, ha. Here's the problem," Hawkman said, pointing at the screen. "Sam can't get through. He'll have to either wait it out or turn around and go the long way. Since kids don't normally listen to the news or weather, he probably didn't know a thing about this fire until he got there."

Jennifer left the computer and stood beside Hawkman as they viewed the scene. "Oh, my word. Well, I guess I better give him a couple more hours before I panic."

Hawkman put his arm around her shoulders. "I think that's a good idea."

About that time, the phone rang and she raced to the counter. "Hello."

"Hi, Jennifer. This is Sam. Sorry I didn't call sooner. My cell phone is charged to the max, but I can't get a signal. I'm calling from a pay phone. Don't have a lot of change, so can't stay on but a couple of minutes. We ran into some difficulty and won't be home for awhile. They've shut Hwy. 96 down because of a smoky fire. We're almost to Happy Camp so I think we'll just wait it out since we're halfway home."

"Hawkman and I heard the news." She frowned. "You said, 'we'. Is there someone with you?"

"Yeah. Maryann Parker." He lowered his voice. "Her dad died."

"Yes, we read about his death in the paper. Would she like me to call her mother and tell her about the delay?"

"No. She said her mom didn't expect her."

Jennifer grimaced. "Really?"

"I gotta go. Don't wait up. We're safe, but have no idea when I'll be home."

"Glad you called. Drive carefully."

"Okay, bye."

After hanging up, she turned toward Hawkman. "How odd."

"What?" Hawkman asked. "I assume you were taking to Sam."

She nodded. "Maryann Parker's with him, but he said there's no need to call Lilly because she doesn't know her daughter's coming home." Jennifer furrowed her brow. "Don't you think that's peculiar under the circumstances?"

"Yes. Obviously, Sam didn't give any explanation."

"No. I've a suspicion Maryann stood within earshot."

❧

Sam stuck the remaining change from the phone call into his pocket and strolled toward Maryann. "See a theater around? We could kill a couple of hours watching the latest release."

Maryann rolled her eyes. "You must be kidding. We're in the middle of no man's land. This hamburger joint is the only place within miles. We can count ourselves lucky it's here."

Sam laughed. "You're right. At least we won't starve. Well, how do you want to kill a few hours? Have a deck of cards on you by any chance? We could play a little poker. Or some other game. I know girls aren't to crazy about Jacks or better."

"Sorry. I only packed the bare essentials."

"I noticed you only had one bag. Are you going back for summer school after the funer... uh, after you've visited for awhile?"

"I haven't decided. My roomies are staying, so my apartment is secure. I noticed a stranger at your place. Did you lease for the summer?"

Sam thought it curious Maryann had noticed, as Dan Williams had only been there since last night. "Yeah. I'm taking a rest. Gonna play awhile, then hit it again in the fall. This is the first time I haven't attended a summer session. Decided I needed a break."

They meandered toward the pickup and Sam kicked a stone with the tip of his cowboy boot, sending it sailing across the parking lot. He pointed toward the direction of the fire. "Looks like the smoke's thinning. One thing about that barricade the police set up, we can see it from here. As soon as they remove it, we'll be able to leave."

"Yeah, but they're not real swift on stuff like fires,"

Maryann said. "They're overly cautious and we could be here for hours."

Sam nodded. "Well, we could take off and go the long route. It's up to you."

She shook her head. "I'm in no hurry."

Resting his arms on the rim around the bed of the truck, Sam stared at her. "Why? Aren't you anxious to get home to your mom? Don't you think she needs you right now?"

She threw back her head and laughed. "Comfort my Mom. Is that what you think I should be doing?"

"It seems the most logical thing."

She shot Sam a look he couldn't decipher. He decided it fell somewhere between evil and mean.

"Oh, Sam, you're so naive," she giggled. "My Mom's probably rejoicing to have that man out of her life. More than likely, she's drunk with happiness."

He felt his cheeks flush and gritted his teeth. This woman made him very uncomfortable. "Tell me, did you ever meet your real father?"

"Several times."

"Do you like him?"

She shrugged. "He's all right."

"Tell me about the man."

"Not much to tell. He came from one of the Shasta Indian tribes. A big man with a yummy physique. Broad shoulders, bronze skin and long black hair." She took hold of a strand of her own. "This color. All in all, a really nice looking guy. He probably would have made a much better father than I had."

"Did you get to be with him much?"

"Not until I got older." She opened the truck door and hopped upon the seat, hanging her feet out the side. "When my old man decided I definitely wasn't his, he could have cared less where I went or what I did. So I had a lot of freedom to roam. That's when I met my real Dad."

"How'd you meet him? Did your mom introduce you or what?"

She laughed. "It's a crazy story. When I was fourteen

and old enough to stay by myself, Mom always took off on a Wednesday, but never told me where she went. We had this old station wagon and it always had a bunch of empty cardboard boxes and stuff crammed in the back. So I found a good hiding place under one of them behind the rear seat."

"Oh, no!" Sam said, slapping his forehead. "I bet you got into a heap of trouble."

"Actually, I thought the same thing when the wagon finally stopped and I sneezed, giving away my hiding place. It scared me to death when this big bare chested Indian man, wearing a pair of slim legged Levi's and cowboy boots, lifted up the box. He reminded me of those covers you see on the front of Romance novels. Standing next to my Mom, he seemed huge. If she hadn't been there, I'd probably have screamed."

"So what happened?"

"He took hold of my arm and helped me crawl out of the car. Then he gently laid a hand on each of my shoulders and looked into my eyes. 'You're very lovely. You shouldn't hide under a box.'"

Sam cocked his head and stared at her. "Is that all? You mean he didn't scold or hit you?"

Maryann twisted a piece of her hair between her fingers and shook her head. "Nope. Of course, later, my Mom gave me hell for hiding in the car. And warned me not to tell Burke or he'd beat us both."

"Did she tell you the Indian was your real dad?"

"No. In my young mind, I figured Mom just bought supplies from him, as he gave her a box of dried beans and vegetables. At that time, it never dawned on me it could be anything else."

"So when did you learn?"

Maryann stared toward the sky. "Let's see, it must have been the next year. A few days after my fifteenth birthday. Burke came home real late in a drunken stupor. I could hear Mom screaming at him from my bedroom. When she lit into him for not being around for my birthday or giving me a present, it developed into a heated argument. He carried on about how that 'damn little squaw wasn't his and he didn't have to give her a gift'. He went on to say, 'no daughter of mine would have long black hair and skin as brown as toast'. That's when it dawned on me." She lowered her head and sighed. "I remember getting up and examining myself in the mirror. I knew then, Burke Parker wasn't my father."

"That must have been quite a shock."

She nodded. "It threw me a bit. But being older, I started putting two and two together. The next day, when Burke left the house, I cornered my mother and she told me the story about how she fell in love with Madukarahat, my real father."

Sam frowned. "Madukarahat?"

"Yes, I call him Maduk. His name means giant."

CHAPTER FOUR

A black and white patrol car caught Sam's attention as it stopped in front of the roadblock. He pointed toward the highway. "Looks like they're removing the barricades. Let's get on the road." He dashed around the rear of the truck and jumped into the driver's seat.

Maryann slammed the door and put on her seat belt, grinning. "There," she said, patting the buckle. "Now you don't have to scold me."

Sam smiled and turned the ignition. "At least we didn't have to wait too long. We should get home by dark, if we don't have any more delays. Continue your story about discovering your father," he said, pulling onto the road.

"Why do you want to know about all that stuff?"

"I think it's interesting and it gives us something to talk about."

"If you really want to hear it, but I can guarantee it's not exciting."

"I'll be the judge. Now, tell me. Did your real dad know all along you were his daughter?"

Maryann sighed and nodded. "Yes. He wanted to introduce me into the tribe at my birth, but Mom wouldn't hear of it. While I was still an infant, she'd take me with her when they met in secluded spots. She said he'd just sit and rock me for a solid hour without saying a word. Once I got older, she stopped the visits, afraid he might take me away."

"Did he ever find out how Burke treated you and your mom?"

Maryann took a deep breath and stared out the window.

Sam shot her a quick glance when she didn't speak for several moments. "Sorry, maybe I'm trodding where I shouldn't."

"Yeah, I think so. I don't want to talk about it any more."

"Understand. Want to talk about school?"

She stuck out her tongue. "Not really. Why don't you tell me what your plans are for the summer."

"I'm going to fish, shoot digger squirrels, take Pretty Girl hunting and, go bike riding with Richard."

She put up her hands. "Wait, hold it. Who's Pretty Girl? And Richard who?"

Sam laughed. "Pretty Girl is Hawkman's falcon. Richard Clifford is the deaf boy who lives up near Topsy Grade."

"Now I remember how Hawkman got his name. Has he always had a falcon?"

"Yep. There was a short time after Pretty Boy died that he didn't have one, but Jennifer found another bird in Washington and had it flown in for his birthday a couple years ago."

"And I remember Richard. He's the guy whose mother and dog were murdered by that old hermit."

Sam nodded. "Yeah, tragic story. He's really a nice guy."

Maryann frowned. "How do you talk to him?"

"He reads your lips. You just make sure he's looking at you and he can answer you. His voice sounds a little strange, but that's because he can't hear the inflections. His mother never allowed him to learn sign language. She wanted him to be able to fit into society. And he's succeeded there and also made such excellent grades in high school that he got a scholarship to college."

"That's amazing," Maryann said. "Where does he live now?"

"Still up in the same little house. Except he and his Uncle Joe have completely revamped the place and it really looks nice."

"Interesting. So, how long have you been friends?"

"Years. We used to ride in the hills together when we

were younger and didn't even know each other's name." Sam chuckled. "I have some fond memories of those rides."

Maryann shook her head. "Guys do strange things."

"So what are you planning for the summer?"

"I'm debating about going back for summer school or staying home. It all depends on the situation."

⌘

Jennifer strolled into the living room and took a seat opposite Hawkman in the matching swivel chair.

"Do you feel better now that Sam's called?" he asked.

"Yes and no." She drummed her fingers on the armrest.

"Why, no?"

"Because of who's with him."

He shrugged. "What's wrong with Maryann Parker? School's out and she probably needed a ride home."

"It's not so much her hitching a ride, but the fact Lilly doesn't even know her daughter's coming home. I'd have thought the girl would already be here with her mother. It just seems strange."

"This whole Parker business is getting more bizarre by the minute. It sounds like a dysfunctional family."

Jennifer sighed and shook her head. "I think you've pegged it. Certainly makes one wonder."

"Let's not make any judgments. We don't know the whole story. The girl could have come home then returned for finals. Granted, it's unusual behavior, but let's find out more from Sam."

She snapped her fingers. "Oh, not to change the subject, but don't let me forget to tell Sam Uncle Joe called. He said Richard tried to text message Sam on the cell, but couldn't get a response."

"That's understandable. But it'll go through as soon as Sam's in an area where the signal's stronger."

Hawkman dropped his feet off the ottoman and sat forward in the chair. "Getting back to the Parkers. I think I'm going to drop in on Detective Williams tomorrow and see if he knows anything about Burke's death. It's out of his jurisdiction, but sometimes Yreka calls on him if they need help"

"You think it might be foul play?"

"Do you know the age of Maryann's parents?"

"I'd say in their forties."

"That seems mighty young for a man to die, unless he had severe health problems. Have you heard Burke had any ailments other than alcoholism?"

"No, but that alone could cause a multitude of illnesses."

"True. The autopsy should give some clues."

Jennifer squirmed in her chair. "How horrible for Maryann if they discover her dad had been murdered."

Hawkman picked up the remote control and flipped on the television to the local station. "Let's see if they have any news on that fire."

Both of them focused on the screen.

"Oh good," Jennifer said. "They've opened the road. Sam should make it home by dark."

CHAPTER FIVE

When Sam pulled into the driveway at Maryann's home, he could hardly believe his eyes. The house had changed drastically from what he remembered four years ago. Paint had peeled from spots on the exterior walls revealing bare wood. One of the gutters on the side of the house hung precariously in front of a window. The grass in the front yard had given up and dandelions grew in abundance. Brown stems of what used to be colorful flowers stood tall in the pots that lined the sagging porch.

Maryann didn't move for several moments, her gaze fixed on the house. "Looks pretty seedy doesn't it?"

"It definitely needs some attention. Maybe this summer Richard and I can help you get this place back in shape. I'm sure your mom doesn't have the money to hire someone to do it, especially now with no money coming in from your da... uh, Burke."

She stared into his face. "I can't expect you guys to spend your summer vacation working on a dilapidated old house."

"I'm serious. The place is small. A bit of paint, a few nails, and some grass seeds will do wonders. Why within a few weeks of hitting it hard every day, we'll have it done."

Maryann sighed and jumped out of the truck. "I appreciate your offer, Sam. Let me see what my Mom's plans are before you even think about it. Who knows, she might have left the country."

Sam climbed out of the pickup and walked around to the bed of the truck. "Is she working?"

"She's been working as a waitress at a greasy spoon

cafe downtown for about six or seven months. I don't even remember the name of the place."

Sam unfastened the tarp and pulled out her suitcase. "Give me a call. If Richard can't help, I'd be more than happy to do what I can." He turned toward the house, but Maryann took the bag from him.

"I can manage. Thanks for the ride."

Sam climbed into his truck and as he snapped on his seat belt noticed a scroungy looking man step from the narrow alley behind the Parker house. He watched for a moment as the vagabond adjusted the plastic bag he had slung over his shoulder before proceeding down the street. Sam shook his head as he turned the key in the ignition and pulled away from the curb. This part of town had its share of outcasts and it made him thankful he didn't live here.

Soon, his sad thoughts of Maryann and her dilemma faded as he drove toward Copco Lake. A feeling of giddiness overtook him and he could hardly wait to see his folks. Even though he'd been home over the Christmas holidays, it seemed like an eternity ago.

༜

Maryann carried her suitcase up the rickety stairs of the porch and dropped it at the entry. She gave Sam a wave as he pulled away from the house. "Mom, it's me. Are you there?" she called, softly rapping on the wooden frame.

When no one answered, she dug into her purse for a set of keys and unlocked the front door. She picked up her bag and stepped into the living room. Tossing the suitcase on the couch, she called again. "Mom, are you here?" Still no answer.

Taking a cigarette from the pack lying on the end table, she lit it, then carried an overflowing ashtray to the kitchen and dumped it into the trash can. The house smelled of stale smoke and food, so she opened a couple of windows to let a breeze blow through. Strolling back into the kitchen, she flipped on the light and let out a sigh as her gaze traveled across a sink full of dirty dishes. Skillets with congealed grease coating their bottoms sat on the stove. When she walked across the room, the soles of her boots stuck to the floor, making a sucking noise. She snuffed out her cigarette in a dirty saucer, left the room in disgust, picked up her suitcase, and headed for the room she called her own.

Not sure what to expect, she hesitated a moment before opening the door. To her surprise, even though a musty smell invaded her nostrils, everything appeared much like she'd left them from her last trip home. The Raggedy Ann doll with the smiling face still graced the pillow on her bed. She dropped her bag on the floor and opened the windows.

While things aired out, Maryann meandered through the rest of the house. When she came to her mother's bedroom, she leaned against the door jamb and stared at the pitiful sight of clothes strewn over the chairs, bed and floor. Her mother had never been very neat, but her housekeeping had gone from bad to worse in just a short time. Things were definitely rough for her mom, but it didn't excuse filth, she thought.

No sense in putting it off. Mother probably won't be home until midnight, since most of the food places stayed open until ten or eleven o'clock on the weekends. And more than likely, she'd stay and help with the cleanup. It will give me time to scour the bathroom and get the kitchen into decent shape so we can fix a meal without the fear of getting sick. Changing into her tennis shoes, Maryann pulled her hair into a pony tail, donned an apron and set to work.

At eleven thirty, she finally finished mopping the kitchen floor. Opening the back door to hasten the drying, she noticed the beam of a flashlight down in the corner of the alley. She let out a disgusted sigh and spoke aloud. "That old vagabond's not about to leave his source of food." Hanging up the apron on a nail in the small pantry, she turned and smiled to herself as she eyed her handiwork. At least the stove, refrigerator and sink now sparkled. A big difference from what she'd walked into a few hours ago. She pulled the rubber band off her pony tail, ran her fingers through her thick hair and let it billow around her shoulders. "That feels much better," she mumbled, shaking her head.

When the front door slammed, she jumped. "Mom, is that you?"

A small, tired looking woman walked around the corner of the room. Her pale blue eyes lit up when she saw Maryann. "Honey, I didn't know you were coming home. What a wonderful surprise." She gave her daughter a hug. "I noticed the lights on in the house, but just figured I'd forgotten to turn them off in my hurry to get to work."

"So you're still waitressing at that cafe?"

Lilly nodded. "There isn't anything else available. Believe me, I've tried. But with Burke giving me less and less as time went by, I had to take what I could get. And now that he's dead, there's nothing coming in and I need to survive."

Maryann nodded. "Can I fix you something to eat or drink?"

Her mother glanced around the kitchen. "Oh my, you've cleaned this place until it's gleaming." Then she waved a hand and shook her head. "I'm not hungry. Had a meal at the restaurant, but I'd love a whiskey and water."

"Sure. Go sit down and take off your shoes. I'll fix us both one and join you in a minute."

Lilly snapped her fingers. "Oh, first, let me put my leftovers out on the porch for Frank."

Maryann shook her head. "Mother, why are you still feeding that old homeless man when you hardly have enough to eat yourself?"

"Frank walks the streets day and night looking for food. Bless his heart, he needs some nourishment. And he's surprised me several times by doing little odd jobs around here when I've been at work."

Maryann put a hand on her hip. "Like what?"

"Last week he raked up a bunch of debris that had gathered under the porch and carport, then put it in the dumpster. But it doesn't matter, the restaurant would have just thrown this good food out anyway." She took the plastic container out of the bag she'd carried into the kitchen and hurried to the front door. Within a few seconds she came back in and flopped down on the couch.

Maryann thought about scolding her mother for the risk she might be taking as a woman living alone, but decided tonight wasn't the time. She wanted to find out more about Burke's death and her dad, Maduk.

The sun had barely set when Sam drove over the bridge, and heard the sound of the Klamath River cascading beneath his truck. The air smelled sweet and pure making him yelp with joy at finally being home. The lights were on inside and he could see Jennifer peeking out the kitchen window as his headlight beams hit the glass. She ran out the door and greeted him before he managed to get out of the truck. He embraced her and gave her a kiss on the cheek, then glanced up at a grinning Hawkman standing in the doorway.

"Glad you arrived safe and sound," he said, giving Sam a big hug and pat on the back.

"Oh, man, I've so looked forward to getting here. That danged fire held us up for a couple of hours."

They unloaded the truck and carried the items to the boy's room.

"This place looks great," Sam said, dumping a load of stuff on the bed.

Hawkman eyed the pile of dirty clothes and grinned. "Yep, there's nothing like coming home."

After dinner, they settled in the living room.

"Catch us up on your news," Jennifer said.

"What do you want to know?" Sam asked.

"Do you have plans for the summer, or are you going to hang around here?"

"I plan on hanging out right here, fishing, riding my bike and relaxing."

Hawkman chuckled. "Sounds like you plan on being down right lazy."

Sam laughed. "Well, it's a nice thought. But when I saw the house that Maryann's mom lives in, I offered my services to help get it back in shape. Maybe I'll be doing a bit of hard labor, too."

Jennifer looked puzzled. "What do you mean?"

"The Parker place is falling apart. I thought I'd talk to Richard and encourage him to help, at least on the weekends."

Hawkman leaned forward. "What kind of repairs are you talking about?"

Sam shrugged. "Oh, painting the outside, fixing gutters that are hanging loose from their brackets. And the porch is sagging, it needs some shoring up or someone's going to get hurt. In fact, the house looks like it's in shambles. Even the lawn is burned to a crisp and taken over by weeds."

Hawkman raised a brow. "You might have offered more than you can do. Sounds like it could take a hunk of money."

"I thought I'd talk to some of the merchants I know in town. Maybe they'd be willing to donate some paint and stuff, if I did the labor. Especially, since Mr. Parker just passed away." Sam sat up straight in the chair and faced Hawkman. "By the way, how'd he die?"

"We don't know," Hawkman said. "They found him in a motel room, and the autopsy report isn't out yet."

"He couldn't have been very old," Sam said.

"Did Maryann say anything about her dad?" Jennifer asked.

"Yeah, more than I really wanted to know."

"I'm sure she's upset."

He shook his head. "Maryann isn't the least bit bothered by his death. In fact, I got the impression, she's glad he's gone and so is her mom."

Jennifer frowned. "That's sad."

"It's what she told me on the ride home." Sam scooted to the edge of the seat and rested his arms on his knees. "You want to hear her story?"

She nodded. "Yes."

After Sam finished relating Maryann's tale, he threw up his

hands. "You can see why it doesn't bother her that Mr. Parker's dead."

Hawkman rubbed his chin. "Her story sounds plausible, but do you really know how much is valid?"

Sam grimaced. "I never gave it much thought. I guess because all the evidence points to the truth. Look at Maryann's skin tone and hair. Obviously, Burke realized she wasn't his daughter."

"How much do you know about the girl?" Hawkman asked.

"Not much really. I dated her a couple of times in high school and she pesters me at college, but she turns me cold. My thoughts went toward her mother living in that rundown house. Guess I felt sorry for her since she doesn't have a man around to do the repairs any more."

Jennifer remained silent for several minutes before speaking. "Do you think Maryann's lying?"

Sam shrugged. "Not sure now. Her story sounded very convincing at the moment. But I don't trust her."

Jennifer frowned. "Why not?"

He scratched his head. "It started back in high school and continued into college. She's fickle. Not so much toward me, but with my buddies."

"How's that?"

"Remember when I asked her to the Senior Prom?"

"Yes."

"I didn't realize at the time, Jim had already asked her and she'd accepted. When I called, she agreed to go with me, then called Jim and broke their date."

Sam shook his head. "I felt really bad for the way she'd treated my buddy and never dated her again."

Hawkman waved a hand in the air. "Women do that all the time."

Jennifer shot him a look. "No respectable female does that to a man." She turned to Sam. "Go on."

"I found out later she'd done this to several of my friends. Eventually no one asked her out, afraid at the last minute she'd turn him down if she got a better offer. She obviously didn't learn from the experience, because at college she developed the same reputation. Even the girls stay out of her way as she's tried to steal their boyfriends. She's just a real bitch when it comes to dealing with people."

"Is she still pretty?" Jennifer asked. "I haven't seen her in several years."

Sam rolled his eyes. "She's one beautiful babe, I kid you not. The guys go nuts when she walks past them going to class."

Hawkman went into the kitchen to get a beer. "My gut tells me she might be trouble, so beware."

"Don't worry, I've got her pegged." At that moment, his cell phone beeped, and he grabbed it from his pocket. "All right! Got a message from Richard."

CHAPTER SIX

The next morning, Hawkman knew Sam would be up early to ready his bike for the impending ride with Richard. He meandered outside, picked up the hose and pretended to focus on watering the flower beds near the garage. Sam stepped out the front door and headed for the tool bench where he had his bike implements stored. Once he had everything laid out in front of him, he pulled the cover off the motorcycle.

"Oh my gosh!" He dropped the tarp and dashed out of the garage. His gaze darted from Jennifer standing on the porch to Hawkman off to his left, both were grinning.

"Th..That's a brand new bike," Sam stuttered, pointing toward the shiny machine.

"Like it?" Jennifer asked.

"Oh, man, it's a beauty. But, what'd you do with my old one? It still worked great and had plenty of riding miles left."

Hawkman raised a finger in the air. "Sold to Uncle Joe. Richard's old bike finally conked out. So now you two can ride the hills without worry of mechanical problems."

"Oh man, what a surprise. How can I ever thank you?"

Hawkman strolled over and patted the boy on the shoulder. "Just work hard and keep up those grades like you're doing."

"No problem," Sam said, smiling from ear to ear.

He went back into the garage, donned his helmet and pushed the Honda XR400R onto the driveway. "I'm not due at Richard's for a couple of hours. Think I'll take a ride and get used to handling this machine."

"Good idea," Hawkman said. "I took it for a couple of

spins. The baby really hums. Keep in mind that's a powerful piece of equipment."

Sam gave a wave and took off down the driveway, then turned left onto the asphalt road. Jennifer ambled down the gravel pathway and joined Hawkman. She put her arm around his waist as they watched the boy cycle toward the old dumping area.

"He's a good kid," Hawkman said, as they strolled toward the house.

"I hope he has a fun summer. You realize this will probably be his last long visit at home?" She blinked her eyes against the well of tears. "This time next year he'll be out in the world making it on his own."

Hawkman gave her a comforting hug. "You can't keep a boy like Sam away from this paradise for long. He loves to fish and hunt too much."

In an hour, Sam rode into the driveway. Hawkman grinned as he watched his son through the kitchen window rub at a spot on the polished metal with his shirt sleeve.

"That's one neat dirt bike," Sam said, entering the house, a smile gleaming across his face. "Smooth as silk and goes up a hill in nothing flat. I can hardly wait to show Richard."

"Glad it meets your approval," Hawkman said.

Sam opened the refrigerator. "Jennifer, you got any sandwich makings? I want to take a lunch so we don't get hungry."

She joined him in the kitchen and removed several different types of lunch meat from the meat drawer. Soon, Sam took off for Richard's place with a backpack full of food and drinks.

Hawkman slapped on his leather hat. "Hon, I'm going into town. Talked with Detective Williams a few minutes ago and he'll be in his office this afternoon."

"Doesn't that man ever take off on Sundays?" she asked.

"Very seldom."

ᥬᕫ

Hawkman parked in one of the visitor's slots at the police

station. The place appeared pretty deserted when he entered the lobby. He waved at the officer attending the main desk and proceeded down the hall toward Williams' office.

He poked his head around the door jamb. The detective sat at his desk, deeply engrossed in reading a report. Hawkman tapped lightly on the inside of the wooden frame.

Williams glanced up and waved him in. "Good to see you. It gets a bit boring around here on Sunday. Of course, you'll probably put an end to the serenity, as I'm sure you're not here on a social call."

Hawkman laughed. "This visit is mostly out of curiosity."

The detective rolled his eyes. "That can spell all kinds of trouble. So, what are you questioning today?"

Hawkman removed the clipped article about Burke Parker from his pocket and handed it to the detective. Wondered if you knew anything about this man's death?"

Williams scanned the article. "You know him?"

"Not personally. Sam's a friend of his daughter, Maryann. They went to high school together and now attend the same college. She rode home with him yesterday and related some pretty weird stories about her family."

Williams stood, stretched his arms, then went to the coffee urn. "Want a cup?"

"Sounds good."

"Yeah, Yreka asked us to help investigate Parker's death. They're a small town and understaffed. The one detective they had in their department moved on to the big city." Williams handed Hawkman a mug of the steaming brew, then sat down at his desk. "We asked the paper to keep the story under wraps until we notified the family. Turns out they must have shoved it aside and didn't figure it any big deal, because the the news didn't come out for almost a week."

"Are you saying the death isn't recent?"

Williams nodded. "Our coroner did the autopsy, but everyone's behind schedule. He's overworked due to his assistant leaving and he's gotten several corpses behind." The detective scowled. "I hope he finds some help soon. It's hard to keep people in these small towns." He raised a hand. "Anyway, I just got the autopsy report last night and it states Parker had been dead several days before they found the body."

Hawkman took a sip from the mug. "Can I see the report?"

"Sure." He pulled a file from under some papers and handed it to him.

After Hawkman thumbed through the photographs of the body, he glanced at Williams. "It definitely appears the man had been dead for some time."

"The coroner figured from four to six days."

"How'd that get by the motel owners?"

Williams shook his head. "Real shabby place. No attendant is ever on duty. The place is full of derelicts and it stinks to high heaven. Doubt anyone even noticed the smell."

Hawkman continued to read and wrinkled his forehead. "It says he died of an alcohol related disease along with a mixture of drugs. But it doesn't explain what kind. The coroner just notes scoring of the mouth, tongue and esophagus."

"Some stuff had to be sent out for testing. You'll notice on the bottom it states, 'incomplete report'. Sometimes it takes weeks to get back the full results."

"Do you suspect he died naturally, accidentally or foul play?"

Williams shrugged. "Right now it's hard to say. There were no traces of anyone occupying the room except Parker. No signs of a struggle. It seems the man just collapsed."

"Were you the one who notified his wife, Lilly?"

The detective leaned back in his chair and scowled. "Yeah, weird lady."

"Why do you say that?"

"She acted strange. I couldn't really tell if she was distraught or angry." Williams waved a hand in the air. "I shouldn't make that kind of judgment. People react differently when they receive personal death news. But when I asked if I could call a relative to be with her, she said it wouldn't be necessary, she'd handle it. That's the last I've seen or heard from her. We've received no calls asking about when she could have the body picked up. Seems sort of odd. You'd think she'd want to make some sort of arrangements."

Hawkman nodded. "Fits the picture."

CHAPTER SEVEN

When Sam arrived at the Clifford place, he noticed how neat and clean the whole area looked. Quite a difference from Maryann's house. He spotted Richard pushing his old bike, sparkling like new, out of the large open door of the freshly painted barn. Midnight, the black dog Richard had rescued from the hermit's place, trotted happily after him.

Sam rode up alongside Richard, hopped off his cycle, removed his helmet and lightly cuffed his friend on the shoulder. "Good to see you."

Richard grinned. "I thought you'd never get home."

Uncle Joe stepped out the back door of the house, hat in hand and waved. "Hey, Sam. How's it going?"

"Real good, Mr. Clifford. Good to see you."

"I'm going into town to get some groceries. You guys have a good ride."

"Thanks."

Richard screwed up his mouth and looked at Sam. "What'd he say? He turned his face away before I could tell."

"He's going in for groceries."

"I knew that," Richard said, laughing.

Sam pointed at the motorcycle. "How's the bike working out?"

"It's great. I'm sure happy Hawkman talked to Uncle Joe before he sold it to anyone else." Then Richard strolled around Sam's new bike and let out a whistle. "Wow, what a beauty."

"I'll let you ride it once we get up into the hills."

Richard cocked his head. "Man, I don't know. I sure don't want to be the first one to put a scratch on it."

Sam shook his head. "I'm not worried. You ready to go?"

With a nod, Richard pulled on his helmet, donned his gloves and jumped on the bike. The two rode off toward the mountains.

After a couple of hours of steep climbs and following deer paths, they came to a stop in the shade of a tall oak tree. They steadied their bikes and flopped down on a flat rock protruding from the soil. Richard pointed up the hill where you could barely see the mouth of a large cave.

"Remember that?"

Sam glanced in the direction and smiled. "I'll never forget. That's where I found you after your escape from Jerome." He pulled some water bottles out of his knapsack and handed one to Richard. "You ready for a sandwich?"

"Sounds great. Glad you thought to bring food."

Sam handed him one. "By the way, do you still work at the stables?"

"Yeah, but they've moved a lot of their horses into town because of the mountain lions, so I'm not as busy. Why?"

"Would you like to help me do a volunteer job on the weekends?"

"Sure." Then Richard held up a hand and chuckled. "I better ask first, what am I getting into?"

"Helping me repair Mrs. Parker's house. Her husband died and the place is in dire need of attention. Mostly minor repairs and painting."

Richard's eyes opened wide. "Is that Maryann's mother?"

Sam nodded.

"I read about the police finding a Mr. Parker dead in a motel room. But I didn't connect the name to Maryann's family. Sure, I'll be glad to help."

Sam glanced at him suspiciously. "You seem awfully familiar with Maryann. What's the deal?

"I like her. We spent Memorial Day together in town. Went to the parade and the church picnic later. She's really nice."

Sam felt his neck hair bristle. His mind flashed back to the conversation he'd had with her on their way home. When he'd mentioned Richard, she gave the impression she barely knew him. And now he finds out she's playing her little game again, this time with his best friend's feelings. A guy who'd probably dated very little, if at all. And with Maryann's looks, if she gave him just a little attention, he'd fall hard. Sam suddenly lost his appetite.

❧

Later that evening, when Sam returned home, he lingered longer than usual in the garage, then finally went inside. Without a word of greeting to Jennifer, he sat down in Hawkman's swivel chair and picked up a hunting magazine.

She glanced over the top of the computer and studied his somber expression. "What's the matter. Didn't the bike perform like you expected?"

"The cycle rode like a dream." He closed the magazine and slammed it down on the table. Turning the chair toward the window, he stared out over the lake.

"Well, something's definitely bothering you."

"Yeah, Richard."

Jennifer moved away from the computer and crossed into the living room to her chair. "Is he okay?"

"He's fine, but very naive about girls."

She reached over and touched his knee. "I'm not following you."

Twisting the chair around to face her, he let out an audible sigh. Then he told her the story about Richard and Maryann on Memorial Day. "She's at it again with one of my friends. This time with a guy who knows little about women."

"Now, don't get upset. It sounds pretty much like an innocent meeting. There probably weren't a lot of kids their own ages around that weekend and they just spent some friendly time together. I wouldn't worry too much."

"I'd like to believe it, but I can tell Richard's already fallen. I could see it in his eyes. He can hardly wait for this coming weekend so we can start working on the Parker's house."

Jennifer shrugged. "Could turn out for the best. He'll be around Maryann and see what's she's really like."

Sam got up and paced the floor. "Now, I wish I'd never offered to do that job." Then he stopped. "Wait, Maryann told me not to even consider it until she knew he mother's plans. Maybe the whole thing will fall through. She said she'd call." He looked at Jennifer with raised brows.

She shook her head. "No calls."

Sam spent the next few days enjoying a life of leisure. He fished with Jennifer off the dock and caught an eighteen inch trout. The next day they took the boat up the river where he caught a nice mess of yellow perch and another good-size trout. On Wednesday, Hawkman came home early and they took Pretty Girl up to the Clifford's for a hunt. Richard accompanied them to the knoll. Hawkman let him put the falcon on his arm and give her the whistle commands. Richard seemed pleased to discover the falcon hadn't forgotten him.

Later that afternoon, Sam, joined Jennifer on the dock to do some fishing and decided to dive in for a refreshing swim. He broke the surface quickly, his teeth chattering. "Man, is this water cold."

Jennifer laughed. "It hasn't had time to warm up yet. Give it until the end of July or August. Then you can really enjoy a dip."

He climbed onto the dock and huddled under the towel for a few minutes. "That gave me a bit of a shock. I'd forgotten how frigid this lake can get." He pointed to the tree across the short span of lake from the dock. "Look, there's Ossy on that limb, just waiting for you to throw him a fish."

She glanced up at the tree. "I wish. I haven't seen Ossy in over a year. That one's either his son or another osprey who found a good hunting perch. I've never been able to coach him down like I did Ossy."

"Do you think he died?"

"I hope not. Maybe he's just relocated to another area."

"Me, too. Oh, by the way, have there been any calls from Maryann?"

Jennifer shook her head. "No."

"I guess I better get in touch with her. See if her mother's going to live there or move. If she's going to stay, I'll need to go into town tomorrow and get supplies. Sure hope the merchants will consider giving me some free paint and stuff."

Jennifer reeled in her line to put on fresh bait. "Once you're sure, let me know. I have some places in mind that just might be willing to help."

Sam's eyes lit up. "Great. It'll save me a bundle."

Jennifer smiled as she cast her line, then watched her son jog up the gangplank and hurdle a large limb on the lawn Hawkman had pulled out of the lake to dry. It made her proud that Sam kept his commitment, even though it didn't make him very happy. That builds character, she thought, as her attention returned to the tug she felt on her fishing line.

CHAPTER EIGHT

Richard finished his day's work at the horse ranch, drove home, showered and changed his smelly clothes. Afterwards, he went outside and strolled toward the gate leading into the larger pasture. Whitey, his devoted steed, who'd shed tears with him when his mother was so brutally murdered, galloped toward the fence, bobbing his head. Richard tried to imagine how the animal sounded.

He lovingly ran a hand down the horse's head and nose. Of course, Whitey always knew his master stored an apple in his pocket and the minute Richard climbed upon the gate, the critter nudged his side. Laughing, Richard pulled out the treat as he grabbed the horse's mane, and hoisted himself upon the animal's back. Whitey chomped the sweet morsel as he turned and trotted toward the river.

Richard guided the horse to one of his special spots overlooking the cascades. He dismounted and left Whitey at the top of the bank. Keeping an eye out for rattlesnakes, he wound his way down the incline toward a favorite rock. He loved the sight of the rushing water. Occasionally, he'd catch a glimpse of a trout leaping above the rapids, making him smile as he remembered the many times he'd fished here.

Taking his buck knife from his pocket and a small piece of wood, he sat down on the rock and whittled the image of a small fish, just big enough to go on the end of a key chain. As he worked on the finishing touches, Richard kept thinking about his earlier bike ride with Sam. He'd thoroughly enjoyed himself, and thought his friend had also, at least in the beginning. Then Sam's mood turned solemn when he told him about being with

Maryann on Memorial Day. He wondered why. Did he have a crush on her, too?

It had eased his mind somewhat when Sam and Hawkman showed up at the house with Pretty Girl. He went with them to the knoll and had a great time with the falcon. She even remembered his way of whistling and didn't balk at his monotone voice. Sam appeared friendly and joyful as usual, and asked again if he'd help him on the Parker place. They made plans and Sam said he would notify him as soon as he'd set a time with Mrs. Parker.

The shadows were deepening and Richard figured he'd better get back to the house and help Uncle Joe with the evening chores. He whistled for Whitey and climbed back up the grade. Richard tapped the horse's chest and the steed lowered himself on his front knees so he could climb onto his back with ease. They rode at a slow gallop and Richard realized how much he loved the farm. It made him happy that he could come home every other weekend.

He'd worked the summer after graduating from high school at the Zankers in exchange for a pickup they'd stored in their garage. It only had a few thousand miles on the speedometer. After Uncle Joe put in new plugs, and tweaked it a bit, it ran as smooth as silk. It gave Richard the transportation he needed for traveling to and from college.

He brought Whitey into the barn and gave him a good brushing and some grain, then turned him loose in the pasture. Strolling toward the back door of the house, he could smell something mighty good cooking in the kitchen.

Uncle Joe had been a blessing. He'd taken charge and insisted upon Richard finishing high school, then going on to college. The whole piece of property had benefited from his touch. Richard could never thank him enough.

"Hmm, something sure smells good," he said, entering the back door.

Uncle Joe grinned and glanced at him as he stirred the big pot. "I've made the stew of stews, my lad. Plus a batch of bread that will make your mouth water. It smelled so good when I took it from the oven, I had to try a slice."

He licked his lips. "Delicious."

Richard washed his hands and set the table. "How long will it be. My stomach is already grumbling."

"About fifteen minutes."

"I hope I can wait that long."

Uncle Joe laughed. "You won't perish."

"Oh, where's Betsy? I didn't see her in the pasture."

"I'm getting her bred with one of Zanker's prize bulls. By the time you get out of school next year, we'll have a new calf. Let's hope it's a bull. Then we might be able to make a little extra money."

"Hey, that's neat."

Richard went into his bedroom and checked his phone. He had a text message from Sam. "Yes for weekend." He grinned. Now, he'd be able to try his luck with Maryann. Then he frowned. What if she's going to summer school. He shrugged. Well, at least she won't leave until after her dad's funeral. This would give him a chance to watch Sam's behavior toward her and clarify whether he had a crush on Maryann too. If not, he'd try to make headway with the girl. Then he dropped the phone on the bed and glanced in the mirror. In his infatuated state he'd forgotten about his handicap. His looks were presentable, but what girl would want to go out with a deaf guy? He took a deep breath and marched into the kitchen. "Is it ready yet?"

❧

Lilly Parker pushed her plate away and sat back in her chair as she watched her daughter finish her meal.

"I enjoyed your cooking very much. You've gotten pretty good over the past few years."

Maryann smiled. "Thanks. I got tired of fast food and the cafeteria at school is horrible. So, I decided to prepare my own meals. Took a while to get the hang of it, but it sure tastes better."

"Tell me about these two boys who want to fix up the

house. I recognized Sam Casey's name, but don't remember Richard Clifford. Even though his name sounds familiar."

After refreshing her mother's memory, Maryann picked up the dirty dishes and put them in the sink. "You have to admit, Mom, this place looks pretty shabby."

Lilly nodded. "True, but what's in it for them?"

Maryann glanced at her mother. "I don't understand what you mean."

"Do they want money? I can't afford to pay them."

Waving her hand and shaking her head, Maryann sat back down. "No, no, they just want to do it as a goodwill gesture. I think Sam feels sorry for you because Burke died and now you don't have a man around to do repairs."

Lilly put a hand to her mouth and stifled a laugh. "Burke never lifted a finger to keep up this place. The little bit of money he gave me hardly paid for food, much less paint or equipment for repairs. I think he spent most of it on booze." Lilly brushed a few crumbs from her uniform. "Where will they get the supplies they need?"

"Sam mentioned asking some of the merchants in town to help out."

Throwing back her head, Lilly chortled. "I wish him luck."

Maryann stared at her. "Why do you say that? You've lived here most of your life. The people in this town know you're a good person. Why wouldn't they pitch in and help?"

"People in small towns love to gossip. Burke blabbed a lot when he got drunk. He spouted off to anyone who'd listen about how his woman had an Indian lover. When you were two or three years old, he made no bones about pointing out your black hair and dark brown eyes. "That sure ain't no kid of mine," he'd scoff. It got to the point when I walked down the street, people crossed the road so as not to brush by me." She let out a sigh. "If I'd had the money, I'd have taken you and left this tacky place years ago."

"Didn't Maduk want you?"

Lilly's gaze dropped to the floor as she wound a loose thread from her dress seam around her finger. "Yes. But I couldn't do that to him. His people were already upset about him consorting with a married white woman. They would never have accepted me. However, they'd have kept you and raised you as one of their own. I couldn't have stood that."

"You must have loved him a lot."

"I did. He treated us with gentle kindness."

"Have you seen him since Burke died?"

"No." Tears glistened in her eyes.

Maryann's eyes narrowed. "Why?"

Lilly glanced at her watch and stood. "Oh, my, I must get ready for work."

Jumping up, Maryann grabbed her mother's arm. "You're already dressed. Answer my question."

She pulled her arm away. "I haven't seen Maduk in six months. One night he watched through the bedroom window and saw Burke beat and rape me. He broke down the front door and dashed into the room with his knife drawn. I had to stand between the two men or Maduk would have killed Burke on the spot. This town would have hung your father from the nearest tree. I pleaded with him to leave. He finally cooled down, and told Burke if he ever laid another hand on me, he'd slice him to pieces. That's the last time I saw him."

CHAPTER NINE

Friday morning, Sam drove into Yreka and stopped at the Parker's, but found no one home. He surveyed the outside of the house and took notes on items that he thought he'd need. While in the back yard, he heard a noise and glanced down the alley. Two houses away, where the corner of a fence jutted out, shadowed by a large tree, he noticed a man with a long beard shaking out a blanket. Sam watched as he folded it into a square and placed it inside a large plastic bag, which he flung over his shoulder. The man looked vaguely familiar and Sam believed him to be the same vagrant he'd spotted on the day he brought Maryann home. He wondered if she knew such a fellow had made his habitat so near their house. Shaking his head, Sam brought his attention back to his notepad and continued his calculations.

After leaving the Parker place, he made the rounds of different paint shops and lumber yards where he'd worked or knew the owners personally. All donated items, but a couple of the proprietors made derogatory remarks under their breath about the Parkers. Sam felt a bit uneasy, but he pretended he didn't hear or understand, and instead, thanked them for their generous contributions.

As he drove back to Maryann's house, he wondered why the townspeople rejected the family. Did they dislike all of them? Sometimes the human race baffled Sam. He chose not to try and figure it out or he'd be frustrated the whole summer.

He hoped one of the Parker women would be home as he wanted to leave the construction items at their place instead of toting them back to the lake. When he got within sight of the house, he breathed a sigh of relief seeing an old Oldsmobile station wagon parked in the driveway. He knew a little about cars and figured it to be a 1988 Firenza. It made him wonder if this was the one Maryann hid in the first time she met her real father.

He parked in the front and before he could get a leg out, Mrs. Parker, dressed in a pale blue uniform with a frilly white apron, hurried out the door of the house and headed for the car. Jumping out of his pickup, he scurried around the rear of the Toyota. "Mrs. Parker," he called.

She whirled around and put a hand to her chest. "Oh, you startled me."

"Sorry," Sam said holding out his hand as he approached her. "My name's Sam Casey. I don't know if you remember me or not. Maryann and I went to high school together and are now attending the same college."

"Yes, I remember you well. In fact, Maryann told me you and your friend were going to do some repairs on this place." She turned around and eyed the house.

Sam shifted his position "Maryann said it was all right with you."

She ducked her head. "Umm, but I can't pay you."

"Don't worry, Mrs. Parker. We don't want money. We're doing this to help you."

She peered into his eyes. "Not many around here have that attitude." Glancing at her watch, she opened the car door. "Oh, my, I better get to work or I'll be late."

Sam pointed toward the porch. "Is it okay if I stack the lumber and supplies under there? Richard and I will be here in the morning to start work.

Hesitating, she lifted a hand and shaded her eyes. "Yes, that'll be okay." Then she glanced at him. "You'll be here tomorrow morning?"

"Is that inconvenient?"

She waved a hand and shook her head. "No, no, that'll be fine."

He turned and headed for the truck.

After she left, Sam backed into the driveway, donned a pair of gloves and unloaded the lumber.

"My gosh, are you going to rebuild the house?"

The voice startled Sam and he bumped his head as he raised up from underneath the porch. "Ouch," he said, rubbing his crown.

Maryann hung over the railing, grinning. "Sorry. Didn't mean to alarm you."

"Hi. I just assumed you weren't here after your mom left." He tugged off the work gloves and stuck them into his back jeans pocket.

"I was in the shower and didn't see you drive up."

Sam scooted a large box of screws out of the truck bed and placed it beside the lumber. He then removed a long span of gutter, along with a couple of sacks filled with brackets and set them under the porch. "Well, that about does it for now," he said, dusting off his hands. He looked up at Maryann. "Richard and I will be here early in the morning."

"Great. Want to come in for a glass of ice tea?"

He shook his head. "No thanks. I've got lots to do. See you tomorrow."

_ϡ

Maryann, fists on her hips, watched Sam drive away. "Well, he certainly wasn't in a friendly mood," she muttered. Heading back into the house, she slowly closed the door, her mind still on Sam. When she turned around, her hands flew to her throat and she gasped. "Maduk, you scared me to death."

"I didn't mean to frighten you."

"How'd you get in? The back door's locked."

"You ask too many questions, my daughter." He circled Maryann, then stepped back and scrutinized her from head to toe. "You've turned into quite a lovely woman."

Maryann felt uncomfortable under his gaze and sat down on the couch. "Why are you here?"

"Where's your mother?"

"She went to work."

"Her hours have changed. Usually she's home now."

"One of the waitresses called in sick and they asked if Mom could come in. She needs the extra money."

His expression turned solemn and he averted his stare to the floor.

Maryann cocked her head and peered at her father. He'd cut his hair and wore a business suit. "You look different."

"I have a new job that requires me to dress this way, but I'd rather be hunting in the woods."

"Does Mom know? She said you hadn't been around much."

"No," he said, pacing back and forth.

Maryann felt her father's tension. "Why are you here?"

"I need to talk to her about Burke."

She glanced at him in puzzlement. "You know he's dead."

"Yes. Murdered."

Maryann stiffened and her mouth dropped open. "The police gave us the impression he'd died in his sleep."

Maduk's glare cut into her like a shaft. "So they say."

CHAPTER TEN

Saturday morning Hawkman decided to go into the office. He figured after he wrapped up the paperwork on a couple of cases, he'd drop by the Parkers' in Yreka and see if he could help the boys with their refurbishing project. Repairing old houses can be quite a chore and more than meets the eye, especially for a couple of young fellows.

He set to the task as soon as he got behind his desk and worked steadily for several hours. Just as he closed the last file, the phone rang. "Tom Casey here."

"Hey, you work on the weekend, too."

Hawkman laughed. "How's it going, Williams?"

"Glad I caught you in town. If you have a minute, thought you might be interested in dropping by the station. Since you showed an interest in Burke Parker's death, you might want to take a gander at these autopsy reports that came in. Don't have them all yet, but they look mighty interesting."

"Are you saying there's a possibility of something other than natural causes."

"Well, let's say it looks mighty suspicious."

"I'll see you shortly."

This news piqued Hawkman's curiosity. He wondered what had been uncovered. He quickly filed the folders and unplugged the coffee pot. Adjusting his eye-patch, he plopped on his cowboy hat and headed down the stairs. When he reached the detective's office, he found Williams' door closed and heard his loud voice booming from within. It sounded as if someone was getting a good bawling out. Hawkman lingered in the hallway until two red-faced young officers exited the detective's office. They headed down the hallway without glancing his way.

Hawkman peeked around the door jamb. "Is it safe?"

"Damn kids," Williams mumbled, waving for Hawkman to come in. "I swear they're graduating them out of the academy earlier and teaching them less."

Hawkman chuckled. "The truth is, we're just getting older."

"Yeah, speak for yourself old man. I haven't aged a bit." Williams wiped a hand across his mouth, suppressing a grin."

The detective took a folder from the top of his desk. "Poisoning is rare and hard to prove. But the State Crime Laboratory doesn't like what they see and are sending some specimens to a private laboratory where there's a toxicologist. Fortunately, we have a good medical examiner and he'd collected several specimens from Burke's body." He lifted a sheet of paper from the file and handed it to Hawkman.

After a couple of minutes, he handed it back. "Looks like Burke could have accidentally overdosed on his own medication?"

"That's a possibility, but they've found traces of something else and want to check it out before they come to any conclusions on the cause of death. He also had blistering on the inside of his mouth, stomach and intestines. And extensive liver damage. Probably from alcohol abuse."

"You ever pick up Burke on any alcohol related charges?"

Williams nodded. "Yep. Several." He pulled another report from the folder. "Over the last five years, we and the Yreka police have run him out of practically every bar in both towns. He tended to get pretty rowdy after several drinks. However, no charges were ever filed, which surprised me."

"Anyone ever talk to his wife about the problem?"

"Only once. It's here in the report. Last summer a neighbor called the Yreka police about midnight and said there was something terribly wrong at the Parker's. She could hear a lot of screaming, then heard a gun go off. When the officers got to the house, they found Burke in the yard with a gunshot wound to his leg. All they could pry out of Mrs. Parker was Burke came home drunk and tried to wreck the house, so she shot at him, but didn't mean to hit him. They had a feeling there was more to it, but she never gave the police any more information about the incident."

"I'm surprised Burke didn't have her arrested?"

The detective shook his head. "Nope. After he sobered up at the hospital, he said he deserved it. Not much you can do if a man won't press charges."

"So how are you going to proceed in this case?" Hawkman asked.

Williams leaned back in his chair and tapped a pencil on his chin. "Not sure. Can't do much until I know the cause of death. However, I might ask a few questions around the neighborhood and see what I can learn about the family. I'll also check out his doctor. We found a couple of prescription drugs in his rented room." The detective pointed his pencil at Hawkman and grinned. "Be more than happy to have your help. Of course, I can't pay you."

Hawkman chuckled. "Why doesn't that surprise me?" He leaned forward, arms resting on his thighs, hands clasped. "Tell me, do you know anything about a Native American man that hung around Mrs. Parker?"

Williams raised his brows. "No. Is this something new?"

"Not sure. Let me get back to you on that."

Hawkman left the police station, his mind whirling with ideas about poisons, herbs, Indians, and a very dysfunctional family. When he parked in front of the Parkers' house, he saw a shirtless Sam and Richard struggling to carry a large piece of lumber from under the porch. He jumped over a sprinkler the boys had set up to soften the hard soil in the front yard and grabbed the end of the plank.

"What are you guys trying to do?"

"We need to replace a couple of boards in the porch or someone's going to fall through one of these rotten spots and break a leg."

"Sounds like a good plan. Hope you bought screws, they hold better than nails."

"Yeah, I've got plenty," Sam said.

He helped the boys take up the rotten pieces and replace them with the new lumber.

When they'd finished, Maryann stepped out on the porch and onto the new area. "Boy, that sure makes a difference. It feels solid now, instead of bouncy."

Sam wiped the sweat from his brow with his tee shirt, then slipped it over his head. "That was the idea." He pointed toward the dangling gutter. "Once we get that fixed, we'll concentrate on sowing a lawn in the front yard, then paint the house. You should have a new looking place in a couple of weeks. You might even want to think about planting something in the front flower beds."

❧

As Richard stood to the side and watched the conversation, he noticed Maryann had eyes only for Sam, but he didn't respond. In fact, Richard thought he saw contempt in his friend's expression.

After Richard slipped on his shirt, he stepped forward. "If you like fresh vegetables, you might consider a small garden. There's plenty of room for one. That is, if you're not going back for summer school."

She turned and gave him a smile. "I'll be here. And you're right. I've never tried my hand at gardening and it might be fun to see if I have a green thumb."

Sam picked up the tools and scooted them under the porch. "Thanks, Hawkman, for your help. I think we'll call it a day."

"You got a lot done." Hawkman waved and walked toward his 4X4.

Sam motioned for Richard and they jumped into the truck. They'd traveled several blocks before either spoke.

"Did you notice that black car that circled the block several times?" Richard asked.

Sam frowned. "Yeah. Did you ever get a good look at the driver?"

"He looked like a Native American male. His shoulders were very broad and his head almost touched the ceiling of the car. No one I've ever seen before."

"Probably Maryann's dad," Sam mumbled.

From the look on his friend's face, Richard knew that Sam had let that last comment slip. "I think you know more about Maryann than I do. Why don't you tell me."

Sam glanced at Richard, took a deep breath and related what he knew. When he finished, he let out a sigh. "It's not a pretty story."

Richard brushed some loose hair off his forehead with his fingers and stared out the windshield. "No, it's not. She's more handicapped than I am."

CHAPTER ELEVEN

Not knowing how to respond, Sam kept his eyes on the road. It bothered him repeating Maryann's story, but now Richard could form his own decision about her.

"Do you think that might have been her real dad in that car?" Richard asked.

Sam shrugged. "It's possible. Now that Burke's dead, he might feel more comfortable showing his face. But seeing us at the house, he probably didn't want to cause Maryann or her mother any embarrassment. In a small town gossip spreads like wildfire."

He turned into Richard's driveway. "Shall I pick you up at the same time in the morning?"

"It's a lot of trouble for you to come all the way out here and waste your fuel. Seems more sensible for me to pick you up. You're right on the way to town."

"Okay, but only if you let me split the gas cost. After all I'm the one who got you into this mess."

Richard threw back his head and laughed. "I didn't have to accept. But it makes me feel good to do something for someone else. So many people have helped me." He climbed out of the truck and waved. "I'll see you in the morning."

Sam made a U-turn and headed home. He felt like a burden had been lifted off his shoulders now that his friend knew the truth. Richard's expression revealed a romantic interest in Maryann and Sam hoped he'd reconsider pursuing a relationship. Perhaps Richard only felt sorry for her. Only time would tell. At least he didn't feel guilty anymore.

He drove into the driveway and parked at the side of the

house. When he entered the kitchen, Hawkman and Jennifer were in a serious discussion about Burke Parker. Their remarks piqued his curiosity.

ᴄᴀ

Lilly Parker had worked over ten hours at the restaurant. Her feet felt like clubs. She still had a young firm body and the skimpy uniform she wore while working at the bar revealed a deep cleavage and trim legs. Lilly hadn't told Maryann about her job as a cocktail waitress on the weekends. The money had really helped. She stashed away her tips and any extra she had at the end of the month, in hopes that after Maryann graduated, she'd have enough to buy a newer car. Or maybe even move away from this dump. With Maryann's two friends working on the house as a gesture of kindness, she didn't have to worry about paying anyone to fix up the place before putting it on the market. And with Burke dead, life looked a little cheerier.

As she drove into the driveway, her eyes filled with tears. What had happened to her Maduk? Had he left her too? She let out a sigh as she climbed out of the car and locked it. When she turned around, a large shadow loomed over her. Before she could scream, a hand clamped over her mouth.

"Hush, Lilly, it's me, Maduk."

She fell into his arms. "Oh, my love, where have you been? I've missed you so much." She smothered her tears in his chest as he held her tightly.

"I want to take you away."

Raising her head, she wiped her cheeks. "We can't talk out here. Even the trees have ears in this town. Let's go inside."

When he hesitated, she took his hand and pulled him toward the house. "Don't worry, Burke will never bother us again. He's dead."

"Yes, I know. That's why I'm here."

Once in the living room, Lilly closed the drapes. "Now, that's better. I feel we have some privacy." Then she glanced toward the bedrooms. "Let me check to make sure Maryann's asleep. Did you know she's home?"

He nodded. "Yes, I spoke to her."

Lilly stopped in her tracks and glanced at him. "When? She didn't tell me you were here."

"It doesn't matter. Maryann knew I'd come back."

She peeked into her daughter's room, then softly closed the door. "She's in dreamland." Lilly sat down on the couch and removed her shoes. "Oh, that feels so much better." She wiggled her toes, leaned back on the couch and patted the cushion. "Come, sit beside me. It's so comforting to have you here. You've been gone a long time. Where've you been?"

Maduk sat down on the edge of the couch, his back rigid and his large hands resting on his knees. "We need to talk."

Lilly knew he had something very serious on his mind, but right now, she just wanted him to hold her. She could see it wasn't going to happen at this point. Rubbing her feet on the carpet, she reached over and touched his leg. "You want something to drink?"

He shook his head. "We need to get out of here very soon."

She frowned. "Why the urgency?"

"I have a job that takes me into other towns. We can't stay here."

Cocking her head, she stared at him. "That doesn't make much sense. You've had jobs where you went to other areas, but you never talked like this."

Maduk stood. "The police are going to ask a lot of questions about Burke's death. They'll come looking for me."

Lilly stiffened. "But I understood Burke died of natural causes."

"The police have asked for numerous lab tests. They wouldn't, if they didn't suspect foul play."

"How do you know these things?"

"I have my sources."

She gazed up at him with pleading eyes. "I'll tell the police you were with me."

His arms rose and dropped to his side. "You can't, my sweet one. The coroner doesn't even know Burke's exact time of death. All they know is he'd been dead for several days when they discovered the body. And with this new job, there were times I traveled all over the area and no one saw me for days."

Lilly got up and paced, her hands clenched into fists. "I'll tell the authorities how Burke beat and raped me when he was drunk."

"Since you never reported the abuse when it happened, they certainly aren't going to believe you now."

She threw up her arms. "If I'd ever told the police what all Burke did, they'd have taken Maryann away from me and put her in a foster home." She hugged herself as tears slid down her cheeks. "I couldn't have stood losing my little girl."

Maduk pulled her into his arms. "Regardless, Lilly. We've been lovers for years and it hasn't gone unnoticed. People can see Maryann isn't Burke's daughter. Once she reached the age where her black hair and dark brown eyes became apparent, Burke made no bones about announcing it in every bar.

I don't know if the police know me by name. But they'll be looking for a Native American as their first suspect. So I can't be seen with you or hang around the area for much longer. Someone will soon spot me."

She threw her arms around his neck. "No! They can't take you away. I've waited too long for this day."

CHAPTER TWELVE

Maryann opened her eyes, glanced at the bedside clock, then stared at the closed door. It was well after midnight, but she could hear muffled voices somewhere in the house. Pushing back the covers, she threw her legs over the edge of the mattress and slipped her feet into the scuffs next to the bed. She shrugged into her robe, then quietly opened the door a few inches. Standing rigid, she listened to her mother and Maduk for several minutes.

Finally, she stepped into the hallway and strolled silently into the living room. Maduk spotted her immediately, and turned Lilly around by the shoulders to face their daughter.

"Oh, honey. Did we wake you?" Lilly asked, wiping tears from her cheeks.

"No, Mom, it's okay." She studied the dark eyes of her father, identical to her own.

Lilly tossed a quick look at Maduk, whose expression didn't change as he stared at his child.

Maryann took a step forward. "Maduk, how do you know so much about Burke's death?"

Lilly's hands flew to her mouth. "Honey, how can you ask such a thing? You act like your father might have done something bad."

"I'm not asking you, Mother. I'm asking Maduk." Her gaze locked with his.

"As I told Lilly, I have my sources."

"If people know Mom has a boyfriend, then why should it bother you to be seen around here?"

"Because no one really knows who I am except you. But

the police have their suspicions and are going to be looking for me as a suspect involved in Burke's death. They'll be looking for a Native American. The only other person who has ever seen me in this house was Burke. And I'd have killed him then, if your mother hadn't stopped me."

"I wish you had." Maryann's eyes narrowed. "But it's hard to believe after all these years living in this little town, no one has ever connected the two of you."

"We were very careful."

Maryann threw up her hands. "Why the hell didn't you take us away from this place?"

Lilly shot her daughter a hard look. "You have no right to ask that question."

"Yes, I do. He's my father."

Maduk stared fixedly at Maryann. "I had no money and no shelter."

She advanced toward him, her shoulders set in defiance. "You could have taken us to the reservation. They'd have made sure we had a roof over our heads and food to eat. And we wouldn't have had to contend with Burke anymore."

His gaze never swayed. "They'd have turned their backs on us."

Maryann frowned. "Why?"

"Because I'd been banned from the tribe."

Her head jerked up. "What! How come?"

Lilly stepped between her daughter and Maduk. "Maryann, that's enough. You're going where it's none of your business."

Maduk put a hand on Lilly's shoulder. "Maybe it's time she knows."

Maryann gave her parents a questioning look.

Lilly clenched her hands together, and moved out of the way. "Do whatever you think best."

Maduk took a deep breath. "I killed one of my own people."

Maryann dropped into the overstuffed chair in the corner of the living room. "I can't believe what I'm hearing." She glanced up at her father. "How and why did you kill a person of your own tribe?"

"He was an evil man and had been harassing me for a long time about going out with a married lady. Even though he came into town regularly to take advantage of the white women in the bars. One night after he'd had too much whiskey, he came back to the reservation, yelling for me to come out of my house. By the time I stepped outside, a large crowd had gathered. He claimed I dishonored our people."

"How did he know?"

"Our people know many things about each other. Not much goes by they don't see."

"So what happened?"

"He walked to the center of the yard waving a long blade and challenged me. I took my knife and met him."

Maryann's eyes were wide. "You mean, you killed him in self-defense."

"The white man called it that, but they never got involved. They let the tribal council handle it. My people said I won because I proved the better fighter. But they banned me, saying, if I killed once, I'd probably kill again and they didn't want me among them."

"That's stupid," Maryann said in disgust. "What if it'd been the other way around?"

"The same thing. The evil one would have been run out."

Maryann rubbed her eyes with the palms of her hands, then shoved her hair behind her ears. "So what are we going to do?"

Lilly stepped forward and took her daughter's hand. "Nothing for now. If you and I disappear, it will look bad. But Maduk must leave until he's cleared of suspicion. When it all blows over, we'll join him." Lilly glanced at Maduk. "Hopefully far away from this place."

Maryann thought she noticed a tic in Maduk's cheek as he contemplated what Lilly said.

"If you think it's the right thing to do," he said. "Then I'll go. When things are safe, I'll come for you."

"How will we stay in contact?" Maryann asked.

"We can't. Any message or phone call can be traced."

"But how will you know when it's safe?"

"I'll know."

Maduk pulled Lilly into his arms and kissed her. "I hope we'll be together soon." He glanced at Maryann. "I'll see you shortly, my daughter."

The two women watched Maduk walk out the front door.

Lilly took a handkerchief from her pocket and wiped the tears from her cheeks. Maryann put an arm around her mother's shoulders and guided her to the couch.

Jennifer and Hawkman glanced at Sam when he walked in the door.

"I heard Burke Parker's name. Have you found out something new?" he asked.

"Well, his death might not have been from natural causes."

Sam sat down on one of the stools at the kitchen bar beside Hawkman. "Did they find a bullet hole in his body?"

Hawkman shook his head. "No."

"So what'd they find?"

"All the tests aren't in, but they've discovered some unnatural things that occurred in his body. Which could mean anything from an overdose to a reaction to alcohol in his system. Or, he could have been poisoned."

Sam's eyes opened wide. "Poisoned?"

Hawkman raised a hand. "Don't jump to any conclusions. And keep this to yourself. Nothing's final yet."

"Oh, man!" Sam rubbed a hand over his chin. "That means Maryann and her mother are going to be involved in a murder investigation. And police will be swarming all over the new lawn we're putting in." He slapped his hands on the counter. "And I thought I'd have a peaceful summer."

Trying to suppress a smile, Hawkman patted Sam's back. "If the reports show a shadow of a doubt that he died of anything but natural causes, Lilly and Maryann will have a few hectic months ahead. Welcome to the real world, son. And yes, family members are the first suspected."

That night, Sam tossed and turned before finally falling asleep. Richard and Maryann kept popping into his mind. If it turned out Burke was murdered, Richard's compassion for Maryann might grow. After all, he'd been a suspect in the murder of his mother, and knew the anguish they'd be going through.

Early the next morning, Sam paced back and forth across the driveway as he waited for Richard to pick him up. He debated whether he should confide in his friend about the latest news on Burke's death. Hawkman warned him to keep quiet until all the tests were in, but it tore at his gut to think the police could converge on the Parker property at any time, and catch Richard off guard.

Sam finally spotted his friend's truck coming across the bridge. As soon as the pickup rolled to a stop, he hopped aboard and they took off toward town. He observed how well Richard had mastered the art of driving by using all the mirrors. They drove a few miles before Sam spoke. He leaned forward so that Richard could see his mouth without too much distraction.

"If they discovered Burke had been murdered and the first suspects investigated were Mrs. Parker and Maryann, how would you feel?"

Richard shot a look at Sam and swerved, but quickly corrected his error. "I'd feel terrible. I've been there. It's not fun. What makes you think Burke might have been murdered? Does Hawkman know something?"

Sam shook his head. "It just crossed my mind as a possibility. Sort of gives me the willies."

"Yeah, me too."

Sam changed the subject to the latest mountain lion attack in the area. A sheep rancher had lost several of his prize ewes before he finally bagged the big cat with the help of animal control.

The boys arrived in Yreka and stopped by a garden

shop where they rented a rototiller. They reached the Parker residence shortly before nine and immediately worked on the lawn, taking advantage of the morning cool air.

Even though they'd watered the ground and left instructions for Maryann to change the sprinklers often, they still found it very hard. But fortunately, due to the smallness of the yard, it didn't take long to turn over the chunks of soil.

They'd just stopped for a cool drink and wiped the sweat from their brow when Sam noticed a white car slow to a stop in front of the house. A uniformed police officer stepped from the passenger side as Detective Williams came around the front of the vehicle. Sam shot a glance at Richard, whose gaze was already glued to the two men strolling up the sidewalk.

Sam grabbed his tee shirt off the ice chest and quickly slipped it over his head, then stepped onto the narrow walkway. "Hi, Detective Williams."

The detective stopped, smiled and put out his hand. "Sam Casey, my Lord, it's been a couple of years since I've seen you. You look great. How's school?"

"Real good." Sam turned and motioned for Richard. "You remember Richard Clifford."

"I sure do." They shook hands. "So what are you guys doing here? Looks like you've been hired to do some rather heavy work."

"We're volunteering to help Mrs. Parker out."

"That's mighty kind of you," Williams said and glanced toward the door. "Is she home?"

Sam shrugged. "I don't know. Haven't seen her or Maryann this morning." He pointed toward the station wagon in the driveway. "Her car's here. So, she must be inside." He frowned. "Is there a problem?"

"Just some loose ends we need to tie up. Good seeing you two." With that, the detective gave a wave, and the two men scurried up the porch steps.

Sam noticed the frightened look that crossed Lilly's face when she opened the door.

"Yes, what can I do for you?" she asked, a slight quiver in her voice.

"Mrs. Parker, we'd like to talk to you and your daughter. May we come in."

She stepped back to let them inside and closed the door.

Richard touched Sam's arm. "What'd he say to her? She looked scared."

"He just said they needed to talk to her and Maryann."

"She's got something to hide. I could tell by her eyes," Richard said, staring at the house.

CHAPTER THIRTEEN

The next morning, Lilly awoke to a loud noise in her front yard.
She peeked out the window and spotted the two young men
taking turns wrestling a rototiller. She didn't dare complain, but
she sure could have slept another hour. Sighing, she padded into
the bathroom and examined her puffy eyes in the mirror. "Oh,
my," she mumbled. "I look awful."

She splashed cold water on her face, then patted her skin
dry with a soft towel. Going to her closet, she selected a loose
fitting house dress since she planned to stay home until work
time. She shoved back the shoe box that rested on the ledge
above her clothes. That shelf must not be level, she thought.
Seems like the box inches itself forward every few days.

Closing the closet, she left the room and moved softly
past Maryann's door. She went into the kitchen and put on
the coffee pot. Not feeling very hungry, she decided on a bowl
of dry cereal. No sooner had she finished her breakfast and
poured herself another cup of coffee, when someone knocked
on the front door.

Thinking it must be one of the boys, it jolted her to come
face to face with two men, one in a police uniform and the other
flashing a badge.

"Yes?" she asked.

"Hello, Mrs. Parker. I'm Detective Williams of the
Medford Police Department. This is Officer McDonnell. May
we come in? We'd like to speak to you about the death of your
husband."

Lilly felt her stomach tighten as she ushered the men into

the living room and offered them a seat on the couch. "Can I get you a cup of coffee?"

"No, thanks. We're fine."

She sat on the edge of the overstuffed chair, her back straight and hands clenched on her lap. "What can I do for you gentlemen?"

Detective Williams straightened his tie. "Is your daughter here? It would be best if she were present."

"Yes, I'm here."

He jerked his head around and eyed the young woman. "Good."

Maryann crossed the room and sat down on the arm of the chair next to her mother.

The detective cleared his throat. "It's never easy to be the bearer of bad news."

"I already know my husband is dead, Mr. Williams. What worse news could there be."

Unfortunately, we suspect your husband didn't die of natural causes."

Lilly put a hand to her throat. "You mean murdered?"

Williams raised a hand. "No, I'm not saying that. It could have been accidental. But we need some personal information about him. Did he have health problems? Was he on medication?"

Maryann stared at him with a piercing gaze. "Why don't you go to his doctor and find out those things?"

"I intend to do just that. But I need to verify the name of the doctor on the prescriptions we found in the room. Was Dr. Clevenger his regular doctor?"

Lilly nodded. "Yes."

"Mrs. Parker, did your husband consume a lot of alcohol?"

Maryann's eyes narrowed. "If you mean, was he an alcoholic? Yes. And an abusive one at that."

Lilly grabbed her daughter's hand. "He probably drank more than he should? Why?"

"Some of the tests have come back showing a high percent of alcohol in his blood. Which could have reacted with the medications." Williams stood. "I will probably have to ask you more questions as we get deeper into the investigation. Please don't leave town."

"Why would I leave? I live here."

He nodded. "Don't get up. We'll show ourselves out. Thanks for your cooperation."

When Lilly heard the door close, she rose from the chair and crossed to the window. Hugging her waist, she peered through the sheer curtains as the two men got into the unmarked car. She noticed Sam's and Richard's heads turn toward the house as soon as the vehicle drove away. Her hands dropped to her side and she glanced at Maryann. "I don't like this. It's just the beginning."

Maryann put an arm around her mother's shoulders. "Maduk will be safe. He knows how to hide."

She nodded. "I wonder what they found that makes them so suspicious? It certainly wouldn't surprise me if Burke died because he mixed his medications with booze."

Maryann moved away from her mother, and headed toward the kitchen. "I need a cup of coffee."

Lilly followed her daughter and poured her cold coffee down the drain and replaced it with the hot brew.

Maryann sat down at the table. "I gathered from the way the detective talked, they don't have all the test results."

She sighed. "Well, once they talk to the doctor, they'll know Burke trod on dangerous ground with all his drinking."

"Do you think the doctor realized how much Burke drank?"

Lilly threw up her hands. "I don't know. But I might as well prepare myself for a lot of questions."

"Me, too," Maryann said, taking a sip of coffee.

"You weren't even here, so the police probably won't bother you."

"Mom, you've forgotten. If Burke had been dead for a few days before they found him, I could very well be a suspect. Remember, I was home over the Memorial weekend. In fact,

I spent most of the day with Richard." She pointed toward the yard. "The deaf boy helping Sam."

Lilly felt the blood drain from her cheeks as she stared at her daughter.

CHAPTER FOURTEEN

Richard broke up the clumps of dirt caused by the rototiller, then raked the ground smooth so they could sow the grass seeds. Sam had taken his truck to return the machine. While in town, he planned to check a couple of the garden centers and inquire if they had any leftover patches of sod from previous landscaping jobs which they might be willing to donate.

Sam had suggested the authorities suspected Mr. Parker hadn't died of natural causes. Richard's gaze drifted to the front door. This worried him, because he knew Maryann and her mother would be questioned extensively, especially if the rumors of Burke's abuse were true.

He wondered if the detective knew anything about Mrs. Parker's boyfriend, in his mind, a prime suspect with a motive. And being a Native American, the man might well know how to mix up a toxic potion from plants. Richard shook his head. Maryann and Mrs. Parker also had a reason to kill the late Mr. Parker.

His thoughts were interrupted when Maryann hurried out the front door, ran down the steps and headed straight toward him. He stepped over some dirt chunks to the narrow sidewalk.

She folded her arms at her waist and smiled. "Hi, how's it going?"

"Real good. We should finish the lawn today. Then we'll start painting tomorrow."

"That's great." She glanced around the yard. "Where's Sam?"

"He'll be back shortly."

She looked down at her feet, then up at him. "Uh, Richard, I'd like to ask a favor."

"Sure, if I can."

"Don't tell the cops I was here over the Memorial Day weekend."

Richard felt a stab of shock at her request. "Why?"

"It's just important they don't know."

"But there were other people who saw you."

"That's true, but I doubt the police will track them down."

Richard frowned. "I won't lie, Maryann. If they ask me, I'll tell them, but I won't volunteer the information. I don't see why it should matter if you've nothing to hide."

She dropped her hands to her side. "Of course, I don't expect you to understand, and your response is fair." Turning on her heel, she hastened back into the house.

Richard always thought he could read faces pretty well, especially eyes, but Maryann concealed her feelings extremely well. Her orbs were like two big black obsidian stones set in a beautiful face, but they reflected no emotion. Deep in his gut, he felt an ominous squirm. He now realized Sam had tried to warn him against establishing a relationship with Maryann, without telling him point blank to stay away from her.

Maryann dashed back into the house and went straight to her room. She flopped down on the bed and stared at the ceiling. Her mind told her she'd just made a big mistake. Thinking Richard had fallen for her, she believed he'd do anything she asked. What a surprise to find his ethics outweighed his feelings. Now she'd raised his suspicions and more than likely he'd tell Sam. She'd made too many blunders in the past week. When Sam offered to fix up the house for her mother, she translated it as his wanting to get closer. But he hadn't made one advance toward her since he'd been coming to the house. In fact, he avoided her as much as possible. Even if she caught him looking at her, his gaze held mistrust. What had she done to make him dislike her so? She hit her fists on the bed. "Dammit," she muttered, "I've got to change his opinion. I don't want his pity."

The aroma of food wafted under her nose. She jumped off the bed and traipsed into the kitchen. "Mom, what the heck are you doing? Looks like you're cooking enough for an army."

Lilly had cut up two chickens and proceeded to drop the flour coated pieces into the large hot iron skillet on the stove. Potatoes were boiling and salad makings were strewn across the cabinet.

"I've got to keep busy, Maryann. I can't just sit around and think about Burke's death. I decided those boys have been working very hard on our place and I'm sure they have big appetites. The least I can do is make them a good meal. And I don't know of any young man who doesn't like fried chicken."

"That's good of you, Mom. I hope you've told them so they don't go get sandwiches for their lunch."

She put a floured hand up to her forehead, causing a white smudge. "Oh, dear, I hadn't thought that far ahead. Will you go tell them?"

Maryann let out a sigh. "Sure."

When she went outside, Sam had returned and the two were unloading what looked like rolls of grass. "What the heck are you doing?" she asked walking toward them.

"I really lucked out," Sam said, huffing, as he carried a large bundle to the edge of the yard and dropped it onto the ground. "Some guy had just finished putting in a sod lawn and had all these left over pieces. When I told him what we were doing, he just loaded them right into my truck without ever taking them inside the garden center. I'm sure we have enough to cover the whole front yard."

Maryann peered into the bed and pointed to a dozen paint cans stacked against the cab. "That says interior paint. You're not going to use that for the outside, are you?"

"No, I already have those under the porch. The paint shop next door to the garden center was going to dispose of that line of colors to make room for a new batch and the owner asked if

I wanted them. Naturally, I accepted. So, if your mom wants us to paint the inside, we can do that too."

Maryann noticed Richard attentiveness, even though he continued to unload the large rolls. She imagined he'd grasped the gist of the conversation.

"Oh, Mom sent me out here to tell you she's making fried chicken for you guys and it will be ready in about an hour. She wants to do something to show her appreciation for all you're doing."

Sam's eyes lit up. "Richard, did you catch that?"

"Yeah," he said grinning. "Makes me hungry just thinking about it."

"Good. I'll leave you alone so you can continue. I'll let you know when the food is ready."

"Tell your mom, thanks," Richard said.

Richard wanted to inform Sam about Maryann's request to keep quiet about being together over the Memorial Day weekend, but realized his monotone voice carried a great distance and he didn't want to risk Maryann overhearing. He decided to wait until they headed home.

They wet down the soil and Sam filled the rented roller with water. It weighed about eight pounds to the gallon, making it one heavy piece of equipment. They took turns running it over the moistened ground, then worked hard laying the sod. They had about half of it down, when Maryann called from the front door.

"Food's on."

Sam patted Richard's shoulder and motioned toward the house. "Time to eat."

The boys removed their heavy work gloves, brushed off their clothes and stomped on the cement sidewalk to knock off as much dirt as possible from the soles of their boots. Then they washed their hands under the hose and slipped on their tee shirts before heading for the house. When they entered the living room, they both sniffed the air.

"Oh, man, does that smell delicious," Sam said.

Lilly smiled and motioned toward the table set for four.

"Sit down. I'll join you as soon as I get the dinner rolls from the oven."

"Wow, this looks like a feast," Richard said. "We won't want to work after eating this, we'll need to take time out for a siesta."

Maryann laughed as she pulled out a chair and sat down. "I think you're right. I'll definitely be stuffed for the rest of the day."

"They filled their plates and ate in silence for several minutes, until Sam broke the quietness. "Mrs. Parker, this is excellent. Thank you so much."

Richard nodded. "It's delicious."

Lilly patted her mouth with a napkin. "Thank you, boys. I'm glad you're enjoying it."

Sam raised his hand. "Oh, Mrs. Parker, before I forget. The paint shop next to the garden center donated some interior paint and there's plenty for several rooms. If you'd like, we can also paint the inside."

She smiled. "Oh, my, that would be nice. But you boys are using up your vacation on my house."

"We don't mind. In fact, we're both glad to help."

Lilly stared at her plate for a few moments. "I guess you noticed the police were here this morning and you're probably wondering what's happening."

Maryann dropped her fork and glanced at her mother. "Mom, I doubt the guys are interested in our private life."

Lilly raised her head and fixed her gaze on Sam. "Your dad is a private investigator and has close contact with Detective Williams. I'm sure he knows there's a question about whether Burke died of natural causes."

"Uh, I'm not sure what he knows," Sam stuttered. "He doesn't confide in me about such things."

She smiled. "Well, I just want you to be prepared while you're here, and see police officers around the house. It's nothing to worry about. They only want information about Burke."

Maryann studied both boys, but couldn't make out what

they thought about her mother's outburst. However, they appeared very uncomfortable and hurried through their meal. They soon excused themselves and went back to the yard work.

Maryann rose from the table, picked up a couple of the plates, then sat them back down and put a hand on her hip. "Mom, why did you bring up the police?"

Lilly shrugged. "Might as well be upfront, so they don't think we're hiding anything. They recognized the detective and officer. And let me tell you." She pointed a finger at her daughter. "That young Sam knows more than he's letting on."

Maryann frowned. "What makes you think that?"

"Didn't you see his expression? Even his face flushed. I have a suspicion he knows about Maduk. Have you ever told him about your father?"

"Yes."

Lilly glared at her. "That's too bad. We may be in for more trouble than I expected."

CHAPTER FIFTEEN

Sam and Richard finished laying the sod and instructed Maryann to keep the ground damp for a few days so it'd take root. The boys drained the roller then dropped it off at the garden center. Both felt they'd had a good workout for the day.

As they drove toward home, Richard told Sam about Maryann asking him not to mention their being together over the Memorial Day weekend.

Sam frowned. "What the heck? Seems mighty weird. She got something to hide?"

"My thoughts exactly."

"Did she give you any type of explanation?"

"No, just said she didn't expect me to understand."

"What'd you tell her?"

"I wouldn't lie."

Sam punched his friend on the shoulder. "Good for you. I'll bet it has something to do with Burke's death." He put a finger in the air. "And you know, I thought it odd her mom mentioned Detective Williams came by just wanting information and for us not to be concerned."

"Yeah, me, too. Why did she think she had to say such a thing?"

Sam raised his hands and dropped them on his thighs. "This whole Burke thing looks mighty suspicious."

Richard nodded. "It's pretty unnerving to be at their house when all this is going down."

Sam glanced at his friend. "Hey, Richard, you don't have to help. I sucked you into this deal, so you're not obligated in any way."

"Hey, buddy, don't take me wrong." A sly grin curled the edges of his mouth. "In fact, I find it rather exciting to be involved in a murder investigation and not be the suspect."

❧

Jennifer noticed when Sam arrived home, he seemed unusually quiet. The only thing he asked was when Hawkman might be home. He didn't even seem interested in dinner. After showering, he walked out on the deck and meandered down to the dock where he stood staring out across the water. She watched from the window, wondering if his pensiveness had something to do with Maryann and the death of Burke.

When Hawkman's vehicle came in sight and rolled across the bridge, Sam hastened up the gangplank toward the house. Jennifer's curiosity piqued and she hoped he'd voice his concerns in front of her and not make it some man-to-man thing.

The minute Hawkman entered the door, Sam hit him with a barrage of questions.

"Did you know Detective Williams and a police officer came by the Parkers' today? Have you heard any more about the cause of Burke's death? The garden center gave me a bunch of sod and the paint store donated a dozen cans of interior paint. So it looks like we'll be painting the inside of the house. too."

Hawkman raised his hand. "Hold it, hold it. One thing at a time, please." He gave Jennifer a peck on the cheek. "Did he hit you with all this when he got home?"

She smiled. "No, he waited for you."

Hawkman hung up his jacket, removed his hat and adjusted his eye-patch. "Think I'll get a beer, then we can sit down and talk."

Sam paced the living room, his hands clasped behind his back. Then he gazed out the picture window until Hawkman strolled in and sat down on the hearth.

"Now, what's this about Williams coming to the Parker's?"

Sam sat down on the couch facing his dad and told him about the day's events. "When Mrs. Parker fixed that big fried chicken meal and told us not to be concerned about the police hanging around, it really set off an alarm in my brain. Why would she say that? It just makes them look guilty. Maryann even tried to avoid it by telling her mom we weren't interested in their private life. It sort of put Richard and me in a spot, especially when she said I probably knew a lot about Burke's death because my dad was a private investigator."

Hawkman raised a brow. "I wonder if she thinks I'm on the case? Did she mention what the detective wanted?"

"No, she never alluded to what they talked about. And it beats me what she meant by the crack about you, but it sure made me uncomfortable. Like she thought we were spying on her. Then coming home, Richard really blew me away when he told me what Maryann asked him to do."

Hawkman set his beer bottle on the brick beside him and leaned forward, resting his forearms on his knees. "I'm all ears."

After Sam related the conversation between Richard and Maryann, Hawkman frowned. "I don't like the idea of her asking him to lie. Why would she care if anyone saw her in town that weekend?" He took a swig of beer. "Unless. . ."

Sam scooted forward. "Unless what?"

Hawkman strolled into the kitchen where he took the hanging calendar off the wall. He brought it into the living room and pointed at the dates. "The police discovered Burke's body in the motel on this day." He tapped the Wednesday square after the Memorial Day weekend. The coroner's report estimated he'd been dead at least three or more days judging by the condition of the body." He then moved his finger over the previous weekend. "It means he died sometime over this holiday."

Jennifer had been listening as she leaned against the back of the couch. "Do you think Maryann had anything to do with Burke's death?"

Sam dropped his head into his hands. "Man, I don't know. She's a weird one, but I never thought her capable of murder." Then he snapped his fingers. "Maybe she's trying to protect someone else."

"Who?" Jennifer asked.

"Maybe her real dad, Maduk. He definitely had a motive. And he'd probably know how to make poisons."

Hawkman raised his hand. "Hold on, you two. Let's not get carried away. Just because the coroner's report stated Burke's death wasn't due to natural causes, doesn't mean murder. He could have died of an overdose of a drug or his own medications mixed with alcohol could prove fatal. We do know his mouth and stomach showed signs of something caustic and unusual in the body. But it hasn't been identified yet."

"You're right," Jennifer said. "But it's still strange Maryann suggested Richard not mention she'd visited the area over the long weekend."

"Yes, it's very intriguing." Hawkman drained the last of his beer and turned to Sam. "By the way, have you seen Maryann's real father around since you've been working there?"

"Richard and I spotted a guy driving by the house several times in a luxury black Buick on the first day we were there. Neither of us got a good look at the driver. But we compared notes and came to the conclusion, he resembled a Native American. It might have been him." Sam shrugged. "Or someone looking for an address."

"But he never stopped and asked directions?"

"No."

"Did you say her father's name was Maduk?" Hawkman asked.

"That's what Maryann calls him. His real name is Madukarahat, or something like that. She said it means 'giant'."

"Has she seen him lately?"

Sam shook his head. "Not that I know of, buy she gave the impression months elapse between their visits. However, I got the feeling her mother sees him often."

"What gave you such an impression?"

"I don't know." Sam shrugged. "Just a feeling from the way Maryann talked."

Jennifer came around the couch and sat down. "It's odd we don't hear much about the affair between Lilly and Maduk.

Probably because many people didn't really blame her. Everyone knew about Burke's alcoholism. And rumor has it, he abused her terribly. I've never heard anyone say they'd seen Lilly with another man, nor ever heard the name Maduk or Madukarahat associated with her. However, the grapevine gossip always referred to her lover as a Native American."

Sam glanced at her. "Well, if there's a murder investigation, they'll have to find him."

CHAPTER SIXTEEN

Sam received a text message on his cell phone from Richard inviting him over to play a new game he'd just uploaded on the computer. He decided to ride his motorcycle and took off shortly after dinner. Soon after Sam left, Hawkman slipped on his shoulder holster and plopped on his leather cowboy hat.

Jennifer eyed him and put a hand on her hip. "It looks like my men are all deserting me. You're obviously going into town to see what you can find out about Burke Parker. Which will probably involve bar hopping."

Hawkman grinned. "When you read my mind, it scares me."

"It's not hard to figure, since the man's name monopolized the whole evening's conversation."

"Hope you don't mind being alone for awhile. I probably won't be real late. The bars close early on Sunday."

"Not really, it'll give me a chance to catch up on my writing. I've fallen way behind since Sam's been home."

He gave her a peck on the cheek and a pat on the bottom. "I'll see you later tonight."

She grinned and gave him a wink. "Don't get any clever ideas of waking me up at two in the morning."

He poked his thumb into his chest. "Who, me?"

Hawkman left the house with a smile on his face. How he loved that woman. He felt sorry for those who didn't have a good wife and stable home. Burke Parker came to mind. If the rumors were true, sounded as if the fellow liked his booze more than his woman.

Next week, he'd stop by Curly's in Medford and ask if he'd

ever heard of Parker. But tonight, since the bars closed early, he'd check around Yreka. He could pretty much count on the old timers frequenting their hangouts nightly.

Most of the night clubs or bars in the small town were located on Main Street. And he remembered chatting with an old fellow named Harley sometime back when he needed information. Long ago, the old guy had hung out with a bunch of motorcycle riders and acquired the nickname Harley only after he'd relinquished his motorcycle for a bicycle in his later years. He lived in a shack on the outskirts of town and had no family as far as Hawkman knew.

He pulled into the parking lot of the bar called The Ranger where he'd found Harley before. Locking his vehicle, he scrutinized the area and adjusted his jacket so his gun stayed concealed. When he entered the bar, he hesitated for a moment inside the door for his sight to adjust to the dim lighting. Music blared from the overhead speakers as he glanced around the room. He noted the bar stools were full, but didn't recognize any of the customers, so he meandered back to the booth area, looking for Harley.

He felt eyes upon him and turned. The bartender stood with his fists on his hips, a big grin on his face. "Hawkman, you son-of-a-gun, where've you been keeping yourself?"

Hawkman stepped up to the counter and held out his hand. "I'll be damned, Skillsaw, the last time we met, you were fighting fires in the Siskiyou County forest."

"Yeah, I'll never forget those days. You were on a case hunting down some missing young girl and we found her body buried up there in the hills while cutting a fire line. It was one of the most gruesome things I'd ever seen. I still have nightmares."

"So have you given up fire fighting?"

Skillsaw nodded and let out a sigh. "Had to. Several of us got cornered in a fire storm. Big burning tree limb fell on me and I lost a foot. I'm lucky. I got out alive. Two of our boys didn't make it."

Hawkman frowned. "Sorry to hear that."

Skillsaw shrugged. "All part of the job. You know the risk when you go in. Now tell me, what can I get you to drink."

"I really stopped by to see if I could find Harley. Is he still kickin'?"

He laughed. "Oh yeah. We're usually on his schedule for Friday night. Try up the street at the Dude or Larry's.

Hawkman touched his hat. "Thanks. I'll stop back in when I have more time. Good seeing ya."

He then drove to the Dude, scouted the interior, but didn't find Harley. The bartender told him the old fellow visited them on Saturday night. Hawkman figured he should keep notes about Harley's rounds in case he needed him again. Larry's bar was located on the next street, so Hawkman hiked over, leaving his SUV parked at the Dude.

A smaller pub than the other two, Hawkman immediately spotted Harley's big round floppy hat in a booth at the far corner. It appeared he and a buddy were engrossed in a game of checkers.

Hawkman ordered three beers and carried them to the table. "Hello there, Harley. Are you whipping your buddy's butt."

A cigarette hanging out of the corner of his mouth, Harley grinned, exposing several empty spaces between his teeth. The ashes fell to his lap when he let out a big whoop and jumped three of his friend's checkers. "Yep. old Frank here, now owes me three beers."

The man shook his head and got up. "Can't take any more, Harley. You're too good."

Hawkman handed Frank one of the beers. "Here's for trying."

"Why thanks, partner." He picked up the walking stick resting against the table and limped away.

"Who's your friend?" Hawkman asked, sliding into the booth. "Don't think I've ever seen him before."

"That's Frank Smith, or so he calls himself. He wandered into the area about a year ago. Says he lost his whole family in a fire."

"Sounds like a pretty sad story. Where's he from?"

"Don't rightly know or where he's staying, but he seems okay. He don't cause no trouble."

"Appears to be nice enough." Hawkman grinned. "Even though he didn't do well on the checker game."

Harley rubbed his chin and studied Hawkman. "I never forget a face. Especially a pirate with an eye patch. I know you, don't I?"

Hawkman scooted a beer in front of Harley. "Yep. About two years ago you helped me break a case."

"The old fellow's bleary blue eyes lit up like sparklers. "Oh, yeah, now I remember. They called you a bird's name." He scratched his sideburn. "But damned if I can remember which one."

"They call me Hawkman."

Harley pointed a bony finger at him. "That's right. You're a private investigator."

Hawkman chuckled. "You're correct."

The old fellow frowned, and the wrinkles around his eyes made deep crevices across his temples. "How'd I help ya?"

"Well, you gave me some great information on a missing person. Without your help, we might never have found the young girl alive."

Harley snapped his fingers. "Got it! That was the guy I spotted putting a little pretty thing into a van. I thought it odd how she didn't want to go, but he forced her inside. I memorized his license plate. But never thought much more about it as kids can do the dangest things. Then you came into The Ranger one night asking questions."

"Yeah, that's exactly right, Harley. You have a good memory."

"I hope they put that son-of-a-bitch away for a long time. I've hurt people in my day, but never a child. They were always my soft spot. I love seeing kids playing and having a good time. Brings back wonderful memories when I was a young whipper snapper." His crooked grin perked up his face as he lit another cigarette. "Now, you must need some more information or why would you be searching for an old fossil like me."

Hawkman smiled. "You're right. No sense in beating around the bush. Did you know a man named Burke Parker?"

Harley nodded. "They found him dead in a motel room, didn't they?"

"Yes. Did you know him well?"

"Naw, a blowhard of a fellow. No one liked him. Couldn't play a decent game of checkers either."

"What do you mean, a blowhard?"

Harley threw a hand in the air. "Didn't hold his liquor well and he had a loose tongue. He blathered on about his wife having an affair with an Indian for years and that she'd given birth to an Indian squaw. People got sick and tired of hearing it. Many wondered why his wife didn't leave him."

"Do you think she knew about his ravings?"

Harley blew out a puff of smoke and gray circles floated across the table. "No doubt. After all those years, she's bound to have noticed her women friends whispering behind her back in the grocery or drug stores. Gossip travels in a small town."

"Do you think people believed the rumors?" Hawkman asked.

"More'n likely, because I saw Parker's daughter a couple of times. A black haired, brown eyed beauty. No way did she belong to him."

Hawkman leaned back in the booth and took a swig of beer. "Wonder why Lilly never left him?"

"Scared and money."

"Scared?" Hawkman asked.

Harley raised his bony hand. "Leaving the bar at night, Parker bragged about how when he got home, he'd have a piece of tail whether she wanted it or not. We also got the idea he beat her. A couple of people seen Lilly with bruises on her face. Then to make matters really bad, when the girl got old enough, he boasted about having his own young squaw. A damned son-of-a-bitch if you ask me." He leaned forward. "But there's a catch."

"What's that?"

He closed one eye and pointed a crooked finger at Hawkman. "No one ever saw Lilly with any man except Burke. Now, you'd think if some affair went on for all those years, someone would have caught her and the lover together. Now wouldn't ya?"

Hawkman nodded. "Yes, you'd think so."

"Well, it didn't happen. There ain't a soul in this town who can swear on a Bible and state they know her lover."

"That's interesting. But there's a man who might help me on that subject, if I can find him."

Harley raised a brow. "Yeah, who's that?"

"Madukarahat"

The old fellow stiffened. His eyes registered fear as he took the cigarette from his mouth and crushed it in the ashtray. "He's one dangerous man to be questioning."

CHAPTER SEVENTEEN

Hawkman shifted his position and stared at Harley. "You're serious, aren't you?"

"You damn right." Harley took a big gulp of beer, then wiped his mouth with the back of his hand. "He carries a long blade, sharp as a razor, and believe me, he knows how to use it. He fights like an old-time warrior, knows the tricks and uses them. He's a big man and his name really comes from the Karok tribe meaning 'giant', but he claims he's from the Shastas, even though they've banned him from the reservation."

Hawkman raised his brows. "Really?"

"Yeah, he killed one of his own people with that knife. The tribal counsel agreed he fought in self-defense, but didn't want him living amongst their people." Harley shrugged. "Guess they figured if he did it once, he might do it again."

"Seems odd they'd ban him for self-defense. Sounds like there's more to the story than just a fight."

"Can't say. The white man is only privy to so much information."

"I still don't get why you call the man dangerous, if that's the only black mark on his record."

The old fellow sighed. "I ain't told ya everything." He pushed up the sleeve on his right arm. A thin even scar extended from his shoulder to his elbow.

Hawkman leaned forward and studied the wound. "He cut you?"

"Yep, but can't say I didn't deserve it. I'm lucky he didn't kill me."

"You want to tell me about it?"

"Hell, might as well. It happened several years ago when I still rode a big bike. Me and a couple of my buddies were haulin' ass up in the hills. We'd bought some white lightening from an old man who brewed the stuff and were feelin' our oats. We came upon this campsite and thought we'd have a little fun. This huge Indian fellow stepped out of his tent. He held a knife in his hand and the blade sparkled like a cat's eyes at night. An awesome sight when you think about it."

"So what happened?"

Harley rubbed his chin,and pulled a smoke from his pocket. He flicked a wooden match against his fingernail and lit the cigarette, then shook out the flame. "We were a bunch of smart asses then and weren't afraid of nothin'. So one of the fellows headed for the guy's tent on his motorcycle, but he didn't make it. That Indian grabbed the handle bars and threw ole Johnson off his bike. Then he slit the tires and tossed it aside like a toy.

Full of booze and feeling no pain, but lots of macho, I decided to git rid of the food he had cookin'. Just as I came upon his campfire, I saw the gleam of the knife when he swung it up like lightening speed. I felt a great big sting on my right side and looked down at my arm. It scared the hell out of me when I saw my blood runnin'. Needless to say, I headed for town." He chuckled. "I had a hell of a time explaining to the doctors that I'd fallen on my bike. They questioned how such a nice even slice down my arm came from glass on the road."

"What happened to your other friend?"

"He didn't like what he saw and high tailed it out of there."

"So you think Madukarahat is dangerous because he protected his belongings?"

Harley shook his head. "No, that just taught me to stay out of his way. Don't get me wrong, he knows how to use his fists too. He used to come into town to do handy work for people and would occasionally drop by one of the bars. Usually the bully of the night tried to take him on. Never worked. He'd beat the pulp out of him. The men soon learned to stay clear of the big man."

"Has he been around lately?"

"Nope. Haven't seen him in several months. Rumor says he's gone to work for one of the Indian casinos."

Hawkman slapped the table with his hand and stood. "Thanks, Harley. Appreciate the information. Another beer's on the way."

"Sounds good to me. Sure you don't have time for a game of checkers."

"Not tonight. Besides, I don't want to break your winning streak."

Harley guffawed. "Yeah, all good hens cackle when they lay an egg. Good to see ya again."

Hawkman left the bar after sending a couple of brews Harley's way. He strolled down the block toward his 4X4, thinking about the information he'd acquired. The stuff about Parker pretty much coincided with Maryann's story to Sam.

The information about Madukarahat came as a surprise. The man appeared to be a loner and possibly dangerous. He'd check with Williams tomorrow and see if the Indian had a record or if any charges had ever been filed against him. If this man turned out to be Maryann's real father, he could very well be under suspicion, if Parker was murdered.

Hawkman climbed into his vehicle and debated about running up to the Three C's casino, but decided against it as there'd be a skeleton crew working and he'd rather talk to the head guy. He'd save the trip for later, after he talked with Detective Williams. The Burke Parker case hadn't officially been declared a murder, but according to the latest test results, something appeared amiss. Whether Parker overdosed on his own medication in his drunken state or someone administered a second drug remained to be seen. He hoped Williams had talked with Parker's doctor. That might shed a little light on the subject.

❦

When Sam arrived at the Clifford's place, Uncle Joe greeted him at the door.

"Richard's in his room. Figured you guys might be hungry after all that hard labor, so I'm fixing some sandwiches and will bring them in a few minutes."

Sam smiled and even though he'd eaten, he wouldn't think of turning down the hospitality. "Thanks, Mr. Clifford."

The two young men settled in front of the computer, but before they could read the instructions to the new game, Uncle Joe brought in a tray heaped with food and a couple of sodas.

Soon, they were laughing and enjoying an exciting game of pitting their skills against each other in a full fledged space battle. After two solid hours of concentration, they both flopped back in exhaustion.

"I think I worked harder at that game than I did on the Parker's yard," Sam said, pretending to wipe his brow. "I had to think about it. Shoveling dirt and pounding nails doesn't take much thought."

Richard laughed. "You're right, this game is quite a challenge." He left the room and returned with two more cans of soda. He sat down on the chair facing his friend, his expression somber. "I've been thinking about Maryann."

Sam felt his stomach squeeze. "Yeah."

"I don't trust her. I've thought about all the things you've said. You were right and I want to thank you for not telling me I'd be an idiot to fall for the girl. You made me see it for myself."

Sam breathed a sigh of relief. He reached over and cuffed Richard's knee. "Good. I'm glad you saw through her. She uses people, then drops them like a hot potato."

"When she wanted me to lie, I immediately knew she didn't respect me."

"I'm glad you came to your senses before you got hurt."

Richard rested his arms on his thighs. "Do you think she had anything to do with Burke's death?"

Sam raked his fingers through his short blond hair. "Boy, that's a good question. Especially, now that we know Burke might have died over the Memorial Day weekend."

"I think she has the guts to pull it off," Richard said.

"What makes you think so?"

"Her eyes are like blank glass marbles and she shows no emotion in her face. Not even happiness. When she smiles, it's like she has to concentrate to make it happen." He waved a hand in the air. "You know, it's not spontaneous."

"You're right," Sam said. "It seems for her, contentedness takes effort. Of course, if what she told me about Parker's abuse toward her is true, I can see why she'd have trouble communicating with people."

Richard reached over and shut down the computer. "And it's a reason for her to kill him."

CHAPTER EIGHTEEN

Hawkman arrived home shortly after twelve thirty. When he pulled into the garage, he noticed Sam's bike, and felt relieved his son had gotten home safe and sound from Richard's, a feeling he hadn't experienced while the boy had been away at college. Seems when they're at school you don't worry about them. The human mind is a strange thing, he thought.

He slipped quietly down the hall and into his bedroom. When his gaze drifted to Jennifer's form under the sheet, his heart raced. The moonlight coming through the sliding glass door played across her body. She lay on her side with one tanned leg exposed on top of the sheet. Her long brown hair draped across the pillow like a fan and glistened in the pale light.

Dropping his clothes to the floor, he slid in beside her. When he scooted closer, he discovered she was naked. His hands roamed over her hips and up to her firm breast. She groaned and turned toward him, wrapping her arms around his neck.

"I told you not to wake me at two o'clock," she said, nuzzling her face under his chin.

"Oh, I didn't, it's only twelve thirty."

"Well, that's even worse, because I'm more dangerous now than ever." She nestled closer, running her hand over his back and down his buttocks.

"I'm going to remember that," he said, loving her every touch.

Not being able to control himself for much longer, he pulled her into his arms, kissing her passionately.

Hawkman awoke early the next morning and glanced over

at his beautiful wife. He smiled to himself as he gently tucked the sheet around her shoulders then slipped out of bed. That's some woman, he thought, grabbing his holster and eye-patch off the night stand, jeans off the chair, then quietly snatched a clean shirt out of the closet. Adjusting his eye-patch, he headed for Sam's bathroom, where he dressed.

Meandering into the kitchen, he put on the coffee pot and thought about what he wanted to discuss with Detective Williams before visiting the Indian casinos. If he had a picture of Madukarahat, it might make finding him easier. Some people in town knew what he looked like. At least that's the impression he got from Harley. And the old biker appeared scared to death of the big Indian. Interesting that no one connected Lilly with Maduk. Somehow those two people had kept their secret well. He definitely wanted to find out more about this Native American.

Maryann had told Sam more than most people knew and Hawkman wondered why she'd confided in his son. Possibly because she had a crush on him, and thought her story of woe might catch his interest. Or, because of Burke's death, she felt more free to tell her story. But according to Sam, she hadn't influenced him. He still didn't trust her.

This girl also piqued Hawkman's interest. Why would she want Richard to lie? Did she have something to hide? He'd look a little closer into her stories and background. But he might have to get Williams to help him out, since the schools were getting a bit finicky about releasing information on former students. He'd probably do just as well talking to some of her past instructors. They'd remember her, as rumors fly in the faculty's lounge. Sam could supply the names of her teachers.

Hawkman poured himself a cup of coffee and turned around to find Jennifer standing in front of him with a sly grin on her face. "Good morning, sexy woman." He took her into his arms and gave her a big kiss. "What are you doing up so early? I thought you'd like to sleep in this morning."

"It's no fun in an empty bed."

"Shall we go back?"

She laughed and playfully pushed him away. "No. I've got lots to do today. And getting an early start will help. By the way, why are you up?"

"I found out some interesting things last night and want to investigate further."

Her eyes grew big. "Tell me."

He chuckled. "Later."

"Oh, Hawkman. You tease me and then make me wait."

"You'll manage to pull it all out of me eventually. But right now, I want to catch Williams in his office. So just be patient."

"That's not one of my virtues."

"I know, but I love you anyway."

She shook her head and smiled. "You're such a stinker. You always have the right answer."

Hawkman downed his coffee, gave her a hug and left the house. When he reached the police station, he parked in the visitors slot and spotted Williams' unmarked car near the door. Good sign he's in his office, unless he'd left in a black and white.

The police station buzzed with activity. Even the part-time assistants were scurrying to and fro. Hawkman speculated the detective might not have time to see him if this indicated a sign of serious police business. When he entered William's office, he found the detective with his head bowed and signing a stack of papers.

"Pardon me, sir, do you have a minute?"

Williams glanced up and motioned him to come in. "Hey, glad to see you." He dropped his pen and flexed his hand. "It gives me time to let my fingers rest. I swear we get more paperwork every day. We can't even scold a man for littering without having to write up a report. It's crazy."

"Guess you have to protect your butts or you'd be sued more than you are now," Hawkman said, pulling a chair to the front of the desk.

"So what brings you here today? I'm sure it's not a social call. You could do that on the phone."

Hawkman nodded. "Any more reports come in on Burke Parker?"

"No. But I expect them this week. Why?"

"I'd like to know the names of the chemicals they find in Parker's body."

"Any special reason you're interested?"

"Yeah, but I'm not going to say just yet. What I'm really curious about is a Native American called Madukarahat, or Maduk for short. Wondered if he's ever been arrested?"

Williams scratched his head. "Name sounds familiar." He rose out of his chair and went to the filing cabinet. After thumbing through several files, he pulled out a slim folder and carried it to his desk. "Let's see if this is the same guy. Of course, I doubt there are many people with that name." He flipped it open, and fingered through the few sheets, then pulled out a photo. "Is this the man?"

Hawkman leaned forward and looked into a very strong and tough looking face. "I'm not sure. I've only heard about him. What's the file say?"

Williams scanned a couple of the sheets and then handed them to Hawkman. "I vaguely remember this incident. Several years ago, he killed a man on the reservation in self-defense. The police never got involved as their chiefs handled it. If I remember correctly, the tribal commune banned him from the reservation. But we've obviously had no problems with him, as there's nothing here except those few pages."

"Is there a chance I could get a copy of this picture?"

"Sure." Williams got up and went over to a copy machine in the corner.

"Say," Hawkman said, "you've come up in the world. When did they allow you that toy?"

The detective laughed. "They presented it to me just last week. Said they were sick and tired of me jamming up the one down in the main lobby."

He returned to his desk and handed the sheet of paper to Hawkman. "Now, tell me why all the interest in this guy. Does he have something to do with Parker?"

"I'd say in a round about way. He might be Maryann's father."

Williams' mouth dropped open. "You mean he's Ms. Parker's lover?" He flopped back in his chair and ran his fingers through his hair. "How the hell did you come to that conclusion in just a few days, when the whole town of Yreka has wondered for years."

Hawkman chuckled. "I'll never reveal my snitches."

The detective leaned forward with a solemn expression. "You know I visited Lilly and her daughter a couple of days ago?"

"Yes. I heard. Sam told me. What's your impression this time?"

"Normal. Anytime police come into your home, people get nervous. First time I'd seen her daughter and she acted a little catty, but hell, she's just protecting her mom. So I didn't think too much about it." He glanced at his calendar. "That reminds me. I have an appointment with Burke Parker's doctor this afternoon. You going to be around?"

"Yeah."

"Well, how about being my unofficial helper. Of course, I can't pay you."

Hawkman chuckled. "Have I ever been paid by this police force?"

Williams furrowed his brow and studied the ceiling. "Yeah, several years ago. I think we paid you to help on a case. Can't remember which one though. I'd have to look it up."

Hawkman grinned and waved a hand in the air. "Don't bother. What time do you go see the doctor?"

"At three thirty. Oh, by the way, when did you grow the mustache?"

"About time you noticed. I've had it for almost a year. You thought I'd gotten a hair cut."

The detective guffawed. "That was during the Jamey Schyler-Gray debacle."

"Yep." Hawkman rose. "Well, I won't keep you any longer. I'll see you at three thirty. Thanks for the picture."

"Let me know what you find out about that Indian. So far we haven't classified the Parker death as a homicide. But things could get sticky."

CHAPTER NINETEEN

Hawkman left the detective's office and climbed into the 4X4.
He sat for a minute holding his cell phone, then decided to give
Curly a call at home. If anyone knew about Maduk, he was the
man. And he could probably give him more information on
Burke Parker.

Curly picked up on the second ring.

"Hey, man. Have you quit screening your calls?"

He laughed. "Hawkman, haven't heard from you in a long
time. What are you up to?

"If you're not busy, thought I'd drop by."

"Never too busy for a buddy. You just get your butt right
over here and we'll have a great cup of java."

"Be there in a few minutes." Hanging up, he thought about
Curly's coffee. A brew so strong it'd grow hair on a bald man. He
chuckled to himself as he drove away from the police station.

Hawkman parked on the street in front of Curly's house,
and strolled up the narrow sidewalk to the small front porch.
Before he could ring the bell, Curly opened the door, greeting
him with a big grin and hearty handshake.

"So good to see you. Where've you been keeping
yourself?"

"Busy."

"Come on in and tell me about it."

Curly had lost his wife several years ago and now with his
son Mark out on his own, the man must be lonely. Hawkman
silently scolded himself for not stopping by the house or bar
more often. "So how's business?"

"Good, in fact, real good. Things have really boomed

lately. Don't know what's caused the big upswing, but I ain't complainin'."

"That's great, glad to hear it. Maybe it's because we've had a big influx of young people move into the area. Which is good news for everyone."

"Yep." Curly placed two mugs of steaming coffee on the table. "Now, I figure when you drop by the house at this hour, you need information. So, what can I do for you?" he asked, plopping down on a chair.

Hawkman laughed. "Boy, do you have me pegged."

Curly guffawed. "Known you long enough to have figured it out. So shoot and I'll see what I can tell ya."

"Couple of questions. Did you know Burke Parker?"

"He's the man they found dead in a motel room, right?"

"Yeah."

"Didn't know him personally, but I had him thrown out of the bar a few times."

Hawkman raised a brow. "Bad dude, huh?"

Curly pointed a finger at him. "One of the worst kind. Couldn't hold his liquor. One drink sent him off his rocker."

"In what way?"

"Spouted off about his personal life and people got sick of hearing it. When someone told him to shut-up, he'd jump all over them. There'd be a big fight and I'd have to throw out several guys or they'd wreck my place. I hated to see that man enter the door. A guy like that just ain't good for business."

"You say he talked about his personal life. In what way? Do you remember any particular event?"

"Yeah, several." Curly related similar stories that Harley had told.

Hawkman shook his head. "Wonder what he thought he'd prove by going on like that? It did nothing but hurt the family image."

Curly threw his hands in the air. "The man was a bum. I got the impression he didn't care a hoot about his wife or daughter."

Hawkman sipped his coffee and drummed his fingers on

the table. "Do you know anything about a Native American called Madukarahat?"

Curly reared back and shot him a look of surprise. "Whoa, you do jump from one type to another."

"Why do you say that?"

"He's one proud Indian. Walks straight and holds his head high. No one messes with him. Don't get me wrong. They used to try, but not any more."

"Does he frequent your place?"

"He's not a regular customer, if that's what you mean. He might drop in once a month and have a beer." Curly cocked his head and looked Hawkman in the eye. "Why are you interested in this man?"

"I'd like to talk to him. Do you have any idea where he lives?"

Curly shook his head. "Not an inkling. He was banned from the Shasta reservation years ago for a killing a man. So I know he's not there. I have no idea where you can find him. In fact, I haven't seen him in a couple of months. Not even sure he's still in the area."

"Do you know anything else about him?"

"Nothing. Very quiet man. He didn't socialize. Sat in the corner when he had his beer and left quietly. You hardly knew he was there."

Hawkman sighed and stood. "Thanks, Curly. Do me a favor. If he comes into your place some evening, give me a call immediately."

"I'll do that."

Hawkman left Curly's, then pulled off the side of the road and called Sam on his cell. He hoped the boy had charged his phone. "Hey, Sam. Are you at the Parker place or home?"

"Home. I'm going to scrounge up some drop cloths for painting. Probably go there tomorrow. Why?"

"Didn't want to talk to you if Maryann might be nearby. Need to ask you a few questions."

"Yeah?"

"Thought I'd do a little background study. What I need are

the names of some of Maryann's teachers in high school. Four or five will do."

"No problem, we were in several classes together." Sam rattled off several.

Hawkman jotted them down on the pad of paper he kept on the dashboard. "That should do it. Thanks. Oh, if you'll look out in the garage, there's a box in the far right corner with some old sheets and a couple of plastic tarps. You're more than welcome to use them."

"Thanks."

After hanging up, Hawkman drove to his office. He might find some of the names listed in the phone book. After checking through the directory, he realized most teachers were unlisted, probably not wanting to take the chance of being pestered or harassed by students. Summer school would be in full swing now, so he might find some of them there.

He checked his watch. Couldn't start the teacher search today, since he'd be meeting Detective Williams at the station in about an hour. It would be interesting to hear what the doctor has to say about Burke Parker's medical history. He just had enough time to grab a sandwich.

❧

Detective Williams and Hawkman entered Dr. Clevenger's waiting room a few minutes before the appointment. Williams spoke with the receptionist, and she glanced at a spiral notebook on her desk.

She looked up at him over her reading glasses and forced a smile. "The doctor will be with you shortly. Please have a seat."

Hawkman noticed everything in the office seemed in perfect order. They sat down on a comfortable couch upholstered in soft earth tones. The walls were painted in a pale green with a pleasing geometric design. Magazines were fanned neatly around a vase of freshly cut multicolored flowers on a small glass top coffee table in the center of the room. A healthy plant with large leaves stood tall and stately in the far corner.

Soon, an older fellow strolled down the hallway, shrugging

on a wind breaker and stopped at the receptionist desk. "He wants to see me again in two weeks."

She flipped the pages of her appointment book, filled out a card and handed it to him. "See you then." Waiting until the patient disappeared out the door, she stood and motioned toward Hawkman and Williams. "If you'll come with me, I'll take you back to Dr. Clevenger's office."

The two men followed her through the small hall passing several examination rooms. At the end, she tapped on a closed door.

"Come in."

"Dr. Clevenger, Detective Williams and his assistant are here to see you."

"Yes, I'm expecting the detective." Still wearing his doctor's smock, a thin man around fifty-five with graying hair and a somber expression rose from the chair and extended his hand. "Detective Williams."

"Hello, Dr. Clevenger, I'd like you to meet Private Investigator Tom Casey. He's working with me today."

"Nice meeting you, Mr. Casey." He waved a hand toward two chairs. "Won't you gentlemen please take a seat."

Dr. Clevenger pulled a file from his side drawer and placed it on his desk. His gaze settled on Detective Williams. "I can't surrender Burke Parker's file without a court order. But maybe I can answer some of your questions."

Williams nodded. "How long had you been seeing Parker?"

The doctor opened the folder and glanced at the first page. "Almost eight years."

"Did he have any major health issues?"

The doctor frowned. "Yes, an enlarged heart, high blood pressure, and showing initial signs of diabetes. Mr. Parker didn't follow my instructions and I could see dangerous problems developing in the very near future. In fact, his death may have come prematurely due to his failure in taking his medications regularly or following his diet."

Williams raised a brow. "Could he have overdosed?"

The doctor sighed. "Unfortunately, yes, it could have happened. Some people tend to think more is better, which can be fatal. Or sometimes they forget they've already taken it and take double doses, equally as dangerous."

"Did Parker have a drinking problem?"

The doctor furrowed his forehead. "I suspected he drank more than he claimed. His abnormal blood work indicated liver damage; his puffy face and slightly jaundiced color suggested cirrhosis. But when I questioned him about his alcohol intake, he swore he only had a glass or two of wine at night, which he'd read was good for his heart."

Hawkman raised a hand. "How did Parker pay his bill?"

"He had to quit his job and go on disability due to his heart, but the fees for his medical services were always paid."

"What medications did you prescribe?" Williams asked.

The doctor checked through the papers and named the heart and blood pressure medications. "I'd just started him on his diabetes medicine and hoped he'd help control it with his diet and exercise. But I should have known better."

Williams removed a paper from his pocket. "The medications you described were found in his room. The bottles have been sent to the lab for testing." The detective stood. "Thank you for your time, doctor. We appreciate it."

"Did you ever prescribe a tranquilizer?" Hawkman asked.

Clevenger ran a finger down a couple of the pages, then shook his head. "No." He glanced up. "Why?"

"Just curious. Are you by chance Burke Parker's wife's physician also?"

"No. I've never seen her."

CHAPTER TWENTY

"Why'd you ask about tranquilizers?" Williams asked, as they drove back to the station.

"Just curious," Hawkman said. "I've been doing a bit of research on medicines and alcohol. Booze reacts with a lot of them, especially therapeutic drugs. Mixing the two can be fatal. It's going to be interesting to see what they find in Parker's body."

The detective pulled into the station lot and parked alongside Hawkman's 4X4. "So you're suggesting, it could definitely show foul play if those types were found in his system."

Hawkman opened the passenger side door. "Not really. If he knew how to order over the internet, he could have purchased numerous medications rather easily." He leaned against the fender of his vehicle as Williams locked the car. "At least we know where Parker got his money." Hawkman raised a finger in the air. "By the way, does Clevenger have access to the coroner's report?"

Williams shoved the car keys into his pocket. "If a physician isn't notified at the time of death, he could request to see it. As far as I know, Dr. Clevenger hasn't asked. Of course, he realized an autopsy would be done, regardless of whether we suspected foul play or not. But I gathered all he knew, or cared about was what he read in the paper."

Hawkman nodded. "I got the same feeling."

"Most private doctors don't like involvement with the police. Not good for business."

Hawkman opened the driver's side door of his vehicle to let out the heat. "Keep me informed on the test results."

"Will do," the detective said, waving as he strolled toward the entry of the station.

❧

The next morning, Hawkman called the Yreka High School and discovered four of the six instructors Maryann had in high school were teaching during the summer session. He'd met each of them during Sam's high school years. If he managed to pull off a meeting, he'd have to be careful approaching Maryann's past, and avoid any reference to Burke Parker's death.

Since classes ended at noon during summer school, he arrived early and sent a note to each of the teachers, asking if they could meet in the lounge at twelve-thirty. He emphasized its importance, promised a short meeting of thirty minutes, and signed it Tom Casey, Private Investigator. The curiosity of meeting with a P.I. might draw them in.

At twelve-fifteen, Hawkman entered the teacher's lounge and rehearsed in his mind how he'd broach the subject. He poured himself a cup of coffee from the urn and waited.

Before long, Mr. Phillips, the math teacher, entered and held out his hand. "Hello, Mr. Casey, it's been awhile since I've seen you. How's Sam doing?"

"Just great. One more year and he'll be out of college. Doesn't seem possible does it?"

Mr. Phillips shook his head. "It seems like he just graduated last year. Time really flies."

"Thanks for coming. I appreciate it. I have a couple more teachers I've asked to join us, then I'll explain my mission."

"Sure, I'm in no hurry." He flopped down on the couch and set his briefcase on the floor beside his feet.

Hawkman turned toward the coffee urn, his back to Mr. Phillips, poured himself some more coffee, reached into his breast pocket and flipped on his voice activated recorder. "Want a cup?" He asked over his shoulder.

"No, thanks. I'm coffeed out."

Soon, Ms. Gardner, Mrs. Cross and Ms. Doyle meandered in, all shaking hands with Hawkman and asking about Sam.

When they'd situated themselves around the room, Hawkman closed the door of the lounge and stood in front of the group. "I've been hired by a large firm back east to do a background study on several students including Maryann Parker. She's a very bright girl and they're looking at possibly offering her a position after she graduates from college. Maryann isn't aware of their interest, as they've been observing her from afar. That's why it's essential you keep this conversation only between the people in this room."

"What sort of things do you need to know?" asked Mrs. Doyle.

"Your honest opinion about this young woman. Is she reliable? Likable? Mostly personal stuff. They know how smart she is, so that's not what they're looking at right now. The person they want to hire has to be congenial."

The four teachers glanced at each other. The women frowned and Mr. Phillips grimaced.

Hawkman rubbed his mustache. "Looks like I hit a sore spot. So what's your opinion, Mr. Phillips?"

"Truthfully, that girl had a hard time getting along with her peers. A beautiful young thing, but she had her problems. Smart, yes. But congenial, no. She never seemed happy."

"Ms. Gardner?"

"I agree with Mr. Phillips. Her conversations always had a cynical touch. Not only with her peers, but also with her teachers. She flaunted her intelligence and turned people off. I definitely liked the girl, but in my opinion she craved attention, just didn't know how to get it."

"Mrs. Cross?"

"I agree with both Ms. Gardner and Mr. Phillips. Maryann was a strange one. When I asked to have her folks come in for a conference her senior year, she wouldn't hear of it. Said they had nothing to do with her future. She'd handle her life and leave her folks out of it. I'm afraid the girl came from a dysfunctional family. And being an only child didn't help. She had no female friends, and came on strong in a suggestive manner toward the boys to the point of frightening many of them away."

"Ms. Doyle?"

Her shoulder's slumped. "It's really sad, Mr. Casey. The girl had so much going for her, but her personality really stunk." She glanced at the other teachers. "Sorry, but that's the way I perceived her. Very arrogant. Girls and boys avoided her like she had a disease. At first, I thought the females were just envious of her mature figure, flawless skin and long beautiful black hair that hung past her waist. She had flirtatious dark brown eyes and lashes that required no makeup. Many girls would kill for those attributes. But then I noticed the boys stayed away too. A siren with no boys panting after her seemed odd. Then one day I overheard a couple of our young men talking. They spoke of Maryann as evil and wicked." She shook her head. "Such a shame."

Hawkman shifted his position and took a deep breath. "I want to thank you all for your honesty. I know it's not easy to give a negative report." He passed a business card to each one. "If you think of anything else, just give me a call. And please keep this meeting to yourselves"

Mr. Phillips sighed and stood. "Don't worry, Mr. Casey. None of us will say anything. These meetings are not fun, but sometimes necessary."

Hawkman dumped his coffee in the sink and threw the styrofoam cup in the trash. Once everyone left the room, he flipped off his recorder and strolled out to his vehicle. Maryann appeared as a devious woman on the exterior. Did she feel that way deep inside or did she have a lot of pain? If so, her outward appearance definitely fooled people. Even Sam said Richard saw her as a cold and calculating woman. As he drove to his office in Medford, he couldn't get his mind off what the teachers said about Maryann.

CHAPTER TWENTY-ONE

Maryann watched her mother pick at the lunch she'd prepared.
"Mom, I thought you liked chili dogs?"

"Oh, I love them. I'm just not hungry."

"You've got to eat something before you go to work. I can tell you're losing weight, you're nothing but skin and bones."

Lilly pushed the plate away. "I've got a lot on my mind. Just put it in the refrigerator and save it for Frank." She slumped back in the chair. "By the way, have you had any luck in finding employment?"

She shook her head. "No. You're right about this hick town, it doesn't have much to offer. Any openings are taken by the residents. But I've got a little saved and a job waiting when I get back to the university, so I should be okay for the summer. And don't change the subject, Mother. What's worrying you?"

"I've been thinking about how stupid I've been by not reporting Burke's beatings." She let out a long sigh. "Now I can't protect Madukarahat. But Burke scared me so much with his threats, I feared you'd be taken away."

Maryann pointed a finger at her mother. "Mom, you're letting your imagination get the best of you. How do you know Maduk had any thing to do with Burke's death?"

Lilly stared at her daughter, tears welling in her eyes. "Just from some of the things he said."

Maryann slapped her hand on the table. "Mother, think about it. If Maduk had killed Burke, he'd have used his knife. I believe Burke died of natural causes. The idiot probably overdosed on his own medications. The test will show it and we'll all be cleared of any wrong doing. If not, you and I will be the first they put under scrutiny. And I don't think that's going to happen."

"I wish I felt as certain as you do. Unfortunately, you told the young Casey lad about Maduk. Now it will be all over the community."

Maryann covered her face with her hands. "Yes, I probably did a dumb thing, but we're just speculating about Burke being murdered."

"Then why are they doing all the testing?"

Maryann rose from her chair and paced the room, wringing her hands. "I don't know. Maybe it's just police procedure when they find a dead body."

"Maduk thinks otherwise. He thinks they suspect murder."

"He's just guessing. Just like we're doing."

Lilly shrugged. "I hope for all of us you're right. When this leaks out, I'll probably lose my job. Then what will I do?"

Maryann narrowed her eyes and stared at her mother. "We'll leave this horrible place and find somewhere else to live. We should have gone a long time ago. It's been hell growing up here."

Bowing her head, tears trickled down Lilly's cheeks. "I know it's been hard on you. And I'm sorry for the pain you've suffered. All I can say is you were born out of love."

Going to her mother, Maryann put an arm around Lilly's shoulders and gazed into space. "I know. But please try to eat. Let me warm up your food, so you'll have some energy for work."

⁂

Sam found the drop cloths in the garage and stuffed them into a big garbage bag, then tied them down in the bed of the truck. He looked over the interior paint colors and thought they'd be quite attractive for the rooms of Mrs. Parker's house. He needed to check with her and find out whether she'd like the outside or the inside painted first. It made no difference to him, except they'd need a whole day for draping the furniture, removing pictures and shelves off the walls. He figured doing a couple of rooms at a time would be best and he could do the preparation without Richard's help. Maybe Maryann would lend a hand. Even though he hesitated about working beside her, he wanted to get this job finished so he'd have some of the summer left to play. He hoped she'd remembered to water the sod.

Jennifer helped Sam gather up paint rollers and other supplies he needed from the storage shed. She handed him some paint hats and several rolls of masking tape. "I hope you haven't taken on a bigger job than you can handle. The way things are going, you're not going to have any free time left to fish or ride your new bike before you have to return to school."

"The house is small. It won't take long. If I can get things prepared before the weekend, Richard and I can get most of the inside painted in a couple of days."

She patted him on the back as he climbed into the cab of his truck. "I admire what you're doing. I hope Lilly and Maryann appreciate your efforts."

Sam shrugged. "I think Mrs. Parker does. Can't tell about Maryann."

He arrived at the Parker home about one o'clock. Lilly's old station wagon sat under the carport and the sprinklers were watering the new grass which appeared healthy. He noticed flowers had been planted in the pots that lined the front porch.

Glad Lilly's home, Sam thought. I'll talk to her before she goes to work. He strolled up to the front entry and picked up a small bouquet of flowers lying on the porch, then knocked lightly. Maryann opened the door.

"Hi, Sam." Her gaze dropped to the drooping stems in his hand. "I think those need water."

"Oh, I found these on the porch."

She rolled her eyes and took them. "I bet they're from Frank. Probably picked from someone's garden."

"A new beau?"

Maryann shook her head and laughed. "No, Mom feeds a

homeless man. I'm sure this is his way of thanking her. Anyway, what brings you here during the week? Thought you guys just worked on the weekends."

"I want to talk with your mom about whether she wants us to paint the inside. If so, I want her to pick the colors for the rooms, plus I need to find out a good time to drape the furniture and remove stuff off the walls. Then it shouldn't take Richard and me more than a couple of days to paint. In fact, If I can manage to get a couple of the rooms ready, I'll start before the weekend. The outside doesn't require as much preparation."

Lilly meandered up behind Maryann and touched the plants in her daughter's hand. "Oh, honey, put those pretty blooms in water before they're beyond help." She then turned her attention to Sam. "It sounds like a splendid idea. Show me the colors you have."

"Sure, come on out to my truck."

Sam jumped up into the bed and lifted the gallon cans to the tailgate, so Lilly could inspect them.

"Oh my, you have quite a variety."

"Yes, but there's at least three gallons of every hue, so it's plenty to cover one room." He thumped the top of one of the cans. "In fact, this one called Oyster has four gallons. So you might want it for your living room. I also thought this pale blue enamel might be nice for your kitchen. And there's another enamel in a light yellow, which would be good in the bathroom. The rest are flat paints in shades of white. Here's an Eggshell, perfect for a bedroom. He waved his hand over the tops. "They're all water based, so it will be easy to clean up."

As Lilly made the choices for each room, Sam took out an indelible marking pen and wrote on the tops of the cans. "I'll start in the living room, if that's all right with you. I need to tape around the windows and remove any pictures or shelves you have attached to the walls."

She nodded, then frowned. "I'm worried about the fumes."

"I'll keep the windows open for ventilation. Fortunately, the weather is mild."

"That's true." Lilly smiled. "This is going to be so nice to have a fresh and clean house." She turned toward Maryann who'd follow them out. "See what you can do to help the boy. I've got to get ready for work."

She left the two young people standing at the back of the truck.

"Let's put the cans of paint on the front porch," Sam said, as he lifted a couple of the gallons and headed toward the entry.

Maryann grabbed two of the cans. "Let me get an old sheet or tarp to set them on. I don't want our nice front porch decorated with paint rings."

"Good idea."

After they'd removed all the cans needed, Sam lifted the bag of drop cloths and miscellaneous supplies from the truck bed. He carried them into the living room and placed them in a corner. Glancing around, he decided the room would be a piece of cake to prepare. Only two pictures on the walls and the rest of the furniture just needed to be scooted toward the center and covered.

To his amazement, Maryann turned out to be a good assistant. She helped him move the couch and bigger items, then took the pictures to a safe haven somewhere in the back of the house. She cleared off the small bookshelf, putting the items into brown grocery bags, and carried them to another room. Taping the windows proved the biggest challenge.

During the midst of their work, Lilly stepped into the living room in her waitress uniform. "Oh my goodness, you kids have already got a lot done."

"What's a good time tomorrow for me to start painting?" Sam asked.

Lilly touched a finger to her chin. "How about noon."

"That sounds fine. I'll see you tomorrow."

She waved and went out the front door. Sam heard the old car engine groan, but then fire up. He glanced out the window and noticed the black exhaust as she pulled into the street. "Wonder how long your mom's car is going to last?"

Maryann laughed. "It's old, but still moves when you put it into gear. The engine sounds rough, but it always starts."

Sam finishing taping the last window and turned around to put the masking tape away. Maryann stood behind him. Her dark hair fell over her shoulders, and her eyes glistened. She held up the beer in her hand.

"Want one?"

He shook his head. "Uh, no thanks. I have to drive home."

"Oh, come on Sam. Loosen up. It's been fun working together." She unbuttoned her blouse, her face glowing with passion as she moved closer to him. Taking his hand, she slid it inside her bra, a sly grin curling the corners of her mouth. "Don't tell me you don't like women?"

Sam yanked his hand away and glared at her. "I love women, Maryann, but I don't trust you."

She stepped back. "What do you mean by that statement? I've never done anything to you."

He dropped the tape into the sack. "It's not what you've done to me, it's how you've treated my friends. You're fickle and can't be trusted. No man wants to get involved with a woman who turns on him." He moved the supplies to the corner and headed for the door. "Thanks for your help. I'll see you tomorrow."

When Sam walked out onto the porch, Maryann slammed the door. "Like hell you will. I won't be here," she hissed.

CHAPTER TWENTY-TWO

Sam jumped into his truck and left the Parker's house. He flipped on the radio, turned up the volume to a loud rock station and tried singing along to wipe the image of Maryann's sexual advance from his mind. But it didn't work. He hit the steering wheel with his fist. Why did she pull such a stunt? It only made him dislike her more. How he wished he'd never offered to fix up their place. He'd see the job through, but he'd learned a vital lesson. Keep your big mouth shut.

As he drove over the bridge crossing the Klamath River where it dumped into Copco Lake, his anxiety eased. He spotted Hawkman's 4X4 in front of the garage as he turned the corner. His thoughts leaped to Burke Parker. Maybe Hawkman had some news.

Parking at the side of the house, so not to block the driveway, Sam hurried toward the front door. But before he reached the entry, the crunch of tires on gravel caused him to glance around.

"Hey, Richard, what's up? You just get off work?" he asked, strolling toward the driver's side.

"Yeah, and I have tomorrow off, as they're taking the horses into town to get them shod and vaccinated against the West Nile virus. It's cheaper than having the vet come out. So, you wanta do something?"

Sam grimaced. "Wish I'd known. I've spent the day at the Parkers' taping and draping the living room. Told her I'd paint it tomorrow."

"Didn't know you were working during the week on the house."

"I want to get it done, so I'll have a little summer left to fish and ride my new bike."

"Okay, I'll pick you up. What time?"

Sam jerked up his head. "Hey, you don't have to take your day off to help me with this dumb project."

Richard threw back his head and laughed. "I don't mind. Guess I'm being selfish, but with two of us working, we can get things done a lot faster and have more time to play."

"If you're sure," Sam said grinning. "Mrs. Parker said come about noon, so pick me up around eleven fifteen. That will give us plenty of time."

"Okay, see ya then." Richard threw the truck into reverse and backed out to the street."

When Sam entered the house, Jennifer and Hawkman were sitting at the breakfast bar talking. A delicious aroma swirled about his nose. Then he spotted the blackberry pie cooling on the cabinet. He bent his head over the pastry and rubbed his stomach. "Oh, man, does that ever smell wonderful."

Jennifer smiled. "I froze those berries last year. Hawkman and I picked them up at the Miller ranch. That's the last batch. I wish we'd get a good crop from our own bushes. They just don't seem to do well." She rolled her eyes. "And the deer love them."

"Heard anything on Burke Parker?" Sam asked, scooting onto the stool next to Hawkman.

"No, but had a nice conference with four of Maryann's teachers."

Sam grimaced. "I'm afraid to ask what they said."

"Not very positive, other than they all agreed the girl is very smart and pretty. But it seems all of them think she's very aloof."

Sam shook his head. "I've already told you that."

Hawkman leaned forward, placing his elbows on the counter top. "I'm sure the girl aches inside. And being on the defensive, she makes sure no one can hurt her."

"Burke did a lot of damage to her mentally," Jennifer said. "That takes years to overcome."

"I don't think she's tried." Sam stood. "I'm going to shower before dinner." On his way back to his room, he'd pulled his shirt out of his jeans, then called over his shoulder. "Jennifer, do I still have those old clothes I left here when I went off to college? I'm going to be painting tomorrow and might as well wear them."

"Yes, they're stored in a box on the floor of your closet."

"Thanks."

☙

When Jennifer heard the shower running, she buried her face in her hands. "I might as well get ready for clothes strewn all over that room tomorrow."

Hawkman laughed. "Now, honey, didn't you raise a neat kid?"

She pointed a finger at him. "Are you kidding? He took after you." Then she glanced toward the hallway. "You notice how he didn't want to talk about Maryann?"

He nodded. "It sort of surprised me that he didn't ask any questions. I'm sure he saw her today, but I get the distinct feeling he definitely doesn't like that girl."

Jennifer frowned. "After what you told me the teachers said, Maryann must have had problems for years. If you checked, you'd more than likely find her troubles go all the way back to the primary grades."

Hawkman nodded. "Especially after what Sam told us about Burke's abuse."

"I can't even imagine that horror."

☙

Madukarahat drove the back roads as much as possible when going to the different areas where he had to obtain reports on the casinos. At this point in time, he didn't want anyone seeing him around Yreka or connecting him with Lilly. He had lots of time to think about what he'd heard through his sources. A tall cowboy with an eye-patch had frequented the bars and asked questions about him. Maduk recognized the description of the man the locals called Hawkman, a well respected private investigator who had once worked for the Agency. He wondered what interest he had in the death of a nobody like Burke Parker? Or did he want to find out something else? Maduk had never met Hawkman personally, but figured he'd have no trouble recognizing him. There weren't many men roaming around Yreka with a patch over their eye.

He also knew that the man's son and the deaf boy had taken on the job of fixing up Lilly's house as a charitable gesture. Having the boys nosing around made Maduk uncomfortable. He couldn't even sneak in a visit, afraid the lads might appear. And the deaf one had sharp senses like an animal. He wondered how much the two young men knew. Did they know about him? He knew Maryann had eyes for the one called Sam. How much had she confided to him?

All these questions made Maduk uneasy. His daughter had almost become a stranger. No longer innocent and naive. She'd grown into a beautiful woman. Any warrior would sell his soul for her. But she had a sharp tongue. And he worried about the coldness in her eyes. He sensed she'd not forgiven him for leaving her and Lilly in the clutches of Burke Parker. He gripped the steering wheel. At least the bastard was dead now and would never lay a hand on either one of his women again.

He turned off the main road and followed a small gravel lane up into the hills where he'd purchased a piece of land with a small cottage. Maduk pulled into the out building next to the house and parked. He'd earned enough money to put on the finishing touches, so he'd soon bring Lilly here. Strolling toward the front of the house, he stood for a moment gazing over the land. Beautiful, he thought. What a breathtaking view. He gazed at the large trees surrounding the house. "They'll make things cool in the summer, and protect the roof from the snow in the winter," he said aloud.

He shook himself out of the serenity of the scene, selected the right key from the ring in his hand, then went up the three steps onto the small porch and opened the front door. Moving into the pine paneled living room, he flipped the switch and the lights came on. He smiled, as the order for power had gone in last week and the electric company guaranteed him service within a few days. He ambled into the kitchen and turned on the water spigot. Water flowed. Again, he smiled to himself. Things were moving right along.

The septic tank had been checked and given the okay two months ago when he bought the place. An inspection of the construction all passed and the only thing needing attention were a few loose shingles on the roof. That created no problem for Maduk; he could tackle that job on his own. The house had been owned by an older couple who could no longer maintain it, and they'd moved into town.

The dwelling consisted of a living room with a large river rock fireplace gracing one wall with an opening large enough to hold a three foot log. A dining area occupied the far end. A small bar separated this room from the kitchen, leaving an open view where someone cooking could still see out the big picture window on the opposite wall of the living room. A full bathroom occupied the short hallway that led to two bedrooms. The master sleeping quarters had its own bath. The total footage of the house wasn't much, but the layout served his purpose and made for comfortable living. Some furnishings were included in the sale price, so each room had a smattering of furniture, which gave the abode a cozy feel. He had no doubt that Lilly and Maryann would love it.

Maduk changed into jeans and a cotton shirt in the master bedroom and hung up his suit. He then went outside to the detached garage. Pulling on a pair of work gloves from the tool bench, he picked a short-handled shovel from the row of hanging tools on the wall. Opening a small box in the corner, he checked the lid on the container inside. After making sure it didn't leak, he picked up the box and carried it out the back door. He meandered out to the border of the property and disappeared into the shadows of the forest.

By the time he returned, the sun had set. He hung the shovel on its respective nail, and tossed the gloves back onto the work bench. Weariness crept over his body. He headed straight to the bedroom, opened the windows, stripped down to his underwear and stretched his long body across the bed. Soon, the crickets lulled him to sleep.

CHAPTER TWENTY-THREE

The next morning, Sam rolled over, stretched and stared at the ceiling. He sure didn't look forward to the job today. Thank goodness Richard offered to join him. He hoped Maryann meant what she said when she slammed the door. She probably didn't think he heard, but a voice laced with fire carries through wood.

He sighed, climbed out of bed and rummaged through the box of old clothes in the closet. Tossing the rejects onto the floor, he finally settled on a pair of jeans with holes in the knees and a white wrinkled tee shirt with a stupid picture of a toothless singer across the front.

When he waltzed through the living room on the way to the kitchen, Hawkman glanced up from the paper and surveyed him from head to foot. "Hope you don't plan on wearing that garb on a date."

Sam couldn't resist laughing. "Ah, Hawkman. Darn, I thought this attire would stack up a million points with the girls."

Hawkman shook his head. "Don't count on one."

Sam grimaced. "Gonna do some painting today at the Parker's. Fortunately, Richard's got the day off and offered to help. He's going to pick me up before lunch."

"You sure don't sound very enthused. Looks like this job has become more of a hassle than you expected."

"I don't mind the work. It's Maryann that drives me crazy. She's always there trying to come on to me."

"Take it as a compliment."

"I would, if it came from anyone but her."

Hawkman folded the paper on his lap. "Sounds like she's definitely gotten under your skin. I really don't know how to tell you to discourage her. It's hard to be rude while working in her home."

Sam through up his hands. "I'll be fine. I hoped she'd get a summer job, but she doesn't seem interested in finding one. Which sort of surprises me, as she works at the university all the time."

"How come you know so much about a person you dislike so much?"

"She makes a big pest out of herself at school, and manages to come over to my apartment for some cockeyed reason once or twice a week. Since she lives in the building next to mine, she's always running out of sugar, salt or bread. Always some dumb excuse to knock on my door. If it's not that, she wants to ask me a question about a class I'm taking. I tell you, if it wasn't so hard to find a place to live near the campus, I'd move and never tell her my address."

"What sort of jobs does she do?"

"Everything from slinging hash at the cafeteria, working with a landscaper to helping a chemist in his lab."

"At least she's ambitious."

"Yeah, I guess."

"Don't you think you're judging her pretty harshly?"

Sam shot him a fierce look. "No," he said, stalking into the kitchen.

Hawkman moved from the living room to the eating bar.

"Where's Jennifer?" Sam asked, opening the refrigerator.

"She had an early morning appointment in town."

He held up a package wrapped in foil. "Do you think she'd mind if I made some sandwiches for me and Richard out of this leftover meat loaf? They'd sure taste better than some fast food stuff."

"I'm sure she'd be pleased that you thought it that good. Help yourself."

"If she gets mad, it's your fault."

Hawkman laughed. "Okay, I'll take the blame."

Sam busied himself making lunches and Hawkman drifted back to the living room to finish reading the paper.

Hawkman heard the beep of Richard's pickup and Sam hurried out the door carrying the lunch bag. After the boys left, he dropped the paper on the coffee table, turned his chair and stared out over the lake. It appeared Maryann had access to all sorts of chemicals. She worked with a gardner who could have introduced her to weed and pest control poisons, and also a chemist. Through those experiences and her classes, she probably learned how the body would react if toxins were ingested. This girl might be one to keep a close eye on. He hoped Sam wasn't in any danger, being in such close proximity to the woman. She obviously had a crush on him and if he riled her, she might feel rejected. The thought sent a shudder through his body. People have killed for less.

Maybe he should drop by the Parker's every now and then to see how the boys were doing. He didn't have any pressing cases right now, so he could do a little spying without looking too conspicuous. Plopping on his hat, he figured he'd go to the office, leave a bit early, then head over to the Parker house.

Driving toward Medford, he wondered how long it'd take before Detective Williams received the results of those tests. His gut told him Burke Parker died of poisoning, either accidentally or by someone else's hand. When he noticed the scoring of the lips and tongue in the photos of the body, it definitely told him something toxic had been ingested. As an agent, he'd seen more poisonings that he cared to mention. But until they had the tests back, he'd have to keep his opinions to himself. An investigation would damn near include the whole town of Yreka. Everyone he spoke to thought the man a scum bag. They all had a reason to kill him. Along with Maryann, Maduk and Lilly.

When he reached the city limits, he suppressed the urge to stop by the police station. Williams promised he'd call when the results arrived. And he'd learned years ago, one doesn't rush the lab. Unless, of course, it was a high profile case, and this wasn't one.

Hawkman spent a couple of hours at the office answering calls and getting his financial statement caught up. He missed Jennifer popping in now and then to keep his bookkeeping updated, but since she'd signed a contract to do a mystery series, she didn't have the time. He glanced at his watch and decided he'd better get going if he wanted to catch the boys before they called it a day.

A block from the Parker's, he spotted Richard's truck parked in front, but Lilly's car was gone. He figured she'd left for work long ago. As he approached the house, he noticed the windows were open and the front door stood ajar. At least the boys were thinking and had good ventilation while painting.

Hawkman pulled up close to the tailgate of Richard's truck and got out. He moseyed up to the front door and poked his head inside. Sam stood on a ladder which rested on a tarped floor. While he rolled paint across the ceiling, Richard sat on his butt and painted the trim board along the floor. "How you guys doing?"

Sam's painter hat had not protected his whole face, white speckles of paint glistened across his nose and cheeks. "Hi, Hawkman. Need a job? We don't pay well, but we could use any kind of help."

Richard stopped in the middle of a brush stroke and glanced up. A large white smudge graced his neck and a streak iced his dark hair

Hawkman laughed. "Looks like you guys have been in a paint fight."

Sam placed the roller in the pan and climbed down the rungs. "Man, doesn't matter how careful one is, you end up with paint all over your body."

"There's always more to a job than meets the eye." Hawkman stepped into the room, put his fists on his hips and surveyed the walls. "You guys are doing a good job. Looks nice."

"Thanks."

"Where's Maryann and her mother?"

"They left together. Mrs. Parker had to go to work, and I heard Maryann tell her she'd pick her up, as she needed the car to run some errands. We haven't seen either of them since." Sam turned his head away from Richard's view. "And that suits me just fine."

Hawkman brushed his hand across his mouth and snickered. "I see." He sauntered toward the kitchen. "Looks like you have this room ready, too. Are you going to try to do it before you call it a day?"

"Yeah, I think we can get them both done by dark. We're almost finished in here."

Hawkman headed down the short hallway followed by Sam and Richard. He glanced into a room where clothes were strewn across the unmade bed and draped over a chair. Several different pairs of shoes were scattered across the floor. A dirty plate and glass sat on the dresser. "May I make a suggestion?"

"Sure," Sam said.

"Do one bedroom at a time. That way if the fumes are strong, then the two women can sleep together or one of them can sleep on the couch in the living room."

Richard nodded. "Good idea. And the smell is strong after the first coat. Having everything open helps. But I doubt they'll want to keep the house unlocked at night."

Hawkman turned toward the other bedroom and shoved open the door. He stood in the hallway and noticed a doll placed on the carefully made bed. In the closet, clothes hung neatly and shoes lined the floor. "Is this Maryann's room?"

Sam turned and headed toward the ladder. "Yeah, I think so."

Quite a difference in the housekeeping, Hawkman thought, as he studied the interior for several moments. He closed the door and strolled back into the living room. "If you guys are going to paint the kitchen tonight, you're going to get hungry. I'm sure you've already eaten those sandwiches you brought. Want me to go grab you some hamburgers before I head home?"

Richard dug into his pocket and handed Hawkman a five dollar bill. "That'd be great."

Hawkman waved a hand. "Put your money away, it's on me."

"Thanks, Mr. Casey."

The boys were taking the paint gear into the kitchen as Hawkman stepped out onto the front porch. He decided to look around the exterior of the house to see what might be required for the outside job. If the boys needed anything, he could pick it up while in town. At least, they wouldn't have furniture to cover. He walked around to the backyard and eyed the level of the roof line. After some mental calculations, he decided the two ladders Sam had brought were tall enough. As he came around to the car port where Lilly parked her car, he noticed a storage cabinet built along the wall. He opened the doors, squatted on his haunches and studied the contents.

CHAPTER TWENTY-FOUR

Sam peeked out the back door as Hawkman rounded the corner of the house. He knew his dad had something on his mind, like scouting the area. That made him a good private investigator when he took advantage of every opportunity. He wondered if there'd been any news from Detective Williams.

As much as Sam disliked Maryann, he didn't want her or her mother to go through any unnecessary trauma. It nagged at him that they might be under heavy suspicion. He felt they'd been through enough.

After several moments, Sam wondered why he hadn't heard Hawkman leave. Placing the paint roller into the pan, he wiped his hands with a rag, then touched his friend on the shoulder. "I'll be back in a minute."

Richard nodded and continued painting.

Sam strolled around the side of the house and spotted Hawkman kneeling in front of the cabinet under the carport.

"What are you looking for?" Sam asked.

Hawkman glanced up. "Nothing in particular. Just nosing around."

"Did you hear anything from Williams today?"

"Nope. Not a word," Hawkman said, closing the cabinet and brushing off his hands. "I'll go get your sandwiches now. Be back shortly."

Sam watched as he drove away, then glanced at the cupboard. His curiosity made him flip open the doors with his fingers. He crouched down so he could scan the inside. Seeing nothing but old cans and bottles, he shrugged, closed the cabinet, and went back into the house.

The boys moved into the kitchen and found painting this small area more tedious than the living room. They were constantly getting themselves into odd positions.

"Man, I bet I'll be sore tomorrow," Richard said, straightening and rubbing his back after leaning over the stove for several minutes.

Sam scooted out from behind the refrigerator. "Yep, we're straining muscles that haven't been worked in a while." He checked the small copper pipe leading into the appliance. "Sure hope we don't cause a leak in the ice maker. That tube is stretched to the max."

Hawkman soon returned with two large sacks. "Okay, boys, break time."

Sniffing the aroma of french fries and hamburgers, both boys immediately set down their painting gear.

"Oh man, does that smell good," Richard said, grinning as he scrubbed over the sink.

They took their food from Hawkman, exited to the front porch away from the fumes, and sat on the steps, where they unwrapped the juicy burgers.

"I'm taking off," Hawkman said. "I'll tell Jennifer you won't be home for dinner. Richard, want me to call your uncle and tell him not to expect you until late?"

He nodded. "Yeah, thanks. That'd be great."

⌘

After Hawkman left the premises, he called Uncle Joe on his cell phone; then his thoughts went to the things he'd observed at the Parker's. Maryann appeared abnormally fastidious for a girl her age. He'd seen the apartments at the college when he and Jennifer had searched for Sam's living quarters between his freshman and sophomore year. They were amazed at the clutter left behind in both the girls' and boys' places. No wonder Jennifer found strange towels and shirts in Sam's laundry. The kids were oblivious to ownership, and grabbed whatever happened to be handy. It surprised them Sam hadn't come down sick more often since the kitchens were definitely not clean. Guess they build up an immunity.

Lilly's room appeared more like a college student's than Maryann's. Strange how they were so opposite. But maybe the girl's mother hadn't always been that messy. She'd definitely not led a life of leisure.

Hawkman wished he could've searched both the bedrooms, but thought it a bit out of line at this point. He really didn't know what to look for, but figured if he'd found anything out of the ordinary, it would be worth noting. For instance, that cabinet outside. Near the back of the first shelf, he'd spotted a clean square area where something had recently been removed. It might be nothing of importance, but he'd remember it just in case.

When he arrived home, Jennifer sat at the computer, but immediately shut down the machine. "I need to talk to you."

He studied her expression. "Everything okay?"

She waved a hand and stood. "Yes. It's about Lilly and Maryann."

He hung up his hat, ran his fingers through his hair, and stood at the end of the kitchen bar. "I'm all ears."

"I went into Yreka this afternoon, and spotted Maryann dropping Lilly off at that greasy spoon restaurant at the end of Carb Street."

Hawkman raised a brow. "So?"

"Why is she working there?"

"Maybe it's the only place she could find employment. Jobs are hard to come by right now."

Jennifer shuddered. "But it's a dive. Does she work there weekends too?"

"I don't know. But more than likely."

"Poor woman. That place is wild from what I understand." She wrinkled her forehead in thought. "Wish I knew somebody who needed help. Maybe they'd hire Lilly."

Hawkman pointed at her. "You stay out of it right now. If Burke Parker was murdered, Lilly's going to come under heavy investigation. And it's best you're not involved."

She moved away from the computer toward him and touched his arm. "Hawkman, anybody in Yreka could have killed that man. No one liked him."

"It's a matter the police will have to sort out. Did you by any chance see which direction Maryann went?"

"No, I didn't even notice. I'd just come out of that little bookstore on the corner when I spotted Lilly in a waitress type uniform getting out of the car and going into that horrible place. I could hardly believe my eyes."

"Don't fret about Lilly. There's nothing you can do. And obviously, she needs the money."

Jennifer sighed. "I guess you're right. Maybe it's just temporary until she can find something better."

Hawkman meandered into the living room and sat down. "Sam won't be home for dinner. He and Richard want to finish painting a couple of rooms before they quit, so I went out and got them burgers. They're doing a good job."

She stood staring at him with a hand on her hip. "How do you know? I hope you weren't spying on the boys."

Hawkman laughed. "I guess I'm guilty." He held up a hand. "Don't get me wrong. I'm not concerned about their work. Just wanted to do a little snooping on my own and with them there, it seemed the opportune time."

Jennifer sat on the edge of the couch, her arms resting on her knees with hands clasped. "Why? Is there something you haven't told me?"

He shook his head. "No, just curious. Trying to stay a jump ahead."

She frowned. "But you don't even know the cause of Burke's death yet."

"I saw the pictures of his body. Fortunately, Williams has a good staff. The photographer didn't miss a thing and neither did the coroner. I think they suspected something from the beginning."

"What did you see?"

"Scoring around and inside his mouth. I'm sure when the tests come back, we're going to find out that Burke ingested poison. And I doubt very seriously his medications killed him."

"Wouldn't he have realized he'd swallowed something toxic?"

Hawkman raised his hands, palms up. "Depends on how much liquor he'd consumed. From what I understand, he didn't hold his booze well. Williams said they found a couple of empty whisky bottles in his room. They've sent those to the lab for evaluation." He stared at the floor a moment. "Wonder if he bought his liquor or someone gave it to him?"

"Are you thinking out loud?"

He glanced at her as if shaken out of a deep sleep and grinned. "I think you've got me pegged."

She smiled. "It doesn't mean he drank a whole bottle the night he died."

"That's true."

"Getting back to you prying around Lilly's place. Are you looking for anything specific?"

"Not yet. I wanted to see how she and Maryann live. It gives me some background on their personalities and what they're capable of doing."

"Come to any conclusions?"

"No. But I can see why Sam doesn't trust Maryann. I think the girl definitely has some deep seated problems. Whether she's capable of murder is hard to say."

"What about Lilly?"

"No opinion. I haven't had the opportunity to talk to her or observe her behavior. I've only seen her messy bedroom. Every time I stopped by to see the boys, she'd already left for work. So this weekend I'm going to hit that greasy spoon where she's employed."

"Why are you waiting until then?"

"Because I want to see if she also works in the bar. It's only open on Friday and Saturday evenings."

CHAPTER TWENTY-FIVE

By the time Sam and Richard cleaned their equipment, capped the paint cans, pulled off the tape around the windows and removed the drop cloths protecting the furniture, darkness had set in. Both boys stretched and groaned at the same time, then laughed at each other.

"Bet I sleep good tonight," Sam said.

"Me, too." Richard stepped back and inspected the walls. "You know the fresh coat of paint really helped lighten these two rooms."

Sam stacked the supplies on the front porch. "Sure did. Tomorrow I'll come over and get one of the bedrooms ready. If you can't help me paint on Thursday, don't worry about it. Maybe I can get the rest of the inside done by Saturday and we can start on the outside."

"Okay. I'll check and see how things are going at the stables. I might be able to leave early. If so, I'll give you a call. Be sure you have your cell phone charged."

"Right." Sam snapped his fingers. "I better leave a note for Mrs. Parker. I didn't mention I'd be over tomorrow." He scribbled on a paper pad he found near the phone, asking Mrs. Parker to call if it wasn't convenient for him to come. He propped it against a small lamp on the end table. "We better close the windows and lock up before we leave."

The boys secured the house and turned out the lights, except the one where Sam had left the message. They hopped into Richard's pickup and drove away from the house. They rode pretty much in silence as Richard couldn't see Sam's mouth in the dark. After a few minutes, Richard broke the quiet.

"Don't look out the back, but check the mirror on the outside. There's been a car following us ever since we left the Parker place."

Sam quickly glanced out the passenger window. They weren't out of town yet, so he touched Richard's arm and made a gesture of getting something to drink, then pointed in the direction of Raley's. Richard nodded and turned at the next corner.

When they arrived in the lighted parking lot, he pulled into an empty space and stopped. They watched the vehicle behind them swerve off onto a side street.

"Did you recognize that car?" Richard asked.

"Yeah. It's the same one we saw a couple of weeks ago circling the block around the Parkers'."

Richard nodded. "That's what I thought. Do you think it's Maduk?"

"Who else could it be?"

"Why would he be interested in us?"

Sam shook his head. "Beats me." Then he frowned. "Unless he thinks Maryann's talked to us."

"About what?"

"Maybe Maryann killed Burke and he wants to protect her. And you were with her over the Memorial Day holiday."

Richard rubbed a hand over his face. "Oh God. He might want to kill me to shut me up."

"You got a tire iron handy?"

"Yeah." He pointed. "Under your seat."

Sam groped the floor until his fingers wrapped around the long piece of pipe. He dragged it out, took a deep breath and slapped it against the palm of his hand.

"Do you want to chance heading home?" Richard asked.

"We can't stay here all night. You got plenty of gas in case we have to detour?"

Richard glanced at the gauge. "Almost a full tank."

"Good. You concentrate on driving and I'll watch our tail."

Easing out of the parking lot, Richard headed for Copco Lake. He checked every intersection and watched the mirrors, even though he trusted Sam to keep a close eye on the rear. They traveled the twenty miles to the turnoff without anyone following them. They both breathed a sigh of relief as Richard made the turn toward the lake. Then, suddenly, Sam touched his arm and thumbed toward the back. Headlights were rapidly approaching.

Richard wiped the sweat from his forehead. His first impulse was to hit the accelerator, but he knew how dangerous that could be if a deer darted in front of the truck on these winding roads. He took several deep breaths to calm his nerves, then gripped the steering wheel. Keeping his gaze straight ahead, he drove at the speed limit.

As the lights grew close, he felt Sam's tension, along with his own. Suddenly, the vehicle started flashing its bright lights on and off. "Can you tell if that's a car or truck?"

Sam shook his head. "The beams are too bright, I can't see the front end."

What the hell does he want?" Richard asked`, glancing into the rear view mirror. "I can't pull over, the shoulder's too narrow and we'd crash down that embankment." Sweat ran down the middle of his back and he could hear his heart pounding in his ears. He shot a look at Sam's profile. His friend motioned for him just to drive straight ahead as he sat rigid, grasping the tire iron resting across his knees.

The vehicle behind them jerked into the left lane and sped past. Empty beer cans flew through the air and bounced off Richard's pickup. As he watched the small sedan go by, a couple of young men hung out the window making obscene gestures.

Richard's hands slipped down the steering wheel and he took a deep breath.

Glancing at his friend, he noticed Sam had dropped one end of the tire iron to the floorboard and wiped his face with the free hand.

Soon, Richard pulled into Hawkman's driveway. Sam shoved the makeshift weapon back under the seat, and motioned for Richard to come inside.

When the boys entered the house, Jennifer glanced up

from the computer, then came to her feet. "Sam, what's the matter, you're white as a sheet. And you don't look much better, Richard."

Hawkman turned off the television with the remote control. "Want to tell us about it?"

They all sat in the living room, as Sam related the story. "We thought for sure Maduk was out to kill us. Then when that car full of drunks showed up; it almost did us in."

Hawkman slapped his hands on his thighs and stood. "You boys might be jumping to conclusions. You can't be sure you were being followed. Could have been a coincidence that someone happened to be traveling the same direction. I think you're letting your imaginations run away over the death of Burke Parker."

Sam stiffened. "Richard and I both swear it's the same car we saw circling the block on our first day we went to the house. It's the same color and make with tinted windows."

"I'm not saying it wasn't the same car. But you don't know anything about Maduk." Hawkman pulled a picture out of his pocket. "Could you tell me if this is the man you saw in the car that first time?" He held it in front of the boys.

"Is this Maduk?" Richard asked.

"Yes."

He took the photo and studied it for several seconds, then shook his head. "All I could see was a dark silhouette, but I don't think the man had long hair. There's no way I could tell what he looked like straight on." He passed it to Sam.

After examining the portrait, he glanced at Hawkman. "I couldn't tell anything about the person inside the car, except he looked big. But I do remember the Buick as it passed the house several times. And I'm sure that was the same car tonight."

"Okay, fair enough," Hawkman said, pocketing the picture. "Now you know what the man looks like. I'm sure it gave you a shock when you saw the same car traveling behind you. Let me know if you spot it again and try to get the license plate number. And I can imagine how a vehicle full of drunks upset you. Did you come across them again before you got home?"

Both boys shook their heads.

"I'd feel much better if you'd spend the night here, Richard," Jennifer said.

Sam playfully punched his friend on the arm. "That's a great idea. I'll call your Uncle Joe and tell him you'll just go to work from here in the morning. Then he won't worry about you."

Richard smiled. "Okay. I sure wouldn't cherish the idea of running into that bunch of goons by myself. And they could well be up in that picnic area living it up."

Sam made a quick call to Uncle Joe. He didn't relate their scary incidents, figuring Richard could tell him when he got home the next day. After he hung up, he turned to his buddy. "You can shower first. Hope that paint comes out of your hair. You look mighty weird with that colorful frosting across the top of your head."

Richard glanced at his reflection in the window and laughed. "Man, I forgot all about what I might look like after painting."

"You can borrow some clean clothes for work."

"It won't hurt for me to wear these. My job at the ranch involves dirty labor, so I never wear good stuff."

The boys hustled off to Sam's room.

☙

Hawkman leaned back in the chair. His thoughts went to the big black Buick. His gut told him Maduk drove that car. But why would he be interested in the boys? He figured the Indian knew Sam and Richard were friends of Maryann. He might be concerned about how much she'd confided in them.

Jennifer sat down on the hassock next to Hawkman's feet. "What do you think about their story?"

"Not sure. They're two young men associated with a possible murder case. Their imaginations can run wild."

"True, but I don't think I've ever seen Sam so pale."

"It definitely scared them both. But don't worry. Nothing happened, except they got terribly frightened. At least they'll be watching their backs."

Jennifer slapped his thigh. "That doesn't make me feel any better."

Hawkman raised his hands and grinned. "Well, it's the truth. I don't think they're in any danger. They were more in harm's way when that bunch of rowdies came hauling down the road."

She pushed her hair behind her ear and grimaced. "You're right. But I sure am glad they're both home safe and sound."

He patted her shoulder. "Me, too. Why don't you split that last piece of blackberry pie between them. If you don't, I'll go eat the whole thing."

She laughed, gave him a peck on the cheek and pinched his love handles. "You don't need it. I'll go do that right now."

When she headed for the kitchen, Hawkman knew he shouldn't worry her about his fears. Because, if her motherly instinct kicked in, she could make it hard for Sam to return to the Parker place.

CHAPTER TWENTY-SIX

After both boys showered and enjoyed their piece of blackberry pie, they exited to Sam's room. He had an older Nintendo system from his high school days and they decided to try their hand at one of the games they hadn't played in years. After an hour of much laughter, they turned off the set.

Richard expression turned solemn. "Do you think it's safe for you to go back to the Parker house alone?"

Sam waved his hand. "Naw, there's no danger, especially during the daylight hours. I'll keep my eyes open, my cell phone charged and will call Hawkman if I sense any problems."

"Good idea. If I can get away from the ranch, I'll join you."

"I'd appreciate it. I'm more anxious than ever to get that job done. It's getting right down scary to be around that place."

"I agree." Richard stretched and yawned. "Think I'll hit the sack."

After his friend retired to the guest room, Sam turned out the light and lay down across his bed. He stared out the window at the star lit heavens and let his mind drift.

He wondered where Maryann had gone for the day, since she never showed up at the house while they were there. Had she met Maduk in some secluded place and told him of her rendezvous with Richard over the holiday weekend, or did she tell him I knew he was her real dad? Both of those stories could put us in danger, he thought. Especially if Maduk or Maryann killed Burke Parker.

Sam took a deep breath and wondered where Hawkman

found the photo of Maduk? He had no doubt something troubled his dad. If Burke Parker died of natural causes, why would Hawkman tell us to get the license plate number if we ever saw the Buick again?

His mind drifted to the picture of Maduk. The face reminded him of an Indian movie star, and the man had shoulders like a football player. He couldn't tell his height, but figured he wouldn't want to meet him in a dark alley. Rolling onto his side, he clenched his arms around his chest and fell into a fitful sleep.

The next morning, light rays danced across Sam's face as the sun rose over the hills. He blinked his eyes and groaned, realizing he'd forgotten to close the blinds. Pulling the sheet over his head, he turned away from the window. He heard Richard's truck roar to a start, then the crunch of gravel as his friend left for work. Sam finally gave up on trying to go back to sleep, got up, dressed and went into the bathroom. After splashing cold water on his face, he brushed his teeth, then headed for the kitchen.

Jennifer glanced up from the computer. "Good afternoon, sleepy head."

"Uh? What time is it?"

She smiled. "I'm only kidding. It's only eight thirty. Richard and Hawkman have already left. Want me to fix you some breakfast?"

He shook his head. "No. I'll just have some toast. I've got to get moving.

Any calls?"

"Nope. Expecting one?"

"I left Mrs. Parker a note to notify me if it wasn't convenient to come in today."

"The phone's been silent, so guess it's okay."

Sam browned some toast and washed it down with a glass of milk. "See ya this evening," he called, dashing out the door.

When he arrived at the Parker's, Maryann answered the door. "Hi, Sam, come on in."

"Your mom here?"

"Yeah, I'll get her."

He waited patiently, wondering how Maryann could act like nothing had happened. But that shouldn't surprise him; typical of her behavior.

Soon, Lilly appeared in her work uniform still brushing her hair. "Hello, Sam. Don't mind me. I've got to go to work early today. So, I'm having to hustle. I love the living room and kitchen. They look absolutely fantastic, so fresh and clean."

"Thanks, Mrs. Parker. I'm glad you're happy with the colors."

Her eyes sparkled. "I'm very pleased. What room are you thinking about doing next?"

"I thought I'd get one of the bedrooms ready and paint it tomorrow. You ladies could either bunk together or one of you might sleep in the living room for a couple of nights."

"Okay, why don't you start with my bedroom. I'm going to be out of here in a few minutes."

"Great. I'll wait in my truck until you're through."

Before long, Lilly came bounding out of the house and headed straight for his truck. "Okay, Sam. I'm on my way. I made Maryann promise that she'd help you with my room. It's a mess and I'm embarrassed for you to see it. But I know you'd like to get this job done and I'm so appreciative, I don't want to slow you down." She patted him on the arm and dashed toward her car.

Sam exhaled loudly. He didn't need Maryann's help, but what could he do? He got out of the car and strolled toward the front door. He poked his head inside. "Okay if I come in?"

"Sure," Maryann called. "I'm in Mom's room trying to decide where to start."

He made his way to the bedroom, stood in the doorway for a moment and watched Maryann hanging up clothes. "Well, I'd advise you not to put things in the closet, as we've got to clear it out so we can paint the inside.

She straightened after picking up a pair of sandals from the floor. "Oh, yeah. I hadn't thought about that. I guess the best thing is to pile the stuff on the bed and cover it."

"First, let's move the furniture toward the center of the room so I can maneuver around it. Then we'll get the pictures off the wall."

"I can see you have a system."

"Not sure how good a plan it is, but it worked for the living room."

"It's a good one." She tossed the shoes onto the bed, and helped him push the furniture toward the middle. Then taking an armful of hanging clothes out of the closet, she dropped them onto the bed. Sam reached above her and took a stack of boxes off the shelf. The top shoe box slid off the pile and plummeted to the floor. When it hit the carpet, the lid flipped off and the contents scattered.

When he reached down to collect the small digital camera and several pictures, he gasped. "Oh my God."

Maryann quickly moved to his side. "What is it?"

He handed her the camera and photos. Placing a hand over her mouth, she stared at the images as tears welled in her eyes.

CHAPTER TWENTY-SEVEN

Sam nervously gathered up the rest of the pictures and dropped them into the box, then flopped down on an overstuffed chair. "I feel like I've invaded your mother's privacy." He glanced at Maryann and noted this was the first time he'd ever seen her display any emotion. Those were real tears flowing down her cheeks.

She took a breath and quickly wiped them away. "I personally showed Mom how to take pictures of herself with this camera. I didn't think she'd ever used it."

"It appears you taught her well. Those are very graphic."

"Burke beat her so bad at times, she wouldn't go out of the house for days because she felt so ashamed. I told her to keep a record of his abuse." She flipped several of the photo's over and checked the backs. "Thank God, she dated them."

Sam stood. "I'm glad you're here. I don't know how I'd have handled this if I'd been alone. What are you going to do with them?"

Maryann replaced the lid. "They're going into a safe place. Who knows, she might need the proof of what he did to her in the future."

Sam pointed toward the closet. "Could you check the rest of those boxes and make sure there's nothing personal inside?"

"Sure." She quickly went through the remaining containers, then examined the inside of the closet. "There isn't anything else here you'd be uncomfortable handling." She picked up the questionable box and headed for the door, but turned before leaving the room. "You can proceed. This will only take me a few minutes."

Sam continued preparing the room for painting. As he taped the windows, his thoughts went to the pictures he'd just seen. Some showed blood oozing from fresh wounds around Mrs. Parker's mouth. Another showed her eyes almost swollen shut. A couple revealed bruises on her chest and back. He couldn't image the horror the woman must have gone through during such a beating. She probably wondered if she'd survive the next one. A chill ran down his back. Suddenly, he realized he'd stopped taping and was just staring out the window. Shaking his head, he got back to work, thankful Richard hadn't made it in to help him today.

࿇

Hawkman entered his office after negotiating with a potential client at a coffee shop downtown. He'd discovered the majority of female customers didn't want to come to his office, put preferred neutral ground for the initial meeting. The exchange he had today proved true to form, as the woman appeared quite comfortable and relaxed.

He stored the new folder in the desk drawer and checked his answering machine. Still no message from Detective Williams. His calendar showed no appointments for the rest of the day, so he decided to make a trip over to the Three C's Indian casino to ask a few questions. The strange encounter the boys had last night bothered him. Even though he'd tried to relieve their fears, he had a hunch someone had tailed them. He needed to find out who and why.

When he reached the casino, he went straight to the manager's office. He'd met Joshua Rainwater on a previous case and found him cooperative. The door stood open and the receptionist, who had the phone to her ear, motioned for him to have a seat.

After she hung up, she glanced his way and smiled. "Hello, Mr. Casey. How have you been? Haven't seen you in a long time."

Hawkman nodded. "Real good, Ms. Nancy. Is Mr. Rainwater in?"

"Yes. Just a moment and I'll check if he can see you right now."

She left her desk and went into an adjoining office, then returned within a few moments. "Give him a minute or two; he's on the phone. He'll come out and get you."

"Thanks."

She'd hardly sat down at her desk before Mr. Rainwater strolled into the outer office and extended his hand toward Hawkman.

"Hello, Mr. Casey. Good to see you. Come on in."

As Mr. Rainwater gave instructions to his assistant not to be disturbed, Hawkman took the chair in front of the large oak desk.

When the manager entered the office, he closed the door. "I'm assuming this isn't a social call, knowing your type of business," he said, settling into the leather chair. "So, how can I help you?"

Hawkman leaned forward, placing an arm on the desk. I'm trying to find a man who works for one of the casinos. I don't know which one, so thought I'd start with yours."

"Is he in some sort of trouble?

"No. I need to contact him for information about another person."

"Do you know his job title or better yet, do you have a name?"

"I don't know his position. And I've only heard him called, Madukarahat."

Rainwater didn't seem a bit surprised at the single title and immediately turned to his computer. His fingers flew across the keys as he studied the screen. "Hmm, don't see anyone on our staff by that name. Let me check the head office." After a few seconds, he smiled. "Ah, here he is. Looks like he's what the white man might call a roving cop."

"Is there an address or phone number?"

"No, not in this file. You'd have to get that data from headquarters."

"What does that job involve?"

"He travels to all our casinos in the area gathering certain reports and statistics. He then transports them back to the main office."

"Then I'd assume he'd get his paycheck from there?"

"Yes, they're located in Medford." He jotted down the address and handed it to Hawkman. "They can probably give you more information."

"Do you know if he's furnished a vehicle?"

He looked thoughtful. "I'm sure they'd give him a car, as that job requires traveling every day."

"When does he hit here?"

"There's no set schedule. We're required to report casino activity every twenty-four hours. If we slack our duty, we could get a big fine slapped against us from headquarters. So, to keep us on our toes, they don't tell us when he might appear." He smiled. "He could hit here today, tomorrow or maybe not until next week."

"Does he report to you?"

"No, I've never met him. He picks up the reports at the financial office."

Hawkman stood and held out his hand. "I won't take up any more of your time. I really appreciate the information. It makes my job a lot easier."

He grasped Hawkman's hand in a firm grip. "Glad I could be of help. Drop by anytime."

Hawkman felt no need to stop by the business office. Mr. Rainwater had furnished enough facts about Maduk to continue his search. He left the establishment and by the time he arrived back in Medford, the casino head office had closed. He took out his cell and punched in Sam's number. When he received no answer, he hung up and didn't leave a message. Either Sam had left his cell in the truck or happened to be in a poor signal area. Instead, Hawkman decided to bypass the cutoff at Hornbrook and go into Yreka. If Sam hadn't left the Parker's, he could follow him home in case he ran into any more problems. Reaching the house, he saw no sign of his son's truck, so he circled the block and headed toward Copco Lake.

When he entered the house, he found Sam and Jennifer in the living room. Their expressions told him, they were engaged in a very serious conversation.

"What's going on?"

Jennifer waved for him to join them. "Come in here and listen to Sam's story."

Hawkman hung up his hat, adjusted his eye-patch, and ran his fingers through his hair. "Don't tell me you've another tale of woe." He grabbed a beer from the refrigerator, then moved to his favorite chair.

Sam quickly rehashed what he'd told Jennifer about the box of pictures in Lilly's room. "Man, it made me feel like I'd ventured into a person's personal domain. I've felt bad all day."

"Don't let it get under your skin," Hawkman said. "The woman kept them for her own protection. If she ever has to go to court over Burke's death, she has proof the beatings occurred."

Sam put his head in his hands. "They were horrible. She looked like some monster with swollen eyes. Her face all puffy and blood running out the corners of her mouth." He shuddered. "How could any man do that to a woman, much less his wife?"

Jennifer reached over and touched Sam's shoulder. "Unfortunately, there are a lot of sick people in this world. I'm afraid Burke Parker was one of them."

"I didn't see all the pictures. I didn't want to. But they also affected Maryann. I've never seen her cry, but she actually shed tears when she looked at them."

"What did she do with the photos?" Hawkman asked.

"I don't know. She put everything into the box, then left the room telling me she would find a safe place to store them."

"At least she didn't throw them away."

Sam shook his head. " Oh, no, I didn't get that impression at all. In fact, she seemed very pleased her mother had taken the shots."

"Are you going back there tomorrow?"

"Yeah," he said, flopping back on the couch. "I want to

get that place finished real soon. I'd like to relax the rest of the summer. This whole ordeal is driving me nuts."

"Did you by any chance see the car again that followed you and Richard?"

"No. Did you hear anything from Detective Williams?"

"Nope. But I did a little sleuthing. I know where Maduk works and I hope to find out more tomorrow."

Sam's eyes grew big. "Where?"

"He works for the Indian Casino Company and travels from one establishment to the other in this area and collects reports, then takes them to the head office in Medford."

"Did you see him?" Jennifer asked.

"No. And it won't be easy, as he's not on any fixed schedule. I doubt seriously if I can get that information out of the head office, as they keep his comings and goings pretty well under raps."

Sam frowned. "That sounds like a high-ranking job. He must have some sort of a security clearance."

"He could very well have cleared for one. There's no blemish on his record."

"But you told me he killed a man," Sam said.

"The tribe took care of it. He was never written up in our police records. So when he applied for a job, that never showed up. And we only heard about it through word of mouth. So it could never be proven in a court of law. It's all considered hearsay."

Sam rubbed his hands across his face. "This whole thing about Maduk is mighty complicated."

Hawkman nodded. "I definitely agree."

CHAPTER TWENTY-EIGHT

Sam received a text message on his cell phone from Richard stating he wouldn't be able to help him the rest of the week because of work at the stable, but he'd pick him up early Saturday morning. Sam groaned at the thought of being alone with Maryann for the next couple of days. But he'd brought this mess on himself and couldn't blame Richard. He'd work hard at getting everything painted on the inside, then maybe they could finish the whole job by the weekend.

Thursday morning, on his way to Medford, Hawkman received a call from Detective Williams.

"More Parker reports arrived from the lab. You might want to stop by. I think you'll find them pretty interesting."

"I'll be there within thirty minutes."

Anxious to see the information, Hawkman pushed down the accelerator. He parked in a visitor space at the police station and hurried inside. When he reached the detective's office, Williams motioned for him to have a seat as he poured them a cup of coffee. When the detective sat down at his desk, he pushed a folder toward Hawkman.

"Take a gander at this. You're not going to believe it."

Hawkman took a sip of the hot brew, then opened the file. After reading for several minutes, he glanced up. "Paraquat? My God, that's potent stuff."

"Thought you'd find it interesting. They found traces around the tissues of his mouth. And toxic reactions were apparent in his lungs, liver, kidneys, the lining of his stomach and intestines."

Hawkman leaned back in the chair. "I had a vicious case in the Agency involving paraquat. It's a herbicide for weed and grass control. Classified in the States as "restricted use" and can only be purchased by those who are licensed applicators. The US adds a blue dye and a sharp odor to serve as a warning. Yet, this report indicates it was in the original form."

Williams leaned forward on his elbows and laced his fingers into a pyramid "How the hell do you think someone got hold of the undoctored stuff?"

Hawkman shoved back his cowboy hat with his forefinger. "It could have been smuggled in from Mexico. We have lots of foreign gardeners in the area."

Williams nodded. That's possible. Its brown coloring could easily be mistaken for soda or coffee. Or any other brown liquid, as far as that goes."

"Did they find any traces of it on the eating or drinking utensils you found in the motel room?"

"Not yet, but the lab noted, since they've identified the poison, it won't take long to run tests on the other items we shipped. We should get those reports within a day or two."

Hawkman placed the papers back into the file. "I imagine with Burke Parker being in such poor health, it probably hit him like a bomb."

The detective sighed. "Yep. I doubt he suffered long."

"Think I'll do a little research on the computer and see what else I can find out about this herbicide." Hawkman stood and stuck his thumbs in the front pockets of his jeans. "Let me know when you get the other reports. I'll be interested to see if those utensils show any traces. My gut tells me they will." He tapped the back of the chair with his fingers. "Appears you have a murder on your hands."

"Yep, sure looks that way."

Hawkman left the police station and drove to his office. Once inside, he immediately booted up the computer and linked to Google where he typed in paraquat. Years ago, while still in the Agency, he remembered a big debate over this toxin because they found it in marijuana smuggled into the States from Mexico. The US eventually banned the use of this particular herbicide for destroying marijuana fields in the United States.

A long controversy brewed about banning paraquat for all purposes, but to this day no action has been taken. At least they'd placed serious restrictions on the poison. Hawkman studied several reports, but didn't come across anything he didn't already know. He printed out a couple of recent articles and put them in a file.

Leaning back in his chair, he tapped his chin with his pencil and tried to figure out how someone could have administered the poison to Parker. Like Jennifer said, anyone in this town might have done it, since no one liked the man. But he wanted to narrow the number of suspects. He'd start by finding out where Parker had been the days before his death, where he'd eaten, and from which liquor store he bought his booze.

The motel where they found Parker's body was akin to a cheap boarding house. He paid by the week and had no maid service. Williams had questioned the head man, who'd stated he didn't know a thing about Parker other than he paid his bill up front and didn't bother any one. Since the place had no vacancies, the manager didn't hang around, and knew nothing of his patron's visitors.

The detective had also talked to the neighbors. They were all drifters or loners and had no idea when Parker came and went. In fact, some didn't even know what the man looked like.

Sam had mentioned the only reason Lilly stayed married to Burke was for the money he gave her every month. So, he must have done some sort of work as he couldn't pay his rent, keep up his booze habit, and still give his wife money on what little he received through a disability check. Parker more than likely did odd jobs and Lilly probably had no idea where he got his money since the two were on such bad terms. She just took it and ran.

The Indian also aroused his interest. His gut told him

Maduk was somehow involved in the whole scenario. He'd like to meet him face to face and ask a few questions. A thought struck him and he rummaged through his pockets. He finally found the slip of paper Rainwater had given him with the casino headquarters' location, but no phone number. Hawkman pulled the directory from the desk drawer, found the listing and punched it in.

Figuring salaries were paid weekly, he took a chance. "Hello. What time will the paychecks be ready? Thank you."

"Now if the rest could be so simple," Hawkman said aloud. Tomorrow's going be a busy day, he thought.

He worked for a couple of hours on other cases, then checked his watch. He wanted to make sure he left in time to swing by the Parker place, just in case Sam got detained and couldn't leave before dark. He felt uneasy about the boy's safety until he learned more about the black Buick. He could call Sam, but didn't want to give the impression of checking up on him. Young men didn't like parents nosing into their business, their egos were sensitive. Hawkman knew if he casually dropped by, he could use the excuse of wanting to see how much they'd accomplished.

He left the office and arrived in Yreka within an hour. When he drove by the Parker house and saw no sign of Sam's pickup, he headed home. Pulling into the driveway, it relieved his mind to see the small truck beside the house. Sam sat at the kitchen bar with a whopping sandwich on a plate and glanced up grinning.

"I'm starved. Forgot to eat today."

"Well, you seem to be in a much better mood than last night."

"Oh, yeah. Things went real good. While I painted Mrs. Parker's bedroom and bath, Maryann prepared her room for tomorrow. It worked out great. Once I get the inside finished, then Richard and I can concentrate on the outside this weekend. Hopefully we'll wrap up the job Sunday night."

"Glad to hear it. That'll give you a few weeks before you have to return to school."

"Did you find out anything today?" Sam asked.

"Eat and then we'll talk." He glanced over at the empty computer center. "Where's Jennifer?"

"I think she's done some fishing today. She's on the dock securing the umbrella and picking up her gear."

Hawkman strolled over and opened the sliding glass door. "Need any help?" he called.

She waved him off and walked up the gangplank with her pole, fishing creel and a big smile.

"You look mighty content. Did you have some luck?"

"Yes, I caught a twenty inch trout. It's in the refrigerator."

"Hey, that's great."

"What a fighter. I had so much fun bringing in that fish. He jumped out of the water several times. I thought I'd lost the little sucker when he leaped up the last time, but I hurried and got the net under him before he shook the hook."

Hawkman hung her rod on the porch rack, then put his arm around her shoulders as they went inside. "Wish I'd been here to share the excitement."

"What?" Sam asked between bites.

Jennifer took the fish from the refrigerator and showed off her catch, then told Sam about how hard the trout fought until she'd won the battle.

Sam munched a few chips. "Fantastic. I'm bound and determined to do some fishing before the summer's over. Hope I have your kind of luck." He then turned to Hawkman. "Okay, what'd you learn today?"

Jennifer jerked up her head. "You didn't say you had any news."

Hawkman hung his hat on a peg in the corner along with this shoulder holster. "I enjoyed your story a lot more." He took a beer from the refrigerator and sat down at the kitchen bar. Jennifer climbed onto the stool next to him.

"Appears Burke Parker was murdered."

CHAPTER TWENTY-NINE

Sam awoke early Friday morning, rolled over and covered his head with his pillow. He sure didn't look forward to going to the Parker's after what Hawkman had told him and Jennifer last night. He'd heard about paraquat in one of his history classes where they'd touched on the agriculture of the Middle East countries and Mexico. Many people became ill handling this herbicide. Some had died from inhaling it or accidentally ingesting the poison. "Bad stuff," he mumbled, throwing the covers aside and sitting on the edge of the bed. He picked up his electric razor from the dresser and ran it over his face as he thought about the murder.

He figured Hawkman had already come to the conclusion Mr. Parker had been poisoned after seeing the pictures of the body. Not much got by his dad. He'd bided his time until they discovered what kind of toxicant caused the damage. Sam had the impression though, it'd surprised Hawkman when the report stated Parker had swallowed paraquat, a poison not generally found in a normal household. He remembered Hawkman snooping around the Parker place and assumed his search had been for a substance deadly enough to kill a man.

More questions entered Sam's mind. He wondered if Maryann put the paraquat in Burke's food or drink during the Memorial holiday? Or did Maduk? Her dad could probably find paraquat in its natural form more easily, because of his contact with foreign laborers. Maybe once Maduk acquired it, he'd given it to his daughter and instructed her on its use. The thought sent a chill down Sam's spine.

He ran a hand over his smooth face, then placed the razor

back on the dresser. Unplugging his cell phone, he sent a text message to Richard. After dressing in his painting clothes, he clipped the phone to his belt. He threw a clean set of clothes into a duffle bag, opened the door of his bedroom and made his way quietly through the silent house to the kitchen.

Plopping the duffle on the end of the counter, he opened the refrigerator and spotted several of his favorite fruit-on-the-bottom yogurts. Jennifer must have gone shopping yesterday. He grabbed a peach one, threw two pieces of bread into the toaster and poured himself a large glass of milk. After buttering the hot bread, he carried his food to the kitchen bar. Just as he sat down, Hawkman meandered into the kitchen.

"Hope I didn't wake you," Sam said.

"Nope. Didn't hear you at all. In fact, I thought you were still asleep."

"I want to get through early so Richard and I can take in a movie over at the Broadway."

"Sounds like a good plan."

"So what are you going to investigate today?"

Hawkman grinned as he put on a pot of coffee. "You sound like Jennifer with all your questions. I'll let you know in due time."

Sam laughed. "Fair enough."

He pointed toward the yogurt. "Any more left?"

"Oh, yeah. There's a bunch in all different flavors."

When Sam finished eating, he grabbed the duffle bag off the counter and headed toward the door. "Would you tell Jennifer I'll be late?"

Hawkman nodded. "By the way, keep what I told you last night under your hat. Let Detective Williams break the news to Maryann and her mother."

"Don't worry, I won't say a word."

❧

After Sam left, Hawkman poured coffee into an insulated mug, placed his shoulder holster on the counter, then shrugged into his jeans jacket. He had his hat in his hand when Jennifer appeared beside him, still in her robe.

"My gosh, you guys were up at the crack of dawn," she said, stifling a yawn.

"Sam wanted to get an early start. He and Richard are going to the movies after they finish tonight. He said to tell you he'd be late."

She took a cup from the cupboard. "Okay. So where are you going at this hour?"

"I've got some surveillance to do. If I don't get going, I could miss my target."

She frowned. "Your target? Are you planning on shooting him?"

Hawkman laughed. "No, just a figure of speech. I've got someone I want to watch. And I'm not sure when he'll arrive at the destination I have in mind."

"That's a very vague explanation."

"I know. But right now I'm not mentioning any names or places. Maybe later I'll let you in on it, if my hunch is right."

She let out a sigh. "You sure know how to leave a person in the dark."

He grinned and gave her a hug. "I'm going to be doing some bar-hopping tonight. So, I'll also be late."

She put a hand on her hip. "Looks like it's going to be mighty quiet around here today."

He shrugged. "Well, you're always complaining we're too noisy. Now you'll have a chance to get a lot of writing done without interruption and work way into the night if you so desire." Giving her a quick kiss, he plopped on his hat, grabbed his gun and coffee, then scooted out the front door before she had time to respond.

Hawkman arrived in Yreka at eight forty-five and headed straight for the courthouse. He slid his gun and holster under the seat, then threw on the alarm before locking the vehicle. He didn't want to explain his weapon when he went through the metal detector.

Taking the stairs two at a time to the second floor, he rounded the corner and entered his friend's office.

Sheila glanced up and smiled. "Well, hello, Hawkman. Good to see you. My goodness, you're up and about early."

"I need some information and hope you can help me locate a piece of property."

"I'll sure give it a try."

He sat down in front of her desk and printed out Madukarahat on a sheet of paper. This is the only name I know of this person. Is there any chance you can tell me if he owns any property in the county?"

"It's common for Native Americans to only go by one name. I'll throw it into the computer and see if anything comes up."

The machine hummed for several seconds as Sheila kept her eyes on the monitor. "This is very interesting."

"What is?"

"Looks like he purchased a small house on a piece of property within the last six months."

"Why do you look puzzled?"

"I don't see a real estate broker or a mortgage company listed. Looks like he paid cash. Of course, the value of these places is not high because of the location."

Hawkman scowled. "Where is it?"

"It's up in the hills with nothing more than a dirt road access. There are a few scattered homes throughout this area, but they're so dispersed that there's usually miles between each piece of property because of the rugged terrain. And it costs a bundle to have a septic tank installed, plus the thoroughfare maintained. However, the electricity and phone lines are in place. I'll print out the map and description."

After she handed him the copy, he stood. "Thanks, Sheila. I owe you lunch."

She laughed. "One of these days I'm going to have to take you up on all those promises. Maybe Jennifer could join us."

"If I can ever get her away from that computer, we'll give you a call."

"By the way, how's her next mystery coming? I love her stories. I wait eagerly for the next book."

"I'll tell her a fan wanted to know. Maybe it will push her to get it finished."

"Great."

Hawkman waved and left. In his vehicle, he slipped on his holster, then drove to Medford to the casino headquarters. He parked across the street and had a good view of the front, plus the small parking area beside the building. If he had Maduk pegged, he'd arrive right at eleven when the clerk said the paychecks would be ready. If he didn't catch him today, he'd have to wait another week.

At five minutes to eleven, a dark black Buick with tinted windows pulled into a parking slot directly in front of the office. Hawkman slipped on his sunglasses. He figured Maduk had his own spies and would know him by sight. Hunching down in the seat, he watched as the Indian climbed out of the car and headed for the front door. Once the man stepped inside, Hawkman slipped out of his vehicle and strolled toward the Buick. Opening his jacket so his gun showed, he leaned against the driver side of the car and waited.

Within a few minutes, Maduk bounded out the front door, but came to a sudden halt when he spotted Hawkman.

"Good morning, Madukarahat."

The Indian pulled himself up straight and sauntered toward the Buick. He stopped at the front end of the car. His hand rested on the handle of the knife hanging from his belt.

"Relax," Hawkman said. "I just want to talk."

"I've been expecting you."

"Oh? How come?"

"You've been nosing around town asking questions."

"Yes, that's true."

"How'd you find out my name? And how'd you know I'd be here?"

"I'm a private investigator; it's part of my job."

Maduk stared at him. "What do you want to talk about?"

"Lilly, Maryann and Burke Parker."

The Indian's dark eyes narrowed. "Let's go for a ride."

Hawkman shook his head. "No, I don't think so." He pointed across the street to a small cafe tucked between two buildings. "How about a cup of coffee. It's on me."

Maduk glared at him. "What's wrong? You don't trust me?"

Hawkman met his stare. "How can I trust a man I don't know? If you have nothing to hide, it shouldn't bother you to join me in a public place."

"You're a wise man." Maduk stepped off the curb and brushed past Hawkman as he headed toward the diner.

Hawkman followed and they sat in a booth near the window. After the waitress set a mug before each man, she placed a coffee carafe on the end of the table.

Maduk's black eyes twinkled as his gaze bore into Hawkman. "I'm listening."

Hawkman poured them each a cup. "I'm not going to beat around the bush. You know I'm aware that you're Maryann Parker's real father."

"Who told you?"

"Your daughter told my son."

His lips curled slightly. "Ah, yes. I should have known."

"Why do you say that?"

"She's sweet on your boy, Sam."

"I don't know about that, but they've known each other for a long time."

Maduk nodded.

"I understand you and Lilly Parker have been lovers for years."

The Indian glowered. "What business is that of yours?"

"The police found Burke Parker dead in a motel room."

Maduk leaned back against the booth. His stare never left Hawkman's face. "Yes, I read about his death in the paper. What does that have to do with me?"

"You had every reason to want him out of the picture."

Maduk raised up out of the seat and leaned across the table, his face within inches of Hawkman's. "You tell me why I wanted him gone."

CHAPTER THIRTY

Hawkman's gaze locked with Maduk's fiery stare. "Sit down and we'll talk about it."

Maduk eased back into the seat and folded his large hands on the table top. "I'm listening."

"Why didn't you take Lilly and Maryann to the reservation when you learned of Burke Parker's abuse?"

"That's none of your damn business."

Hawkman leaned forward. "Your people banned you from the reservation because you killed a man from your own tribe. Isn't that right?" he hissed.

Maduk clenched his hands into fists. "That happened many years ago."

"Doesn't matter. The police will soon find out. Then, they're going to hunt you down and ask many questions."

"Why?"

"Because they've discovered someone murdered Burke Parker."

"Oh yeah? How?"

"You know the herbicide paraquat?"

"Isn't that a man-made poison to kill weeds?"

"Yes. Do you know where to get it?"

"I don't like that question." Maduk said, rising. "I hated Burke Parker with a passion, and had many opportunities to kill him. But I didn't. If I had, it would have been with this."

Hawkman jumped as Maduk's knife stuck in the table in front of his chest. He felt beads of sweat form on his forehead when he realized he could've been a dead man in a matter of seconds.

Maduk reached over and pulled the knife from the surface. "I'm through talking to you today. Maybe we'll meet again at another time."

Hawkman watched the big Indian walk out the door.

A flustered waitress hurried toward him. "Sir, are you okay?"

He wiped his face with his hand. "Yeah, I'm fine." He pulled a ten dollar bill from his pocket and handed it to her. "Keep the change and keep quiet about this incident."

"Oh, thank you, sir. I'll say nothing."

Hawkman rose and left the diner. He didn't believe for a minute the young waitress hadn't hightailed it to the back room to tell her fellow workers what had just happened, but he really didn't care. By the time he reached the street, the Buick had disappeared.

He climbed into the 4X4 and settled on the seat. Resting his hands on the steering wheel, he wondered how he'd missed Maduk's hand reaching for the knife. Having one eye covered didn't help. It'd been a long time since he'd met a man who had such dexterity with a blade. Harley had warned him. He should have paid more attention. Taking a deep breath, he felt lucky to be alive.

He picked up the papers on the passenger seat and studied the map to Maduk's new home. It appeared he could make it there and back before nightfall. He'd be taking a chance if Maduk decided to go home early. If the road had little traffic, the Indian would spot him immediately. Checking the gas gauge, he decided to top off the tank, just in case he needed to make a fast getaway over unknown terrain.

❧

Sam reached the Parker home early and it eased his mind to find Maryann out in the front yard watering the garden she'd planted.

"Look, Sam." She smiled, pointing toward the wet ground and gesturing toward the flower pots on the porch. "Little green shoots are popping up all over."

He glanced at the new forming plants. "Looks like you have a green thumb."

"Thanks."

"Is your room ready?"

"Yep. Everything's covered, closet is clear and I even taped the windows for you. Don't worry about making any noise, Mom had to go into work early again today. I hate to see her working so hard, but she says she needs the money."

"Thanks for telling me, I wouldn't want to disturb her. By the way, I'm grateful for your help."

"No problem. I'm sure you'll be happy to get it all done."

He nodded, picked up the small ladder from the porch and lugged it into Maryann's room. Slapping on the stiff painter's hat, he pried open a new gallon can, stirred it, poured the paint into the pan, then carefully adjusted it on the ladder before climbing the rungs. He soon finished the ceiling without any interruptions and moved the equipment to one of the corners. His back to the door, he suddenly realized the house had become deathly quiet. An uneasy prickling of his spine made him glance toward the hallway. He almost dropped the paint roller. A huge man stood in the doorway staring at him.

"Hello, Sam."

He gulped, recognizing Maduk from the picture Hawkman had shown him and Richard. His words fumbled from his mouth. "Uh, do I know you?"

"My name's Madukarahat."

"Hello Mr. Madukarahat."

"You may call me Maduk."

Sam took a deep breath, climbed down the ladder and approached the Indian. "I'd offer to shake hands, Mr. Maduk, but mine are covered in paint."

"No problem. Thought I'd let you know I spoke with your father this morning."

Sam felt his mouth drop open. "What about?"

"A number of things. He's a good man, but he needs to learn how to use a knife."

Swallowing hard, Sam felt his stomach constrict. "Is he all right?"

Maryann stepped up beside her father. "Don't let him frighten you, Sam. I'm sure he's fine." She glanced at Maduk. "Isn't he?"

"Of course. He gave no reason for me to kill him at this time." He turned his attention back to Sam. "But you might tell your dad I don't like getting pushed into a corner."

Maduk turned to Maryann. "Tell your mother I'll be back. I need to talk to her." Then he walked out of the house.

Sam hurried to the door and recognized the car as the big man drove away. So it was him in the Buick, Sam thought. He went outside to his small truck and retrieved his cell phone from the glove compartment. Punching in Hawkman's number, he held his breath for several seconds before he breathed a sigh of relief. "Hawkman, are you okay."

"Yeah, I'm fine. Why?"

"I'm at the Parker's house and Maduk just paid me a visit. He told me you needed to learn how to use a knife."

"Oh, really."

"It scared me. Did he try to cut you?"

"No, but believe me, I'll be careful around him."

"He also told me to warn you that he didn't like being pushed into a corner."

"That's interesting."

"When did you see him?" Sam asked.

"I'll tell you about it tomorrow. I'm heading into the hills and my cell will probably cut out. Is Maduk still around?"

"No, he left in that same Buick Richard and I saw the other night."

"Keep on alert while roaming around town. If you spot him again, call me. If I don't answer, leave a voice message."

"Okay."

After Sam hung up, he took a big swig from the water bottle he'd placed on the seat. Then glancing at the container, it dawned on him his truck had been unlocked. What if Maduk had doctored the water with poison. It tasted okay and didn't appear discolored. He wiped a hand across his face. Don't let your imagination get the best of you, he thought. Settle down. He locked up the vehicle and strode back into the house.

Maryann stood in the living room, her arms wrapped around her waist. "Did Maduk really talk to your dad?"

Sam nodded. "Yeah." He brushed past her and headed for the bedroom.

She followed on his heels. "Where did they see each other and what did they talk about?"

"I don't know, Maryann. Hawkman didn't say. He doesn't talk to me about his business," he lied.

She stopped at the door of her bedroom and stared at Sam as he climbed the ladder and picked up the paint roller.

CHAPTER THIRTY-ONE

After Hawkman hung up, he felt anger toward Maduk for scaring Sam. He didn't like it a bit. At least tonight, he planned on being in Yreka and if his son needed help, he could get there quickly.

Since Maduk had just left Yreka, he might have time to search the man's house, but he couldn't bet on it. He'd have to be extremely cautious to avoid getting caught by an Indian who could carve him up like a jack-o-lantern.

Hawkman's attention settled on the area he approached, figuring the cut off must be close. He soon spotted a dirt road that swerved up into the hills where he could barely see the outline of a building nestled among tall trees. This must be it, he thought.

A large padlocked gate barred his way. He studied the road ahead, and decided to drive past the house, find a place to hide his vehicle, then hike up to the property from the rear. It would give him a better opportunity to escape if necessary.

He accelerated over the small crest and found a clump of trees off to the side of the road where he parked his 4X4 deep in the cluster. Perfect, he thought as he climbed out of the truck. He reached behind the seat where he kept a small duffle bag of things he might need, and pocketed the lock pick, then stuck a buck knife into his boot. The house should almost be in a straight line from here, he thought, climbing up the embankment.

When he reached the top, he could see one of the walls of the small cottage. He liked the way it sat nestled in the middle of the trees. The forest bordering the property gave him good cover from anyone looking out. Staying within the shadows, he made his way toward the building. The area seemed well maintained. Scrub brush had been cleared for several yards around the structure, leaving a nice area for a yard and a good fire break if necessary. Fresh paint made the sides of the house gleam in the bright sunlight.

Nice place, Hawkman though, as he moved closer. He saw no signs of life except a blue jay chasing a squirrel across the roof top. Crouching, he flipped up the flap on his shoulder holster, then approached the side of the garage that had no windows. Cautiously, he made his way around to the rear where he spotted a door. Keeping his back against the wall, he reached over and tried the knob, it turned and opened. Slipping inside, he found it empty of any vehicles. Garden tools were neatly arranged on the shelves with several shovels, rakes and other implements hanging on the wall underneath. He noticed one of the spades had remnants of soil clinging to it as if it'd been used recently. Quickly checking a small enclosed cabinet, he found no poisonous herbicides or sprays of any kind.

Hawkman peered out the window where a covered walkway led to the house. He tried the side door, and found it unlocked. He assumed when one lived this far out in the country, you didn't worry much about people breaking in. He smiled to himself as he moved forward in the breezeway, his gaze on the long driveway in front.

The door to the house didn't budge, so he used his pick and within a matter of seconds found himself in a nice sized kitchen. A large recessed window sat over the sink where one could view a breathtaking scene of the forest as far as the eye could see. He moved quickly, opening the doors of the cabinets and small pantry, scanning their contents. Finding nothing lethal, he moved to other parts of the house. The master bedroom, although rather small, seemed ample. Only men's clothing hung in the closet and most of the dresser drawers were empty except for one, which held a few pairs of boxer shorts and a couple of tee shirts. In the bathroom, male toiletries cluttered the counter. The cabinet underneath the sink contained only a couple of cleaning agents.

Hawkman quickly checked the rest of the house, but found nothing indicating any sort of toxins. He moved into the living room and glanced out the front window. A dirt cloud rising from the road indicated someone approaching. He scurried out the back door and ran toward a grove of trees. Jumping behind a large oak, he peeked around the trunk just in time to see the Buick pull up in front of the garage. He exhaled in relief and headed deeper into the woods toward the direction of his own vehicle.

He almost tripped when his his foot sunk into a soft mound of dirt. On closer observation, he came to the conclusion something had been recently buried. Possibly a dead animal. His curiosity aroused, he found a strong limb and dug into the ground. Within a few minutes, the shallow grave revealed his worst fears. Not touching anything, he tossed the dirt back into the hole. He took his buck knife from his boot and marked the tree trunks on each side of the spot so he'd be able to find the exact area. Once he estimated how far he'd come from the house, then calculated the distance back to the road, he figured he could find the spot again without much trouble.

Hightailing it back to the road, he jumped into his 4X4. By the time he reached Yreka, darkness veiled the area. While checking his cell phone to see if Sam had left any message, his stomach rumbled and he realized he hadn't eaten all day. It was still too early to drop in at the bar where Lilly worked and he certainly had no desire to eat there. Having plenty of time and wanting more than fast food, he stopped at one of the local restaurants. He waved at several familiar faces before the waitress led him to a booth. While eating, he thought about Sam and hoped he'd left the Parker place by now. The boys would work Saturday and Sunday on the outside of the house, and hopefully they'd get the job finished. He predicted his son had learned a lesson about volunteering his services.

Sam would definitely have a lot to tell Richard tonight. It

pleased him that the boys got along so well. And Sam certainly had no problem communicating with his deaf friend.

After eating a big steak, baked potato and salad, Hawkman felt his energy returning. He left a hearty tip, then moseyed up to the cashier's counter.

"Great meal, Susan,

"Thanks, Hawkman," she said, counting out his change. "Come back soon."

He took a toothpick from the container and gave her a wave. "Will do."

Hawkman drove down to the end of Main street, found a parking spot under a street light, then walked a half block to the place where Lilly worked. No wonder only low life patronized this place. The lighted sign above the door hung precariously on a few bolts and part of the lettering had burned out. It appeared no one had bothered to sweep the litter of wadded empty cigarette packs and used butts from the front sidewalk for days. A half bottle of beer perched precariously on the window rim next to the front door. When he stepped inside, the loud music ripped at his ear drums. His eye soon adjusted to the interior and he spotted the eating area on the left, the bar to the right. An old fashioned juke box rested in front of a tiny dance floor where several couples were juggling for positions.

He strolled up to the bar and straddled a stool. Glancing around, he spotted Lilly in a skimpy uniform revealing most of her breasts and buttocks. He had to admit, she still had the figure to wear such an outfit. She slapped a couple of hands when they reached out and patted her on the behind. The men then burst out laughing.

"Ah, come on Lilly, be a sport."

"Just keep your damned hands off me or I'll call the bouncer," she retorted.

It appeared she only waited on the tables; the patrons at the counter were served by the bartender. This suited Hawkman as he could observe her without being noticed.

He studied the contents of the bar and spotted a group of less than half full bottles setting to one side of the working area. About that time, a guy wearing a trucking uniform came from the back pushing a dolly piled high with boxes. Once the cartons were stacked at the end of the counter, he left and the bartender began removing liquor bottles from the containers. Hawkman watched with interest as he stocked the booze. He'd put a new bottle under the counter, then remove a partly filled one and placed it to the side with the others. About that time, one of the young waitresses from the restaurant come around the corner.

"Hey, Gus, I'm off duty now." She pointed to the partially filled bottles. "Are these for us?"

"Yeah, take whatever you want."

She gathered about three of the fullest, then headed for the door.

Hawkman slid off the stool and followed her. Once outside, he cleared his throat. "Man, that's mighty nice of Gus giving you that booze."

She glanced up and smiled. "Oh, yeah, on Friday night when he gets the new stock, he lets the help have the leftovers." She held up one that contained about a cupful of whiskey. "It's understood we can take up to three, since they only have a little left in them. But if I save the bottles for a couple or three weeks, I can have a nice little get together." She giggled and batted her eyelashes. "Wanta come to one of my parties, big man? They're the talk of the town."

"Thanks, but don't think my wife would approve."

She turned her mouth down in a comical grimace. "Ah, darn, you're married."

"Yeah, afraid so."

"Well, if you ever get tired of being tied down, just ask for Charlene."

He smiled. "I'll try to remember. Oh, does Lilly ever take her share of the bottles?"

The girl furrowed her brow. "I don't know. I'm usually gone before she leaves on Friday night. And there's the rule we can't take any before we're off work or we'll get in trouble. Why not ask Lilly, she's working tonight."

"I didn't want to ask her right out because my wife and I wanted to get her a little gift. You know since her husband died. But we don't know what kind of liquor she likes."

"Oh, that's nice. Ask Gus. He might know."

"Okay, thanks, Charlene, I'll do that."

He walked back inside and slid onto the stool.

"What can I get ya, partner?" the bartender asked, swishing a wet towel across the surface.

"I'll have a beer."

Since Hawkman was the only patron at the bar, Gus hung around him making small talk.

"How's business?" Hawkman asked.

"Could be better."

"Yeah, I hear that all over."

"People aren't spending as much on a good time nowadays. They have to save their money for food and rent."

"It's bound to get better. Say, isn't that Lilly Parker over there?"

"Yeah, she's one that's had a hard time."

"I heard her husband died."

Gus snorted. "Some husband. He'd beat her to within inch of her life. Barely gave her enough money to live on. That's why she had to take this job. He was a real loser. When he found out that she could get free booze, he'd make her nab as many of those partial bottles she could manage. Then if he didn't think it was enough, he'd slap her around. I felt so sorry for her, a few times I gave her a couple of full bottles, just so he wouldn't hurt her. But since the old man died, she seldom takes any of them. Maybe a bottle of scotch when her daughter's around."

"Well, Gus, it's getting late, I better get myself home. Thanks for the chat."

"Yeah, come on back anytime. Glad to have your business."

"Sure thing," Hawkman dropped some bills on the counter and left.

Driving toward Copco Lake, his mind drifted to the bartender. He didn't even have to ask any questions. The man told him all he needed to know.

CHAPTER THIRTY-TWO

Maryann paced the floor until midnight when she spotted the headlight beams of her mother's vehicle pull into the carport. She quickly went into the kitchen and made a scotch and water. When Lilly entered the door, she practically staggered as she dropped onto the couch. Letting out a sigh, she removed her shoes and rubbed her feet.

"I'm beat."

"Mom, I know you're working as a bar maid over at that horrible place. You're going to work yourself to death trying to hold down two jobs. And you're only making yourself vulnerable to trouble in a liquor joint."

"The tips are excellent, and the extra money comes in handy. Don't worry, I know how to handle vulgar men. I've been around a long time."

Maryann threw up her hands in frustration. "I hope you're not doing this for me."

Lilly smiled. "I'm doing it for both of us. One of these days I'm going to have to purchase a newer car. Mine's about shot." Then she noticed the drink on the end table. "Oh, honey, thank you." She took a sip and smacked her lips. "This will help me sleep."

Maryann sat down on the overstuffed chair next to her mother. "I don't think you better go to bed just yet. I have a feeling Maduk will be here shortly."

Lilly glanced at her daughter. "Really? When did you talk to him?"

"He stopped by today and told Sam to tell his dad he didn't like being backed into a corner."

She frowned. "Why would he say that?"

"I guess he spoke with Mr. Casey and isn't too happy. Anyway, Maduk said he wanted to talk to you and that he'd be back. I don't know if he meant tonight or when."

Maryann thought she saw a flash of fear in her mother's eyes. "Mom are you keeping something from me?"

"I'm worried about Maduk. If anything happens to him, then all my dreams are smashed."

"Mom, he hasn't taken you away yet. When are you going to give up on him?"

Lilly pointed a finger at her daughter. "Maryann, how can you say that? He's stuck by me all these years."

"Yeah, on the sidelines," she said, slapping her hands against her thighs.

"I forbid you to talk like that about your father," Lilly said, her voice quivering.

Maryann closed her eyes and raised her hands. "Okay, I'm sorry. I'm just trying to be realistic. But I think you've been living in a fantasy world too long."

Her mother sighed. "You might be right, but I feel in my heart things are going to change."

"I hope so, Mom. For your sake." Maryann jerked her head around at the sound of footsteps on the porch. "I think he's here."

Maduk opened the door and stepped inside. He glared at the two women with ferocity.

Lilly came out of her seat. "Maduk, what's wrong?"

"The police discovered Burke Parker was murdered."

Her face paled. "Are you sure?"

"Yes. The big man called Hawkman told me."

Lilly slumped back down on the couch. "How?"

"Poisoned by paraquat."

Maryann stared at him wide-eyed and stepped back against the wall. "Dear God, that means we'll all be under investigation."

"That's right. Lilly, I need to talk to you privately. Let's go for a ride."

"Let me get on some comfortable shoes, " she said, heading toward her bedroom.

Maryann watched out the window and made sure the car had turned the corner before she grabbed the flashlight from the pantry and dashed out the back door. Making her way around to the carport, she knelt down and opened the cabinet doors. Shining the light inside, she sucked in her breath, as she frantically searched the shelves. Finally, she slammed the doors and stood up. Leaning against the cabinet, she ran the beam around the area. "It's gone," she mumbled. "But who took it?"

"What's the problem, child?"

Her heart skipped a beat as she whirled around and shined the light into a man's face. "Frank, you scared me half to death. What are you doing here?"

"Just checking to see if your mom left me any food."

"Not tonight. Sorry."

"That's okay, she's a good woman."

Her heart still pounding, she hurried into the house and locked the back door. "That guy gives me the creeps," she said aloud.

❧

Early Saturday morning, Hawkman received a phone call from Detective Williams.

"Called your office yesterday, but didn't catch you. More of the lab test came in and traces of paraquat were found in the liquor bottles that we confiscated from the motel room. Looks like someone tampered with Parker's booze."

"Any fingerprints?"

"A thumb print. We're running it through the system now."

"What's your next step?"

"Going over to the house in a couple of hours and talk to the two women. Want to join me?"

"Yeah. I'd like to talk to you before we go. Are you busy right now?"

"Nothing that can't wait."

"Okay, I'll see ya shortly." Hawkman grabbed a thermos of coffee and locked up his office. He wondered if he should warn Sam so he could cancel painting the house today. On the other hand, the interview with Lilly and Maryann might not take long. And the boys wanted to finish this project.

When Hawkman reached the station, Williams had a couple of officers in his office, but waved Hawkman in. "I've told these guys I want them to accompany us. I don't think we'll need them, but I'd like the back-up just in case."

Hawkman agreed.

Williams turned to the policemen. "Wait for us outside." Once the officers left, he turned to Hawkman. "Now, what do you have to tell me?"

"There are several things you might find of interest." Hawkman scooted a chair up to the desk and unfolded the map showing the location of Maduk's new home. He proceeded to tell Williams what he'd found buried in the woods. Then he related how he'd visited the bar where Lilly worked and discovered the owner gave his help the partially filled bottles of liquor before each new supply arrived. "Lilly started work in that bar about five or six months before Parker's death. When Burke discovered she got free booze, the bartender said Parker insisted she get some for him."

Williams ran a hand through his hair. "Sounds feasible. So you think Lilly could have spiked them with paraquat?"

"Either that, or she passed them on to Maduk and let him do the dirty work."

"Then how'd he get it to Parker without arousing suspicion?"

"I thought about that. Parker lived in that run down motel for months at a time. Maduk could have slipped into the room when Burke wasn't there, switched the bottles, or poured the concoction into the ones already there. I doubt Parker would have even noticed in his state of inebriation."

"So you think Lilly and Maduk planned this?"

Hawkman scratched his chin. "Hard to say. I'm more wary of Maryann. When she figured out where those partial bottles of booze were coming from and discovered her mother passing them on to Parker, she could have doctored them up."

"This is all getting very interesting. I'm going to ask a lot of questions today, and I'd like to search that house. But I'll have to get a warrant first. Which may take a day or two."

Hawkman changed positions and faced Williams. "I had a chance to scout around the Parker house while the boys were there. Now this is just speculation, but while searching through a cabinet under the carport, I spotted a space on one of the shelves where a small box or something square had been sitting. I felt it had been removed recently because the area was still clean. It looked to be the same size as the box I found in the woods behind Maduk's house. I realize this is all circumstantial, but it might give you ammunition for questions."

Williams stood and shrugged into his jacket. "Yep. And everything points in the direction of the family as our suspects. So let's go."

CHAPTER THIRTY-THREE

Sam paced in front of the movie theater until he spotted Richard's truck. He waited for him to park, then hopped into the passenger side. After he told his friend about Maduk approaching him at Maryann's house, Richard smacked his forehead with the palm of his hand.

"Oh, damn! And you still stayed there and finished painting? You're braver than I am."

Sam laughed. "You make it sound funny; but let me tell you, when I saw that big Indian standing there, I thought my heart would jump right out of my chest."

"You still want to go over and paint tomorrow?" Richard asked.

"Hell, yes. The police will probably be swarming the place. At least we won't miss anything."

Richard guffawed. "Okay, I'll plan on picking you up. Now, let's go take in a movie."

❧

The next morning, Sam and Richard arrived at the Parker place about nine and prepared to paint the outside of the house. Sam took the taller ladder and Richard rested the shorter one several feet away.

"I don't want you splattering me with paint," Richard said, as he placed the bucket on the ladder shelf.

Sam grinned. "Don't tempt me. I liked your hair all different colors. Makes you resemble a skunk" He flicked the bristles of the dry paint brush toward him.

Richard ducked and they both laughed.

The boys painted for about an hour when Richard spotted a man standing a few yards away near the street staring at the house. "Hey, Sam," he nodded his head toward the street. "There's an old guy over there watching us."

When both boys turned to look, the fellow advanced toward them with a big grin on his face. "Howdy there. You boys are doing a nice job for a gentle lady."

"You know Mrs. Parker?" Sam asked.

"She leaves me food almost every night on her porch. Takes care of me like family. Even gave me a blanket to keep warm at night."

"You know her husband died?"

The man's expression changed to an angry scowl. His odd colored light blue eyes even turned paler until he looked unnatural. "A very evil person. Good thing he's dead. Now Ms. Lilly can have peace."

At that moment, a look of fear registered on the man's face as he glanced toward the front of the house. He turned quickly and scurried away.

The boys looked to see what frightened him. A patrol car, plus Detective Williams' unmarked vehicle pulled in front of the house. They climbed down their ladders and walked around the corner just as Hawkman climbed out of Williams' car.

"Hello, boys. Making good progress?"

"Yeah, we're moving right along." Sam edged closer to Hawkman. "What's happening?" he whispered.

Hawkman placed a hand on his shoulder. "Nothing for you to be concerned about. Go on about your work."

Sam reluctantly headed toward the side of the house. Richard followed. When they were sure they were out of earshot, Sam nudged his friend. "Something's going down," he mouthed.

Richard glanced down the street. "Where'd the old man go?"

"Don't know, but he's a crazy, that's for sure. Did you notice his eyes?"

"Yeah, gave me the creeps. The color changed when you

mentioned Mr. Parker to the point that he looked like an alien. And I caught his body odor clear up on the ladder. What'd he say, anyway? He had so much hair growing around his mouth I couldn't read his lips."

Sam grinned. "He definitely needed a shower and hair cut." After relating to Richard what the stranger said, they moved their ladders to the back of the house. "Guess we better get busy."

❧

A reflection bounced off Lilly's bedroom window, causing her to glance out. Her hand on the sill, she leaned forward, staring through the sheer curtains at the two cars parking in front of her house. Sucking in a deep breath, her hand fell to her side and she went to the closet. She slipped into a house dress, then ran a brush through her hair and secured it with a hair clamp at the nape of her neck. She sat on the edge of the bed, put on her shoes, wrapped her arms around her waist and waited. Maduk had warned her last night the police might be here today.

Her senses seemed extremely sharp, as she swore she could hear the brush strokes through the walls as the boys painted the outside. Soft footsteps alerted her that Maryann was coming down the hallway. She twisted around when her daughter entered the room.

"Mom, the police are here. Do you want to talk to them right now?" Maryann sat down beside her mother and took her hand. "You don't have to, you know. If necessary, we can get an attorney."

"I can't afford a lawyer." She patted her daughter's knee and rose. "How many cops are out there?"

"Just the detective and Hawkman. The other two officers are still in their car. I think they're just back ups in case we give them trouble."

Lilly chuckled. "I guess they figure we're two dangerous women."

Maryann stood in front of her mother. "Mom, you'd

definitely qualify for a court appointed lawyer and it wouldn't cost you a dime. You don't have to talk to these men."

"I have nothing to hide. If they get overbearing, I'll tell them I won't answer any more questions without a lawyer present." She studied her daughter's face. "You'll be in there with me, won't you?"

"Absolutely."

Maryann led her mother into the living room and had her sit on the overstuffed chair before she invited the detective and Hawkman into the house. She then immediately went to her mother's side.

Lilly gestured toward the couch. "Have a seat, gentlemen. How can I help you?"

"Mrs. Parker, most of the lab tests on your late husband have come back. It appears Mr. Parker died of paraquat poisoning."

"What's that?" she asked.

"It's a very toxic herbicide used for killing or controlling weeds, and can only be used by a licensed contractor, so therefore it's not sold to anyone without proper credentials."

"How in heavens name could Burke have gotten ahold of such stuff. He never did any yard work."

"We need to know if Mr. Parker associated with anyone who might be able to obtain this poison."

Lilly threw up her hands and shook her head. "I haven't the vaguest idea." Then she scooted to the edge of her seat and clasped her hands together. "Detective Williams, Burke and I had not lived together for some time. He tried to molest my daughter and I threw him out."

"We had a suspicion something had happened as we have it recorded in our records that you shot your husband in the leg one night. Is that because of his abuse?"

Maryann stepped forward. "She didn't shoot him, detective. I did."

Williams raised his brows? "You shot your father?"

"Yes." Her eyes narrowed. "He tried to hurt me. I had a gun under my pillow and chased him out of my room. When mother heard my screams, she ran out the door behind me. When I shot him, she pulled me back inside and took the gun. He was a horrible man."

Lilly dropped her head into her hands. "Don't believe her, detective. She's only trying to protect me."

"Mrs. Parker, we'd like to search the house. If you don't give us permission, I'll get a search warrant."

Maryann glared at Hawkman and Williams. "Then that's what you'll have to do. If you think you can pin his murder on me or my mother, you're completely wrong. Just because we hated the man, doesn't mean we'd stoop to killing him."

"What about Maduk?" Hawkman asked.

Lilly' jerked up her head, then dropped her gaze to her hands as she fiddled with the material of her dress.

Maryann shot a sharp look at Hawkman. "Are you insinuating that he had something to do with Burke's death?"

"What do you think?"

"I think it's time for you to leave unless you plan to arrest one of us."

Hawkman stood. "Maduk paid a visit to Sam in this house and in so many words threatened him."

"Not really, Mr. Casey. He asked Sam to relay a message to you. I heard the whole thing."

"Why is he worried, if he's innocent of any wrong doing?"

"None of us like to be pushed into a corner. And that's what happens to a family when a mysterious death occurs. The closest people to the victim are the first suspects. Isn't that why you're here? I've decided we're not answering any more of your questions without an attorney present. And since we can't afford one, I'm requesting a court appointed lawyer for me and my mother."

"That can be arranged," Detective Williams said, as he followed Hawkman to the door. "I'll have a lawyer get in touch with one of you within the next few days."

After the two men left, Maryann knelt down in front of the chair and took her mother's hands. Tears rolled down Lilly's cheeks. "Mom, we need to have a serious talk."

CHAPTER THIRTY-FOUR

When the two men walked out of the Parker house, Hawkman glanced over his shoulder, but the boys were nowhere in sight. They must be at the back, he thought. He wondered if he should suggest they call it a day, but decided against interfering with their project. After all, they were young men now and should be able to handle any problems. He didn't want to interfere with their job. At the rate they were moving, they might finish painting the outside by tomorrow and wouldn't have to return.

Hawkman and Williams rode in silence for several minutes, then Williams broke the stillness. "I didn't expect that reaction. I thought the women would be a bit more cooperative."

Hawkman shifted in his seat. "Look at it this way. Maryann's no dummy. She's educated, knows where this investigation is heading, and is going to protect her parents. I can't blame her."

"You're right," the detective said. "That gal is one hell of a spitfire. It sure makes me consider what you said about watching her. She could very well be guilty of murdering Parker."

Hawkman let out a sigh. "I wish I knew the answer. I want to take another look at at those reports and autopsy pictures."

Williams shot him a look. "What's on your mind?"

"Not sure yet. I'll let you know."

When they reached the police station, Hawkman followed Williams into his office. He scooted a chair to the front of the desk, as the detective slid the Parker folder in front of him.

"I've got a meeting down the hall. If you spot something we've missed, hang around. I won't be long."

Hawkman gave him a wave. "Will do."

After Williams left the room, Hawkman opened the file.

He slowly picked through Parker's autopsy pictures, turning them over one by one. When he reached the head shots, he carefully lined them up side by side on the desk, rubbing his chin as he studied them.

Once he located the coroner's reports, he sorted through the pages until he found the one listing Parker's stomach contents at the time of death. He fumbled in his pocket for the small paper pad he carried and jotted down the items.

His attention shifted to the lab reports. He thumbed through the sheets of paper until he found the one he wanted, took some notes, then set that one aside.

He glanced at the inventory sheet of things sent to the lab. The item he wanted to see hadn't been checked off as received. Leaning back in the chair, he thumped the pencil against the desk. He'd ask Williams about it when he returned from the meeting.

Soon, the detective strolled into the room with several sheets of paper in his hand. He dropped them on his desktop, and took off his jacket, hanging it over the back of his chair. "Okay, got the daily meeting out of the way. Now, let's get down to business." He flopped into the cushioned seat and swiveled around to face Hawkman. "So what'd you find?"

Hawkman took his pencil and pointed to a picture depicting the scoring around Parker's mouth. "I'm interested in how these got there."

"The lab reports state that's the effects of the paraquat."

"Yes, I understand, but if he'd only ingested the paraquat through booze and even if some had dribbled out the corners of his mouth, how come there'd be this much damage around his outer lips, under the nose and across his chin?" Hawkman picked up another picture. "And I noticed here on Parker's right hand, there's some odd looking markings, almost like burns."

"What are you getting at?"

He reached over and thumped the coroner's reports. "It says here, the stomach contents indicated chicken and potatoes for his last meal. Let's say it was fried chicken he'd eaten with his hands."

Williams eyes lit up. "So you think the poison was in the food, too?

"I think it's very possible. Do you remember what you took out of the trash can in that room?"

The detective closed his eyes for a moment and counted on his fingers. "Let's see, there were four items, if my memory serves me right. A big roll of wadded foil, an empty plastic container, which looked like it could have come from a home. An old newspaper and one more item. Oh yeah, a plastic fork."

"Did they have any identifying labels on them, like a sticker label or anything that might identify where they came from?"

"No."

"Did those items go to the lab?"

"Everything went."

"Hopefully, you'll get those results Monday. I have a hunch traces of paraquat will be found on all the food containers."

Williams leaned back in his chair and scratched his head. "So, if someone laced his food with the toxin, we need to find out where he got his dinner."

"It won't be easy. If he got this food from a restaurant, I'd suspect they'd give it to him as a take out in a corrugated box, or possibly in foil. But what stumps me is the plastic thing. That sounds more like it came from a private home where they might have put mashed potatoes or potato salad in a used butter bin. Now, to find out who that kind soul may have been. This is not going to be an easy case to solve."

The detective let out a sigh. "You got that right, if we ever do unravel it. I think it's time to visit Maduk's place and dig up that box you found."

Hawkman put up a hand. "Not today. If Maduk isn't working, he could be out at his new place. He'd spot us for sure. Let's wait until Monday, when we can be sure he's not there."

"Good idea."

❧

Sam and Richard climbed down their ladders at the same

time. Sam arched his back and stretched. "You want to change places when we go around the corner?"

Richard grinned. "Sure, reaching up under the eaves is getting to you isn't it?"

"Yeah, little tough on the neck and back." He stepped back and gave Richard the thumbs up. "We work well as a team. Look at that beautiful job. And we've already got one side and the back done."

Richard pointed toward the opposite corner. "The hardest is still ahead.   That wall includes the carport, then there's the front of the house with the porch."

"That's true, but we'll make a big dent in it today." He rubbed his stomach. "Let's eat. I'm starved."

After capping the paint cans and wrapping their brushes in plastic bags, they strolled toward the pickup.

Richard pointed down the street. "Why don't we go over to that little park we passed. It's only a couple of blocks away. Maybe we can find a free table and eat in the shade."

Sam climbed into the cab. "Sounds good. Let's go."

Richard hopped into the truck and made a U-turn. When they reached the recreation area, they found a vacant table under a large oak tree. It took both of them to lug the ice chest Uncle Joe had packed that morning.

"Good grief," Sam said. "What the heck's in here?"

Richard laughed. "Beats me. But I have a feeling more food than we'll be able to eat."

Raising the lid, Richard rubbed his hands together. "Would you look at all this." He dug out four huge sandwiches, a big container of potato salad, a jar of canned plums, two big bottles of juice and a whole peach pie. On the top were several paper dinner plates and plastic eating utensils. Also a couple of frozen cartons to keep everything cool. "No wonder this thing was so heavy."

Sam stared at the food with wide eyes. "Oh man, what a feast. Let's dig in."

They scarfed down a sandwich, a helping of potato salad and a piece of pie before they slowed down. Then Richard placed his fork on the plate and wiped his mouth with the back of his hand.

"Hawkman and the detective didn't hang around long? Were you able to eavesdrop?"

Sam grimaced. "Yeah. There's a window in the kitchen that's stuck and won't close all the way. Their voices were loud enough to hear. Maryann sounded pretty mad and demanded a lawyer."

Richard leaned forward and stared at his friend's mouth. "Tell me what you heard."

Sam related the conversation between the four people. When he finished, he shook his head. "I'm guessing Maryann's protecting someone."

"Maybe herself." Richard said.

"I don't know, it's possible. But the two most important people in her life are suspects. If Maduk did poison Burke Parker, and Lilly knew he did it, Maryann wouldn't want her mom to say something that might incriminate either one of them. She stated she wanted a lawyer present before they'd answer any more questions. And truly that's the only way to go."

"I agree," Richard said, as he packed the uneaten food into the ice chest. "Guess we better get back to our job, so we can get as much done as possible before dark."

"Yeah. I'm so full right now, I'd like to take a nap. Thank Uncle Joe for me, the food was great."

"If we get hungry mid-afternoon, we have enough for a nice snack."

Sam laughed, as he threw the dirty paper plates and utensils into the trash can. "You got that right, we've got lunch for tomorrow."

When the boys returned to the Parker house, the two women were in the car. Maryann rolled down the driver's window. "I don't know when we'll be back. Just make yourself at home if you need anything."

"Thanks," Sam said, watching as they pulled out of the driveway. He wondered where they were going.

CHAPTER THIRTY-FIVE

Maryann slowed the car and glanced at Lilly sitting rigidly in the passenger seat, her gaze fixed straight ahead.

"Mother, we need to talk."

"Couldn't we have discussed whatever it is at the house?"

"No, I didn't want to risk being overheard by Sam."

"I have to go to work this evening."

"I'll have you back in plenty of time."

"Well, then, get started."

"There are a couple of things I want to ask. One is, where's that weed killer that used to be out in the carport cabinet."

Her mother twisted her head around and stared at Maryann with a puzzled expression. "What are you talking about? I don't even know what's out there. Burke used it for his stuff. I never even bothered looking inside it."

Maryann slapped the steering wheel, making her mother jump. "Don't play games with me."

Lilly let out a sigh. "I've had enough questions. I want to go home."

Gritting her teeth, Maryann pulled to the side of the road and stopped. She glared at her mother. "I know there was a bottle of paraquat in that cabinet. Now, it's gone. I want to know where it went."

Lilly stared into her daughter's eyes with concern. "How did you know that?"

"It doesn't matter how I knew. But it's not there any more."

"Why were you snooping?"

"Mother, I've lived in that house all my life. That bottle had been there for years."

Lilly threw up her hands then let them fall to her thighs with a slap. "Maybe Burke destroyed it."

Maryann reached across and grasped her arm. "I saw it in that cabinet after Burke died."

Rubbing her head with her hands, Lilly looked out the window. "You're giving me a headache, Maryann."

"Are you protecting Maduk?"

Lilly narrowed her eyes. "Maybe I'm protecting you and Maduk. You seem to know an awful lot about a bottle of paraquat."

Dropping her hand from her mother's arm, she bit her lower lip and turned the key in the ignition. "I'm taking you home."

When she pulled around the corner, Sam and Richard were standing in the driveway talking and gesturing toward the house. Maryann noticed their ladders resting against the wall and wondered if they'd looked inside that cabinet. She stopped in the driveway as the boys scooted out of the way.

Jumping out of the car, she slammed the door and stormed into the house. Lilly climbed out slowly and moved toward the front of the vehicle.

Sam watched Maryann march toward the entry, then turned his attention back to Lilly, and pointed toward the carport. "Mrs. Parker, we thought we'd just paint the outside of that cupboard. Unless you want us to paint the inside, too."

She shook her head. "No, don't worry about the inside. It's an old, make-shift piece and just holds junk." She leaned against the fender of the car and folded her arms at her waist. "Looks like you're almost through. You've really helped the looks of my place. I want to thank you two very much."

Sam and Richard smiled.

"You're more than welcome," Sam said. "We hope to wrap it up tomorrow."

She brushed some loose strands of hair from her face, then proceeded into the house. The boys went back to their job.

Lilly hesitated at her daughter's closed door, sighed, then went immediately to her room, undressed, showered and put on her working uniform. She took a few minutes to fix her hair and put on a bit of make-up. Going into the kitchen, she quickly made herself a baloney sandwich and poured a glass of iced tea. She sat down at the table and glanced toward the hall. The low sound of music floated through the air. As she ate, she thought about the conversation with Maryann and it worried her.

Later that night, Lilly stayed after closing time to help out her fellow workers. Everyone pitched in to help each other and she enjoyed the camaraderie. Leaving the restaurant through the back door, she headed for her car thinking how Maryann had never understood why her mother did such dirty work. But it felt nice to have a few friends who appeared to care. Deep in thought, she reached for the door handle when suddenly a large hand clutched her arm. A scream almost escaped her lips before she heard his voice.

"It's me, Maduk."

"Why do you do that to me," she scolded, jerking away. "You scared me half to death."

"I'm sorry. But it's important I see you tomorrow. Can you get away without drawing attention to yourself?"

"Yes. I think I could arrange it. Where do you want to meet?"

"Remember that old broken down barn on the east side of town?"

She grinned. "I'll never forget it."

"About ten o'clock in the morning. I'll have you back in time for work."

He disappeared into the shadows and Lilly climbed into her car. As she drove home, her heart sang with joy.

∽♪∾

The next morning, Lilly arose early and hummed as she showered and dressed. She put on a fresh pair of jeans, and the blue silk shirt that Maduk always liked because he said it made her eyes light up like stars. Slipping into her sandals, she went to the kitchen, tied on a full apron and fried enough bacon for herself and Maryann.

She stopped singing and glanced toward the closed door of her daughter's bedroom. Gnawing on her lower lip, she decided not to tell Maryann she'd be meeting Maduk this morning. The girl had grown rather skeptical about her father. True, he hadn't been around much, but she understood why. Young girls don't know the first thing about true love.

Lilly fixed herself an egg and a piece of toast. When she finished eating, she cleaned up her mess, and left the bacon draining on a paper towel for Maryann. About that time, she heard the boys drive up. She knew she'd better get rolling before Maryann got up and asked a bunch of questions. It would take her about thirty minutes to get to the deserted barn in her old car.

She hurried back to her bedroom, gave her hair one more check and applied some gloss to her lips. Examining herself in the mirror, she decided she still had that pretty look of a young woman and it lifted her spirits. Grabbing her purse off the dresser, she headed outside, waved at Sam and Richard, then left in her car.

When she reached the designated spot, she pulled into the small field and drove around to the back of the deserted barn. The dark Buick sat in the shadow. She felt her heart skip a beat as she parked beside it and the big Indian stepped out to greet her. She ran to him. He picked her up and whirled her around as if she only weighed a few pounds. Then he enfolded her in his arms and kissed her passionately.

"I've missed you so much, my Lilly."

"Oh, Maduk. You have no idea how much I love you."

"Get in, I've got a surprise."

"Where are we going?"

He smiled and his black eyes twinkled. "You'll see very soon."

They drove in silence for several miles as Lilly stared out the window. "It's beautiful up here in these hills."

"I thought you'd like it." He soon stopped at a chained gate and got out.

As he unlocked the padlock, Lilly glanced up the hill and spotted a small home tucked in among the trees and her heart beat wildly. Had her dream finally come true.

Maduk parked outside the garage, went around and helped Lilly from the car. He took her hand and led her to the front door. Picking her up, he carried her across the threshold. "I'll do this again when we're married."

When he put her down, Lilly's hands went to her cheeks and tears welled at the lovely sight before her. "Oh, Maduk, this room is beautiful. Is this house yours?"

"It's ours. I had a few things to do before I could bring you out here."

She rubbed her hands over the rock on the fireplace. "This is so lovely." Then he led her to the kitchen and pointed out the view from the window, she sucked in her breath. Running her hands across the smooth counter tops and opening the cabinets, made her feel like a child with a new toy.

He put his arm around her shoulders and led her down the hallway where he pointed out the main bathroom, then the room he thought would work for Maryann. Pushing the door open to the master bedroom, he took her in his arms and placed a tender kiss on her lips. "This is our room." He gently lifted her and placed her on the bed. His hands caressed her shoulders and breasts, then made their way down unbuttoning her blouse.

Lilly closed her eyes. "Dear God, don't let me wake up if this is a dream."

CHAPTER THIRTY-SIX

When Lilly returned home, her uplifted mood fell when she encountered her daughter in the living room.

Maryann had her hands on her hips and stared at her mother with blazing eyes. "Mother, where have you been?"

"Out and about. Why?" she asked, brushing past her and heading for the bedroom.

Maryann followed at her heels. "Your boss called. He wanted you to come in early. I had no idea where you were or when you'd be home."

Lilly sat on the bed as she removed her jeans and blouse. "They'll survive. They don't have much business on Sunday afternoon." She went to her closet, hung up her clothes, and removed a clean uniform from the hanger. "Looks like the boys finished the house. Sure looks nice. They did a good job. Wish I'd been here to thank them in person before they left." She glanced at her daughter. "Write down their addresses and I'll send them each a personal thank you."

"You're changing the subject and you look different."

"I slept well last night. I feel wonderful."

Maryann narrowed her eyes. "You're lying. You've just come from seeing Maduk, haven't you? You're cheeks are even rosy, like you've been making love."

Lilly chuckled as she checked in the mirror. "My goodness, they are sort of pink aren't they? I told you I felt good. Even shows in my face." She smoothed down her uniform and picked up her purse. "Guess I better get to work."

Maryann blocked the doorway. "You still haven't told me where you've been."

Lilly glared into her daughter's face. "Young lady, I don't have to tell you anything. Just remember, I'm the mother and you're the child. So step aside and let me through."

Letting out a disgusted sigh, Maryann moved out of the way.

Going out the front door, Lilly called over her shoulder. "Get those boys' addresses for me, okay?"

❧

Sam and Richard packed the painting supplies into the bed of Richard's truck and left the Parker place. When they were out of town, Sam gave Richard a playful slug on the shoulder and threw up his hands in glee.

"Hallelujah, we got it finished. Thanks for helping me or I'd have been there another week."

Richard laughed. "No problem. I'm glad it's done. Now maybe we can spend some time fishing and riding in the hills."

Sam ran a hand over his hair. "Man, that sounds wonderful."

Then Richard's expression turned grim. "What do you think will happen to Maryann and her mother?"

Sam sighed. "I don't know. Hawkman said they're still waiting for the rest of the lab tests to come in."

At Sam's house, the boys were unloading and putting away the painting gear when Jennifer stepped out the front door.

"Looks like you guys finished the job."

"Yep. And it really looks good. Even the lawn's growing. Also, Maryann's flowers and garden are flourishing."

"I'll have to drive by the next time I'm in town. Come on in for some refreshments. I think you deserve it."

"Thanks, Mrs. Casey," Richard said, as they went into the house. "I can only stay a little while. Uncle Joe is going to go get Betsy from Mr. Zanker's place tonight and he'll need me to help him."

"Betsy?" Jennifer asked.

"That's our cow. He decided to breed her this year and Mr.

Zanker offered his prize bull. So we should have a nice calf in March or April."

"Hey, that's great," Sam said.

The boys sat down at the kitchen bar and Jennifer placed a platter of lunch meat and cheeses in front of them with a loaf of bread.

"Sam told me your Uncle Joe sent a feast with you yesterday. So you might not be very hungry if you finished that off today," she said.

Richard grinned. "You're right. There was plenty left, but we ate it at lunchtime."

"Where's Hawkman?" Sam asked, smearing mayonnaise on a piece of bread.

"He's in Yreka working on the Parker case."

Sam held the knife in the air and glanced at her. "Did they find some new clues?"

"I'm not sure."

After Richard left, Jennifer sat down at her computer. Sam exited to the bathroom and jumped in the shower. He let the warm water flow over his sore muscles for several minutes. When he finished, he came back into the living room and flopped down in Jennifer's chair. He punched on the television, but before long his eyelids felt heavy. Forcing them open, he hoped Hawkman arrived before he fell into a deep sleep.

A streak of light flashed across the kitchen window. His eyes shot open and his attention focused on the front door.

Hawkman walked in and hooked his hat on a peg of the coat rack. Rubbing his chin, he smiled at Sam. "Hey, painter guy, did you get the job finished today?"

"Yes. And it looks great."

Jennifer half rose from her chair. "Want something to eat?"

Hawkman waved for her to sit back down. "No thanks, hon. I grabbed a sandwich in town."

"I think Sam is waiting to hear the latest news about the Parker case."

Hawkman went into the kitchen and grabbed a beer from

the refrigerator. "Still need those last lab results, but I did make a discovery or two on my own."

Sam's punched off the television with the remote. "Get on with it. Don't leave us hanging in suspense."

Hawkman laughed and sat down in his chair, then took a swig of beer. He told about what he'd seen in the autopsy pictures. "I think Parker's food may have been contaminated. We know the booze bottles showed signs of paraquat. Now we need to find out about the food wrappings found in the trash can."

Sam turned pale. "You said the coroner found chicken in his stomach?"

"Yes."

"Maryann told me that her mother's specialty is fried chicken. That's what she fed Richard and me that day. And I have to tell you it was delicious. I could have eaten my weight in it."

"I questioned some of the neighbors and restaurants today. I didn't find one person or place that had ever given Parker free food. He'd eaten at some of the cafes, but never asked for a handout. So, it'll be interesting to see what we find from those tests."

"Didn't you say that Maryann vehemently refused to let the police search the house without a warrant?" Jennifer asked.

Hawkman nodded. "Right, it doesn't look good for the Parker women."

Sam leaned forward in the chair. "What about that homeless guy that lives in the alley behind their house. Did you ever question him? He might have seen something."

Hawkman frowned. "What homeless guy?"

CHAPTER THIRTY-SEVEN

Monday morning Hawkman met Williams at the police station and they headed for Maduk's place.

"You know anything about a homeless man living in the alley behind the Parker's?" Hawkman asked.

The detective shook his head. "No, but it's not surprising. They're all over the area. Is he causing a problem?"

"No, I don't think so. Sam told me about him and said maybe he saw something. Just wondered if you'd questioned the guy."

"Didn't realize one of those vagabonds had set up housekeeping so close to the Parker's. But it's a thought." He grinned. "That boy of yours going to be a private investigator?"

Hawkman chuckled. "Who knows what these kids will end up doing. Just want him to get that sheepskin."

"I hear ya."

As they neared the house, Hawkman happened to glance out at the passenger side mirror and stiffened. "When you reach the driveway to Maduk's house, don't brake. He's behind us."

Williams glanced in the rearview mirror. "Damn! I thought you said he'd be working."

"I assumed." Hawkman pointed ahead. Drive over that crest and we'll be hidden from view. Then we can use the trees for cover."

"Good idea."

Hawkman directed the detective to the area where he'd parked on his previous visit. The two men got out of the car and Williams unlocked the trunk. He took out a small folded shovel, pulled a large heavy-duty plastic bag from a box, then handed Hawkman some thick rubber gloves and stuffed a pair into his own pocket.

The two men climbed up the embankment alongside the road. When Hawkman glanced over the top, he ducked and quickly signaled for Williams to drop down. He waited a few moments, then peeked over the edge and watched Maduk get out of the car and go into the house.

"Okay, he's inside," he whispered, and gestured for the detective to follow.

They stayed in the shadows and Hawkman kept a wary eye on the house. Going deeper into the forest, he scanned the tree trunks. After several yards, he wondered if he'd gone too far, then spotted the marks he'd made with his knife on the barks of the big oaks.

He measured off three long steps then motioned for Williams to hand him the shovel. Within minutes of digging into the soft dirt, he uncovered the box. Williams slipped on the gloves he'd brought, squatted on his haunches and carefully removed the container from the hole.

Heedful not to damage any evidence, the detective took his pen and flipped back the cardboard lid so he could see the bottle. "Yep, it says 'poison' and 'paraquat'. I'll have the lab check to make sure that's what in the bottle."

Hawkman slipped on the rubber gloves and held open the plastic bag for Williams as he slid the box inside. "The only problem is, there's no evidence that Maduk buried this out here. Even if he did, there could be a very valid reason."

"True," the detective said. "But we know he's connected to Lilly and he's the father of Maryann. Right now it will just serve as circumstantial evidence."

He sealed the bag with an identification tag and stood. "Oh, by the way, did I tell you I received a call from the lab and they'd found a clear print on the plastic container? The report will be with the next batch of test results. Maybe the packet will be waiting when we get back to the office."

"I've been thinking about the liquor bottle with the print

on it. If that came from Lilly's work place, any number of people could have handled it."

"Boy, you're one pessimist."

"Just looking at all the angles. We have nothing concrete on Maduk. Yet, he seems the most likely suspect. Of course, Maryann and Lilly also had reasons to want Parker dead."

Hawkman scooped dirt back into the hole, then scattered some branches over the top so the ground appeared undisturbed. Satisfied, the two men headed back through the forest to the detective's car. When they passed Maduk's place, Hawkman noted the Buick still parked in the driveway.

Driving back toward town, Hawkman told Williams the story about how Sam and Richard figured the old guy living in the alley must have been crazy as he went ballistic on them when Sam mentioned Burke Parker had died."

"That's very interesting. I think I better check him out."

"You never know, he might have seen something."

When the men arrived at the station, they threw the rubber gloves into a container for contaminated items, then Williams filled out a report sheet requesting tests he wanted done. He had the poison placed in a metal container to be transported to the police lab.

When they entered the detective's office, Williams glanced at his desk. "I don't see any new mail. Guess the reports didn't make it today."

Hawkman rested his hand on the door jamb. "I'll check with you tomorrow. Maybe the police lab will have something for us, too."

"I'll give you a call."

Giving a wave, Hawkman left the office.

Lilly gnawed her lower lip as she drove to work. She worried about how hostile her daughter had become, almost to the point of being frightening. And it also concerned her that Maryann knew for some time about a bottle of paraquat in the carport cabinet. Why did the missing poison bother her?

Wishing to avoid these thoughts before work, she concentrated on the time she'd spent with Maduk. She adored the home he'd purchased in that beautiful country setting. To think she'd finally be able to share her life with the man she'd loved all these years. The thought sent chills of happiness down her spine. She prayed her dream would come true soon.

When she arrived at work, she stored her purse under one of the counters and put on a frilly apron. She'd no more clocked in when one the other waitress told her the boss wanted to see her.

Lilly walked down the short hall that led to his office and knocked on the door.

"Come in."

She entered the room. "Mr. Thomas, did you want to see me?"

He glanced up. "Yes, Lilly. Please close the door."

Lilly felt her stomach flutter at his grim expression. "What is it? Have I made an error on my tally?"

He shook his head. "No. A Detective Williams and his partner came in to see me this afternoon. They're investigating the murder of your late husband."

She quickly took the chair in front of his desk. "Why are they questioning you?"

"It seems the liquor bottle they found in the motel room with your husband's body, came from this establishment."

Lilly stared at him wide eyed. "How could they tell?"

"We're one of many bars who puts small coded stickers on our booze. It's a way we keep track of our sales, and make sure no one's stealing our liquor. If we find missing gaps in the numbers, we know something isn't right. They're not positive it came from our place, but he showed me a picture of a liquor bottle with an incomplete stamp and number. It looked suspiciously like one of ours."

Lilly put a hand to her mouth. "Oh my."

"I told him we give the partial bottles to our employees at the end of each week. I'm questioning each of the employees, so don't feel like I've just picked you out of the group because it's your husband who died. But I need to know the truth. Did you ever take any of those bottles?"

"Why, yes. When Burke was alive, he told me to bring home what I could." She lowered her eyes. "He was an alcoholic."

"Yes, we all know about Burke's problems. Do you remember any of the brands you took?"

Lilly fiddled with the lace on her apron. "He told me any of the dark stuff, so I only chose those. I don't know anything about liquor. I'm not much of a drinker." She held up a hand. "Don't get me wrong, I'm not a teetotaler. I like a little snort now and then."

"That's not what concerns me. They found traces of poison in the bottle."

Lilly jerked up her head. "Oh my God! Do you think I might have gotten hold of a contaminated one and given it to Burke?"

"It's possible. Or someone added poison to it later."

Lilly stood, her hands trembled as she gripped the back of the chair. "Oh, my, the police are going to suspect me or my daughter of murdering my husband."

Mr. Thomas raised his brows. "Did you, Lilly?"

She looked him straight in the eye. "Good Lord, no!"

CHAPTER THIRTY-EIGHT

Tuesday morning, Hawkman walked into the living room and found Sam sitting in his chair, staring out over the lake. "Don't tell me you couldn't sleep in."

"I received a voice message on my cell phone from Maryann. She says it's urgent and she needs to talk to me. I'm debating about calling her back."

"Maybe you left something at the house."

Sam shook his head. "I don't think so."

"Instead of sitting there brooding, call and find out what she wants."

"My gut tells me it's about Burke's murder and she won't want to talk about it on the phone. She'll want me to come into town."

Hawkman strolled over beside him and looked out at the water. "You know that might not be a bad idea. You might be able to find out something that we can't."

Sam glanced up at him and scowled. "Like what?"

"Did Burke eat at home after Lilly kicked him out? Or did she ever give him food or liquor."

"Why would she give him booze? He beat her when he got drunk."

"Perhaps she had no choice. He might have insisted she bring him some of those almost empty bottles from work. If she refused, then he might have knocked her around a bit."

Sam let out a sigh. "So, you're telling me to go in and see what I can drag out of Maryann?"

Hawkman chuckled. "I think she'll talk freely. She needs to unload and you're really the only friend she has."

Dragging himself out of the chair, Sam headed toward the front door. "I think I'll call her, and the only place I can get a good signal on my cell is out in the middle of the street."

Hawkman nodded, as he ambled into the kitchen. "Yeah, I know."

Jennifer had set the coffee pot on the timer and the scent of the fresh brew filled the air. Hawkman poured himself a cup and watched out the window as Sam made the call. Maybe he'd get an insight on the cause for murder.

Jennifer waltzed into the kitchen. "Good morning. Looks like a beautiful day. Hmm, that coffee smells so good." She poured a mug full. "What are you looking at?"

"Sam. He's making a phone call to Maryann."

She glanced outside. "I didn't think he wanted to see that girl again."

"I talked him into it."

"You what?"

"She wants to talk. He might be able to find out more than we can."

Jennifer frowned. "You shouldn't put our son in that position."

"Why not? He's a grown man. He might even be a private investigator one day. He needs to learn how to get information from a person."

She glared at him. "You're using Sam."

"He knows it. I told him so."

"Well, you've just ruined my day."

"Sorry about that. You'll get over it."

Stomping into the dining room, Jennifer booted up the computer. "When are you going to work?"

"As soon as I find out what he's going to do."

Hawkman watched his son, shoulders slumped, trudge up the driveway toward the house. He knew the boy would be going into Yreka.

When Sam came through the door, he clamped his cell to his belt. "She wanted me to come by for lunch. I told her no, we'd go someplace and eat. I don't want to be alone in that house with her again."

Hawkman patted him on the back. "Sounds good. I'll be anxious to hear what she has to say. Give me a call after you've taken her home."

"Sam, you don't have to do this," Jennifer said.

"It's okay. I like helping out. I just wish it wasn't Maryann. Every move I make, she takes it wrong and thinks I'm interested in her, even if she's made the advances." He let out a sigh. "I'm sure Hawkman's had cases that weren't pleasant."

"Yes, but he's experienced in these things and you're not."

"Yeah, but he had to start somewhere."

Sam soon left the house and drove toward Yreka. He didn't push it; he wasn't in any hurry. He wondered why Maryann wanted to see him. What did she have to say that appeared so urgent? She'd indicated on the phone that she had to talk to someone and told him to come after lunch when her mother wouldn't be there.

It seemed he'd arrived in Yreka much too soon, even though he'd kept well under the speed limit. He took a deep breath when he pulled in front of the Parker house. Maryann stood outside hosing down the garden and had a sprinkler set up on the lawn. When she saw him drive up, she turned off the water and hurried toward his truck.

"Hi, Sam," she said, jumping into the passenger side. "Thanks for not turning me down. I'm sure you'd rather be fishing."

Sam bit his lip to keep from making a comment. "You sounded pretty desperate." He pulled away from the house. "Where would you like to have lunch."

"A fast food place is fine. Let's get it to go and take it someplace private so we can talk."

"Sure."

They ordered a couple of hamburgers, fries and sodas.

"How about that little park near your house?" Sam asked.

"Okay."

They found a vacant table in the shade and proceeded to unwrap their burgers. Maryann took a couple of bites in silence, then put her sandwich down on a napkin.

"I'm really worried, Sam."

"What about?"

"I'm afraid Maduk murdered Burke."

Sam grimaced. "Why do you think that?"

She took another bite of her hamburger and swallowed. "Before Memorial weekend, I only had one class on Friday, so I decided to cut it and come home Thursday evening. Richard probably told you I was here. I really didn't want anyone to know, but now I don't care. Well, Burke came pounding at the door about one o'clock Friday morning. He was drunk and threatened my mom, telling her he was moving back in. She told him he'd never step foot in that house again. Well, he grabbed her by the shoulders and was going to hit her, but I walked into the living room with my gun. He backed off, but yelled that the house was in his name and he'd have us evicted."

Sam stared at her with a stunned expression. "Boy, he was one mean dude."

Maryann cocked her head and looked him in the eye. "Do you know how that devastated my mother? That house is all she has to her name. There's no way she could afford to rent an apartment. By the time she gets through paying the bills, she hardly has enough money to keep food on the table. His threat would've forced her out on the street as a homeless person."

"That's terrible. But I don't understand how that points to Maduk."

Maryann shifted on the concrete bench, then folded a napkin around the remainder of her sandwich. "Mom left that Friday morning and stayed gone most of the day until time for her to go to work. I think she went to Maduk and told him what happened. You can pretty well guess the rest."

He shook his head. "No, I can't. Because it doesn't make sense. Maduk couldn't get close enough to poison Burke's food and drink without him being suspicious."

She slapped her hands on the surface of the concrete table. "A bottle of poison is missing from the cabinet in the carport. He's the only one that could have taken it."

Sam stared at her, puzzled. "What are you talking about?"

She rubbed her hands over her face. "A bottle of paraquat has been in that cabinet for ages. I have no idea where it came from. I looked for it after we found out Burke had been poisoned. It's disappeared. I asked mom about it and she almost accused me of killing Burke."

Sam narrowed his eyes. "Did you?"

CHAPTER THIRTY-NINE

Maryann's dark eyes blazed. "How dare you imply such a horrible thing." She slapped her sandwich back into the bag and stood. "You can take me home now. I don't think I care to see you anymore."

Sam crunched up his food wrappers and stuffed them into the sack, then scooted off the bench. "Fine with me."

She stomped toward the pickup and climbed inside. Sam took his time and threw the debris into the waste can, then meandered to the truck and slid into the driver's seat.

Leaning against the steering wheel, he faced Maryann. "I don't know what to think. Someone close to Burke poisoned him. You, your mom and Maduk are the most likely suspects. And if paraquat was accessible at your house, that makes it even more believable."

"Do you actually think I could resort to murder?" she spat.

"I don't know. You know how to use a gun and you just told me you'd threatened Parker."

She stared out the window. "You know, I think I could have shot him. But poisoning him. . .I don't think I'd know how."

"You worked at school for a chemistry teacher. And you've had classes; you'd certainly know about poisons."

She shot him a fierce look. "Well, sure. Just like you. But they certainly didn't teach us how to kill people."

Sam frowned and turned the key. "I know that. But we learned what happens if a person ingests certain kinds. Some toxicants are more deadly than others. And I remember learning about paraquat and its irreversible damage done to people in Mexico and the Middle East. Also many deaths were caused from using the pesticide. I don't recall an antidote."

Maryann rode in silence. When they reached her house, she jumped out and turned to Sam. "Maybe you'll come and visit me in prison." Then she slammed the door.

Sam watched her march up the sidewalk. For some odd reason, he didn't feel bad.

❧

Maryann stormed into the living room, mumbling to herself. When Maduk stepped out of the kitchen, her hand flew to her throat. "This is the second time you've almost scared me to death. What are you doing here?"

"I want you to call your mother at work and get her home. We've got to get out of here."

"Why?"

"Sit down, Maryann. I've got something to tell you. Then you'll understand."

When Maduk finished, Maryann went to the phone, her hand trembling as she lifted the receiver. "Mom, you need to come home right now. It's urgent."

"I can't just leave."

"Tell your boss your daughter's been in an accident and you're taking the rest of the day off."

"It's that serious?"

"Yes."

After hanging up, she turned to Maduk. "She'll be home in about twenty minutes."

Maduk nodded. "Good. Pack a couple of bags for you and Lilly. Enough for a few days."

Maryann flew to the bedrooms and had the luggage ready when her mother drove into the driveway.

Lilly dashed into the house, her face contorting into fear when she saw Maduk. Then her gaze shifted to her daughter with the two suitcases. "What's happened?"

"The police are coming to arrest you and Maryann for the murder of Burke. I want to get you out of here."

Her face paled. "I don't understand."

"I'll explain later. We don't have much time. My car's out back."

The three hustled out the door and climbed into the Buick.

❧

Hawkman received a call from Sam telling him the about his conversation with Maryann, and how she feared Maduk had killed Burke. He told him what she'd said about the paraquat in the carport disappearing. "However, she got mad at me and I never did find out if Lilly ever fed Burke or if she supplied him with any booze."

"You've done a good job, Sam. You found out information we didn't know."

"Yeah, but I blew it when I asked her if she'd killed Parker."

"No, you let her know she's under suspicion. The girl has to realize her actions have been questionable."

"I shouldn't have said it so soon, though, because then she got mad and clammed up."

"Those answers might turn up through other sources."

"How?"

"I'll let you know later."

About that time, Hawkman's landline rang. "I'll talk to you tonight; got another call coming in."

After hanging up from Sam, he punched on the speaker phone.

"Tom Casey here."

"Hawkman, Detective Williams. The tests results are here. Also the ones from the police lab. Think you better get your ass down here as soon as you can."

"I'm on my way."

He hung up, quickly stashed away his work and was out the door. When he arrived at Williams' office, he met a somber faced detective.

"Sit down and take a gander at these." He shoved the file in front of Hawkman.

After going through the sheets of paper, he glanced up. "I had my suspicions. Everything I've discovered pointed in that direction."

"Why didn't you say something?"

"I wanted to see these tests first. My hunch was right." He placed the folder back on Williams' desk. "Looks like the box I found did contain paraquat. I figured the bottle wouldn't have any prints on it. So we definitely can't pin anything on Maduk."

"But he could well be an accomplice."

Hawkman picked up the folder again and glanced at one of the reports. "It states Maryann's print was found on the liquor bottle. For some odd reason, I expected Lilly's."

"Yeah, me too. There were several of the bartender's prints and some smudged ones. But they lifted her print off the neck of the bottle. Then on the outside of the plastic food container, they found a nice clear thumb impression of Lilly's and traces of paraquat inside. The aluminum foil held some bones, which appeared to be remnants of fried chicken. They were laced with poison."

Hawkman scratched his sideburn. "You've definitely got some evidence that points to Lilly or Maryann. However, it's all circumstantial. They obviously gave Burke the food and liquor. But someone else could have doctored it after he had it in his possession. No one knows when he ate the food. He might have eaten in the car and carried the trash inside, or it could have sat in his room for several hours."

Williams groaned. "Do you have to be the devil's advocate?"

"It's a good start. You might be able to get a confession out of Lilly. I have a feeling she might crumble under interrogation."

"We've at least got enough to make the two arrests. You with me?"

Hawkman sighed, slapped his thighs and stood. "Yep, it's got to be done."

Before leaving the station, Williams alerted the Yreka police, then called in a couple of his officers for back-up.

Hawkman pointed toward his 4X4. "I'll take my vehicle since we're heading for Yreka."

Within an hour, they pulled in front of the Parker home.

Hawkman got out and joined Williams beside his car. He gestured toward the driveway. "Lilly's station wagon is here. She must be home."

Williams nodded. "Let's go."

They stood at the front door and the detective knocked several times. "That's odd," he said, trying the knob. The door opened, and he poked his head inside. "Mrs. Parker, police."

When he received no answer, Williams motioned for the officers to go around back. Pulling his gun, he stepped into the living room. Hawkman followed with his pistol poised.

Williams called out several times, but heard nothing. Hawkman silently made his way down the short hallway and cautiously opened Maryann's bedroom door. He noted the made bed, but several dresser drawers stood ajar with clothes dangling over the edges. The closet revealed empty hangers and garments dropped or tossed to the floor. Remembering Sam had told him the girl had a gun, he ran his hand under the pillows of the bed, and opened the drawers of the small bedside table, but found no weapon. Without searching any further, he assumed she either had it with her, or possibly didn't have one at all.

He slipped back into the hallway and met Williams standing outside Lilly's cluttered room. "This area's a total disaster. Do you think there's been a scuffle?"

Hawkman peeked inside. "Hard to say. It looks more like messy housekeeping."

"Find anything interesting in the other room?"

"No, other than it appears they left in a hurry."

The detective moved toward the front door. "Let's go check Lilly's work place."

As the two men hurried down the steps of the porch, the back up patrol rounded the corner of the house.

"See anything suspicious?" Williams asked.

"No, just an old vagrant making his rounds of the garbage dumpsters."

Hawkman's interest piqued. "Did you ask him if he'd seen anything?"

"Yes. He said he'd just gotten here and hadn't seen anybody around the area, except us."

They left the Parker house and headed for Lilly's work place. When they arrived, one of the waitresses led them to Mr. Thomas' office.

She knocked softly on the door. "Mr. Thomas, two men here to see you about Lilly."

"Show them in."

When Williams stepped into the room, the manager came out of his chair, his face pale. "Is Lilly's daughter okay?"

"Why do you ask?"

"A call came in reporting that Maryann had been involved in an accident this afternoon. Lilly dashed out of here in a flurry."

"Who made the call?"

"I don't know. It didn't come through my office."

"Could you find out who took it and what time it came in."

"Sure, just a moment."

When Thomas left the room, Williams quickly called the station to see if any accident had been reported this afternoon. He shook his head at Hawkman, then hung up before the boss returned.

"It turns out Lilly answered the phone about three this afternoon."

Williams handed him a card. "Thank you Mr. Thomas. If she calls in, notify us immediately at this number? It's very important."

Thomas placed the card on his desk, then clasped his hands together atop his large belly. "Certainly."

They stood outside Williams' car and Hawkman studied the ground in thought. "Think I might see if I can catch that homeless guy in the next day or two and ask him a few questions. Sam seems to think he lives in that alley behind the Parker place. Hawkman strolled over to his SUV and placed his foot on the running board, then dropped it to the ground and raised a hand. "Oh, by the way, who else had access to those lab reports?"

Williams threw up his hands. "The sealed envelope arrived about two o'clock. I read the results and called you. The only other people would be at the lab facility. Why?"

"It's interesting how those two women have just up and disappeared before we got there. It's like they found out you were coming. Someone picked them up."

"Maduk?"

Hawkman nodded. "He's my first guess."

CHAPTER FORTY

"You think Maduk has a snitch at one of the labs?" Williams asked.

"Or on the Yreka police force. He's been around a long time and knows a lot of people."

"Thanks, you have a way of making my day." Williams climbed into his car, turned on the radio, and reported to the Yreka police department that they'd reached the Parker house and found no one home. They had a clue to check out and would report back later."

"You need a back-up?"

"Don't think so. I have Hawkman and a couple of officers with me. But stay tuned in case we run into trouble."

"Will do."

Hawkman jumped into his 4X4 and Williams gave him the signal to move ahead. It took them close to thirty minutes to reach Maduk's driveway. Hawkman pulled up to the gate, climbed out of his vehicle and walked back to Williams.

"The gate's padlocked."

Williams stepped out of the car, pulled his gun, aimed and shot off the lock. The blast echoed off the surrounding hills, making it sound like more than one shot. "Well, if Maduk hasn't spotted us by now, he'll know we're here."

Hawkman tossed the chain aside and opened the gate. He drove through, followed by the other two cars.

❧

When Maryann heard the shot, she jumped out of the

chair and ran to the window. "It's the police. What are we going to do, Maduk? Shall I get my gun?"

He strolled over to the window and looked over her head at the parade of cars coming up the driveway. "Absolutely not."

Lilly grabbed his arm. "They're coming to arrest me."

He pulled Maryann away from the window and raised a finger to his lips. You two get to the back of the house and stay out of sight unless I call you."

Once the two women had left the living room, Maduk opened the front door, and moseyed out onto the porch.

Hawkman got out of his 4X4 and glanced up at the big Indian who appeared as a towering giant. His gaze went immediately to the knife dangling from the man's belt and the gun poked in his waistband. "Hello, Maduk. Nice place."

"Thank you. This is private property and may I ask what urgency caused you to destroy the lock on my gate?"

Detective Williams came forward and flashed his badge. "We're here on police business."

"I'm listening," Maduk said, folding large arms across his chest.

"We're looking for Lilly and Maryann Parker."

The Indian glared down at the detective. "Why?"

"For the murder of Burke Parker."

Maduk raised a brow. "Both women?"

"Yes. We have reason to believe they are responsible for the man's death."

"That's a little hard to swallow."

"May we search your house?"

"You have a warrant?"

"No. But we're asking for your cooperation."

"You don't have it without a search warrant. Good day, gentlemen." Maduk turned toward the door.

Hawkman stepped forward. "Maduk, have you seen Lilly or Maryann?"

He glanced over his shoulder. "Not for several days. I expect you and these officers to get off my property within the next five minutes."

He entered the house and shut the door, then stood at the window watching as the men piled into their cars and drove down the driveway. Maduk could see the dust rising on the road, and once they'd disappeared from his sight, he called to Lilly and Maryann. "You can come out now."

The two women hurried into the living room. "I heard you tell them we weren't here," Lilly said. "If they find out, you could be in serious trouble."

Maduk chuckled. "My dear, my dear, they wanted Lilly and Maryann Parker. Remember you're no longer Lilly Parker. You are now Lilly Madukarahat." He winked. "How soon you've forgotten we were married this afternoon in the home of Rita Randahl, the Notary Minister? And Maryann, as far as I'm concerned has never been a Parker."

Maryann shook her head. "Maduk, you know that isn't going to make any difference. And I don't understand why they want me? I had nothing to do with Burke's death."

"Your fingerprints were on the liquor bottle they found in Burke's motel room."

She gasped. "Oh, my God. They're probably on every one of those bottles. Mom would bring them home, set them on the counter and I'd put them away."

Tears ran down Lilly's cheeks. "I can't let them take her away. She had nothing to do with it."

Maduk put an arm around Lilly. "I know. They have no proof either of you administered poison to Burke's food or drink, even though your prints were on the plastic container. They're just guessing. Hawkman discovered the paraquat I'd buried out in the forest and they ran some tests on it. No fingerprints were evident."

Maryann jerked up her head and scowled at Maduk. "Where'd you get the paraquat?"

He pulled Lilly around in front of him and held her at arm's length as he stared into her face. "I found the poison in the cabinet under your carport. If the police found it first, they'd pretty much have you in jail by now. I had to get rid of it."

Lilly moved out of his grasp and collapsed in a fit of sobs

on the couch. "We're all going to end up in jail for the rest of our lives."

Maryann paced the room, gnawing on her lower lip. "Get hold of yourself, Mother. It's hard to think when you're making so much noise." She grabbed her father's arm. "So how did Hawkman know you'd buried the poison?"

Madux shrugged. "That, I can't tell you. But, he's a smart investigator and learned I'd bought this place. When I found evidence someone had been snooping around, I figured it was him. I didn't realize he'd been out in the field until one of my sources told me they were testing a bottle of paraquat they found on my property. I went out and discovered it'd been removed. But there's no way they can prove I buried it. I'd wiped it clean of fingerprints. The only thing they have to go on is the stuff they found in the motel room."

She glanced at her father. "Do you think the police will be back tonight with a warrant?"

Maduk nodded. "Yes. As soon as they can get a judge to okay it. And this time I won't be able to stop them from searching the house. So, get your stuff together. I'm going to take you to a safe place. We'll be going out the rear way, so we won't be running into them. Tomorrow, I've made arrangements to meet with a lawyer. He can help us plan what to do next."

Maryann raised a brow. "How do you know all this stuff before it actually happens?"

"I have my sources."

"You've said that before. It doesn't answer my question."

"Don't worry your pretty head, my daughter. It keeps us a jump ahead, and that's important. Now, let's get rolling."

Lilly got up immediately, went to the bedroom, and returned in a few seconds pulling her suitcase. "I didn't unpack anything, so I'm ready." She placed a hand on Maduk arm as he waited by the kitchen door. "Are you coming back here?"

"Yes, it has to look like I never left."

As they drove away, Lilly looked longingly at the house. "If I'd only known you'd bought this lovely place."

On the way to town, Hawkman thought about the encounter with Maduk. He'd watched the windows while Williams talked with the Indian, and swore he saw the curtains move in the room at the far corner of the house. His gut told him the women were there. But no way would Maduk allow them inside without a search warrant.

Williams would have to go through the Yreka authorities, and Hawkman didn't know how well he knew the judge. Having no more evidence than fingerprints on food containers, he might have trouble getting one. If he couldn't get permission to search the premises tonight, they might as well forget it. Hawkman figured, the chances of finding Lilly and Maryann at the house were probably nil, as Maduk would have them out of there in a matter of hours.

CHAPTER FORTY-ONE

Maduk loaded the two women's luggage into the trunk, then had them climb aboard. He drove down the driveway to the fence line where he replaced the blasted padlock and rebolted the chain across the gate.

When he climbed back into the car, Maryann let out a sigh. "What good will that do? The police will only shoot it off again."

"I expect them to. It will warn me they're coming."

Maduk drove back to the house, and circled to the rear where he took what looked like a cow path across the field which led to an asphalt road. Lilly sat erect in the front passenger seat and stared straight ahead. "Where are we going?"

He patted her arm. "Someplace safe until I can decide what we're going to do." Then he turned his head slightly toward Maryann. "Do you have those pictures?"

"Yes."

Lilly twisted around and looked at Maryann. "What pictures?"

"The ones you took of yourself after Burke beat you. I found them in the closet when Sam and I cleaned out your room to paint."

She closed her eyes and rested her head against the seat. "What good will those do now?"

"Lilly, anything that shows what Burke did to you will help," Maduk said. "Maryann also told me about taking you to the hospital in Medford after one of his beatings. I want to get the record of that visit."

"I never told them my injuries were due to Burke's abuse. I claimed I'd fallen down some stairs."

"Maryann said the hospital staff didn't believe it and she saw them write the word 'suspicious' on the chart."

Lilly threw her hands in the air. "That could mean anything."

Maduk shook his head. "I don't think so."

Lilly's tears glistened with the colors of the dashboard lights as they rolled down her cheeks. "I hated that man with a passion. And when he told me he was going to move back into the house, and evict us, I couldn't believe it. I knew if I showed any resistance, he'd have killed me on the spot. Instead, he cruelly threw back his head and laughed. You should see your face, he said." Her chin quivered and a few soft sobs escaped her mouth.

Maduk reached over and took her hand. "Did anyone ever see you with bruises or injuries? It's important you tell me."

She took a deep breath. "Once I went to work with a black eye that I couldn't conceal very well with make-up. No one asked any questions. I think they knew about Burke. But before I started working, I'd stay in the house after one of his brutal beatings. However, there were times when I had to run errands or go to the grocery store. People would stare at me, probably knowing full well what had happened. If anyone asked, I made up some story, which, of course, they didn't believe. They weren't stupid." She raised her hands and let them drop to her lap. "I tried to hold my head high, but it was hard."

"But Mom, you still gave that horrible man food and liquor."

"I didn't really have much of a choice. Once he found out I could get partial liquor bottles from work, he threatened to make me sorry if I didn't get him some. Also on the weekends, he insisted I fix fried chicken so he could have a good home-cooked meal. He said it was the only meal I cooked that he liked, then he'd complain about it. Made me laugh. I couldn't please the man."

Maryann leaned forward and squeezed her mother's shoulder. "Mom, you're a great cook. He was just mean."

Lilly put her hand over her daughter's. "Thanks, dear, I appreciate that. But I figured if it kept him away from me, I'd take the time and effort."

"When did he pick up the food and liquor?" Maduk asked. "You worked late every night, especially on the weekends?"

"He'd come by around midnight. But I finally got to the point where I'd just leave it on the porch, because he always came to the house roaring drunk. I lived in fear of him hurting me again."

Maduk furrowed his brow. "You say you left it outside?"

"Yes."

"Did you always do that?"

"As often as I could. But there were times I didn't have everything together before he pounded on the door."

"So anyone could have come by and doctored that food."

Lilly gnawed her lip and stared out the passenger window. "Yes, I suppose."

Maduk turned onto a narrow dirt road and drove a couple of miles before heading up a rough driveway. A small home, smoke curling from the chimney huddled in a nest of trees. An old rattletrap pickup sat at the side.

Maryann sat forward. "Who lives here?"

"Someone very dear."

With suitcases in hand, Lilly and Maryann stood behind Maduk as he knocked loudly on the old oak door.

A toothless man with long gray hair peeked out. He squinted at the group standing before him, then broke into a big grin. "Madukarahat, my son. Come in, come in." The old gentleman stepped back and waved the three inside.

The house felt warm and smelled of food. Maduk sniffed the air. "Ah, you're cooking rabbit stew."

Grabbing the cane leaning against a chair, the old fellow hobbled over to the wood burning stove and raised the lid on the pot. "Aah, it's doing nicely, should be ready in about an hour." He took a long handled wooden spoon and stirred the ingredients.

"I can't stay, but my wife and daughter will enjoy the cooking of the master." Maduk turned to the two women. "This is my Father. Call him Happy, I don't think the man has ever had a sad day in his life except when mother died."

Maryann stared at the steaming kettle. "I've never had rabbit stew."

Maduk smiled. "It'll be a wonderful experience."

Lilly touched his arm. "Does he know we're going to spend the night and why?"

"Not yet. I will talk to him. But he'll be thrilled. He's quite a storyteller and will keep you entertained. Come and I'll show you where you'll be sleeping. The two of you will have to share a bed."

Lugging their bags, the two women followed him into a small but immaculately clean room filled with the aroma of roses. Lilly noticed the fresh cut bouquet on the top of a small chest in the corner of the room.

"What beautiful flowers."

"Before it gets too dark, take a peek out back at his garden. It's quite a wonder. Now, I'll go talk to my father, and then I must leave."

Maduk left the two women sitting on the edge of the bed. They could hear the male voices echoing through the thin walls, but couldn't make out the words. Maryann and Lilly glanced at each other questioningly, then grinned, realizing the men were talking in their native tongue.

"We'll never know how much Happy knows," Maryann said, as she stood and walked around the barren room. She pushed back the sheer curtain and looked out the only window. The sun had dipped in the horizon and early evening would soon be upon them. She sighed and sat back down. "What's going to happen to us?"

❧

Hawkman hung around the police station, waiting for Williams to return from negotiating with the judge. When the detective finally arrived, he entered the office wearing a sullen expression. "I take it the news isn't good."

Willams shook his head. "The judge says there isn't enough evidence to search Maduk's home."

"So what's your next move?"

The detective flopped down in his chair. "I'm sending a man out to keep a watch on the house."

"Would you like my opinion?"

"I'd appreciate it."

"I think it's a waste of man power. I'm sure the women were there, but once we left, he hustled them to another hiding place."

"What's his game?"

"Time. My guess is he'll get a good lawyer. Then the women will turn themselves in."

"How do you figure? This is a murder rap."

"Maduk knows you can't prove that either one of those women poisoned Burke Parker."

"Do you think he did it?"

"No. But he'll cover for either of them."

CHAPTER FORTY-TWO

Hawkman left the police station and drove back to the Parker place. Stopping in front, he let the engine idle as he surveyed the property. The old station wagon hadn't moved and the house stood in darkness. Nothing appeared disturbed since the police invaded the dwelling.

He slid his foot off the brake and slowly drove around to the alley. Sam seemed to think the vagabond had made his habitat somewhere behind the Parker's. He eased his vehicle onto the dirt and let the headlights play along the back fences. In the beam of light he soon spotted a mound of blankets piled in the corner where two yards came together at an odd angle. He shut down the motor, turned off the headlights, and removed a flashlight from the glove compartment. Getting out of the 4X4, he flipped open the flap of his shoulder holster so he could reach his gun quickly. One never knew what sort of a reaction you might arouse from a destitute person, especially if they'd been drinking or on drugs. He approached cautiously. "Anyone here?" he said, moving the light over the pile of blankets.

The lump moved, and a waving gnarled hand pushed above the covers. "Go away. I ain't botherin' nobody."

"I want to ask you some questions."

A head of dirty gray matted hair emerged from under the blanket, followed by a bearded face. Light blue eerie eyes studied Hawkman. "I seen you before. One don't forget a face with an eye patch. You talked to Harley at Larry's bar, didn't ya? You a cop?"

"No, I'm Tom Casey, a private investigator. And yes, I'm the one who talked to Harley."

"So whatcha investigatin'?"

"A murder case."

The old fellow's eyes narrowed as he slowly climbed out of his bedroll. "What's that have to do with me?"

"I'm trying to find someone who might help me out. By the way, what's your handle?"

"Frank."

"Well, Frank, we're actually looking for Lilly Parker and her daughter. Seems they've disappeared."

The old man furrowed his brow. "Who's 'we'?"

"Me and the police."

Frank's eyes grew wide. "Why do they want Lilly?"

Hawkman scratched his chin. "She's a suspect in the murder of Burke Parker."

The old fellow jumped up and grabbed a walking stick resting against the fence.

Hawkman stepped back, not sure what to expect.

Frank jabbed the cane into the ground. "My Lilly didn't do nothin'. That old man of hers deserved to die."

Hawkman frowned. "What do you mean, 'your Lilly'?"

"Just what I say. She's the only family I have. Makes sure I'm fed and warm." He rested the cane against his leg as he picked up the blanket from the ground and caressed it, then held it toward Hawkman. "See this?"

"Yeah. What about it?" Hawkman asked as he watched the man fold it neatly, then slip it into a plastic bag.

"Lilly gave this to me last winter when it got really cold. She told me to keep it dry and I'd stay toasty warm." He looked at Hawkman with a crooked grin, showing gaps of missing front teeth. "And you know what? She was right." Then he frowned, slapped on an old floppy leather hat and spit to the side. "Enough talk, I gotta find her."

"Did you by chance notice any unusual activity going on around the Parker house this afternoon?"

He slung the plastic bag over his shoulder and using the cane limped toward the street. "Ain't seen nothin' but a bunch of cops swarmin' around."

Hawkman hurried to catch up. "Frank, you said Lilly fed you. What did you mean?"

"Almost every night, but occasionally she didn't have nothin'. The woman barely had enough food for herself and that no good husband. But she always managed to give me somethin', even if no more than a slice of bread." He again spit, then continued. "She had a good heart, and I get mad every time I think of her old man hitting her."

Hawkman took hold of Frank's shoulder. "You saw him hurt her?"

He stopped, stiffened, and eyed the hand on his shoulder until Hawkman removed it. "Yeah, more than once. Parker was a mean devil. Glad he's dead."

Hawkman noticed the man's eyes had turned a light gray color, giving him a ghostly appearance. "When did you see him abuse her?"

Frank turned toward Hawkman and stared into his face. "You ask a lot of questions for not being a cop. Not sure why I'm answerin'. But you look like a mean sucker with that patch over your eye. You've been around, ain't ya? But how do I know you won't shoot or arrest me?"

Hawkman cocked his head. "Well, Frank, for one thing, I'm only mean when I have to be, and the other thing, I'm not a cop, so I can't arrest you. Oh, sure, I could make a citizen's arrest, but you haven't done anything that would warrant it. I look at it as two guys talkin'."

"I think I've said my say. Maybe I'll talk to you again, maybe not. Right now I have business to take care of."

"Thanks for your time, Frank."

The old man waved his cane, then moved down the side of the road. The echo of the wooden stick clanked with each step as it struck against the blacktop.

Thoughtfully, Hawkman made his way back to his vehicle. He pulled a toothpick from his shirt pocket as he drove through the alley. His gut told him Frank knew a lot more and probably held some key evidence. Williams needed to question this fellow.

Maduk stared at the television screen, but concentrated on outside sounds. He figured the cops should have returned by now, unless the judge didn't think the detective had enough proof to issue a search warrant.

He rose from the overstuffed chair and strolled to the window. Staring out into the darkness, he thought about his two women. Neither had confessed to poisoning Burke, but one of them might be guilty, a conclusion he had difficulty accepting. While looking for a mousetrap in that outdoor cupboard, he'd found the paraquat and suspected the worst. You rarely find that stuff in its original form any more. He knew he had to get rid of it before the police discovered the poison on the premises.

The family members are the first suspects and the police were usually right. Maduk suspected Maryann. He'd seen the change in his daughter. Her eyes were full of hatred and at times he felt she directed her scorn toward him. He doubted Lilly killed Burke after putting up with his abuse all these years. But he couldn't rule her out after hearing about Burke's threats to move in and take over the house. That could have pushed her over the edge. He felt like kicking himself for not telling her about buying this place.

Maduk let out a long sigh and turned from the window. If Maryann poisoned Burke Parker, he knew Lilly would protect her to the end. Even if she had to confess to the crime herself. He'd have to be very careful the way he proceeded. Then he noticed the shoe box on the table and remembered Maryann had brought the pictures. He meandered over and lifted the lid. He picked up several of the photos and placed them on the table. Even though he'd already been through them, his heart wrenched again when he saw the damage that evil man had done to his sweet Lilly. She at least healed well. These would definitely go to the lawyer. He dropped them back into the box and replaced the lid.

Glancing at his watch, it surprised him to see both hands on twelve. The detective obviously didn't get his search warrant. Maduk breathed a sigh of relief, flipped off the television and headed for the bedroom.

CHAPTER FORTY-THREE

Hawkman took his cell phone from his belt and punched in Detective Williams' number.

"Williams, here."

"Are you still on the road?"

"Yeah, thought I'd head home and try to catch a few winks. Not much more I can do tonight on this case. What's going on?"

"Just had an intriguing conversation with the vagabond I told you about."

"I'm listening."

"I think he knows something. He calls himself Frank, and I had him going for a while, but he's a stubborn old cuss, and turned me off before I got much information. But he's worth questioning."

"Think he saw something?"

"Possibly. He envisions Lilly as a saint because she gave him an old blanket and food."

"She fed him?"

"Often, so he says. And when I mentioned the police were looking for her, it really upset him. Then, when I mentioned Burke Parker's name, his whole demeanor changed. His eyes took on the most ghastly color I'd ever seen. I thought he was going to turn into a monster right before my eyes."

"You okay? Sounds like you need more sleep than me."

Hawkman laughed. "Yeah, it sort of spooked me when it happened. I thought I'd slipped into a fantasy world. Sam said it occurred when he and Richard talked to the old buzzard. I doubted his story, but not any more."

"So this fellow makes his home in the alley behind the Parker place?"

"That's where I found him today. But I'm sure since I talked to him, he'll figure the police will be next and he'll change locations."

"All depends. If these old boys find a nice, comfortable, safe spot, they'll migrate back to it in a day or two."

"No sense in trying to find him tonight. Get some rest. We'll see if we can locate Frank tomorrow. I'll meet you at the Parker's house early in the morning before he has time to move his belongings."

"Might as well check out what he has to say. Doubt we'll find Lilly or Maryann for several days if Maduk has taken them up into the hills."

"Are you posting a warrant for their arrest?"

"Not yet. I've gone ahead and sent one of my men to watch Madux's place. Even though you think it's a waste of time. At least if he goes to the women, we'll know it."

"Sounds like you've done about all you can for now. I'll talk to you in the morning." Hawkman hung up, clipped the phone to his belt and headed for Copco Lake.

When he reached home, Sam and Jennifer were out on the deck enjoying the balmy weather. The familiar squawk of Pretty Girl echoed through the open sliding door. Hawkman slid the screen back and poked out his head. "Are you two teasing my falcon?"

Jennifer laughed. "No, but I think she's telling us she'd like to go hunting. You better plan on taking her out soon. She's getting awfully restless."

Hawkman glanced at Sam. "You think you could take her over to Richard's tomorrow?"

He grinned. "Sure. Richard loves that bird. But do you think she can wait until he gets off work?"

Walking over to her cage, Hawkman checked her tray. "She has plenty of food for tonight, so don't feed her in the morning and she'll be ready for a good hunt by tomorrow afternoon. The timing will be perfect."

"Why can't you go with them?" Jennifer asked.

"Williams and I are going to question Frank."

She raised a brow. "Frank?"

"There's a homeless guy who lives behind the Parkers'."

Sam whirled his head around. "Really. You think the old guy had any thing to do with Burke's murder?"

"Not sure he had any major role, but he might have seen something."

"Can you believe the old guy? He acted and sounded like a nut case."

Hawkman shrugged. "Hard to say. I questioned him a little while this evening and he appeared pretty lucid."

Sam's eyes widened. "Tell us. What'd he say?"

Hawkman reviewed the highlights of his talk with the vagabond. "He referred to Mrs. Parker as 'his Lilly'.

Jennifer frowned. "That doesn't sound lucid. It appears he's embraced her as his own."

"I gathered more in a protective way than an emotional one. She'd done some nice things for him and he seemed appreciative."

"Sounds mighty odd to me," Jennifer said, as she went into the house.

꙰

The next morning, Madux arose early. Dark clouds covered the sky. Thankful he'd taken the week off from work, he quickly dressed and took his binoculars to the front window. About a quarter of a mile down the road, he spotted a suspicious parked car. Expecting this might happen, he'd left the Buick at the rear of the house. He'd again have to take the back route to his father's. Stepping out the kitchen door, he surveyed the area with his glasses and found it clear. Fortunately, neither the police nor Hawkman had discovered this remote path.

Not sure how much time he might have before the police converged on his place, he grabbed the box of pictures, locked up and left the premises. He drove slowly over the dirt road hoping to keep down any dust cloud that might draw attention to his departure. Once around a bend in the road where he could no longer see the house, he picked up speed.

When he reached his father's house, his stomach tightened. No smoke drifted from the chimney and Happy's old truck was gone. What had happened? Hurrying to the front door, he dashed inside. Rushing from room to room, he discovered Lilly's and Maryann's suitcases open with clothes dangling over the edges. In his father's room, he found an unmade bed, missing the decorative blanket his mother had made years ago. He ran back to the kitchen where a note placed on the table, held down by a cold cup of coffee read, 'Happy sick, taking him to hospital in Yreka, Love, Lilly'.

Maduk ran out of the house and jumped into the car. The tires squealed as he yanked the steering wheel into a U-turn and sped out of the yard. It didn't appear they'd been gone long, and the old truck wouldn't travel over forty miles per hour, or you'd have a problem. And he imagined as soon as they got onto the main highway leading into town, they'd get stopped. The truck hadn't been registered in years because they never used it on the main road.

Sweat beaded Maduk's forehead as he thought about the dangers involved. He could foresee some young rookie pulling the vehicle over to get his quota of tickets for the day and discovering Lilly and Maryann in the car along with a sick old man.

His heart beat faster when in the distance he spotted the old truck off to the side of the road. He could see his house now and pushed the accelerator, then came to a screeching stop alongside the vehicle. He jumped out of the car, rushed to the pickup's side and threw open the door. His pulse pounded as he found the cab empty except for a pair of old slippers resting on the passenger side floorboard.

He glanced toward his house, but knew in his heart someone had picked them up. Madux's mind raced as few people traveled this route, especially this time of the morning. His gaze shot up the road where he'd seen the surveillance cop. The car had disappeared.

CHAPTER FORTY-FOUR

Hawkman awoke to a dark dreary day. Gusty winds buffed against his vehicle as he drove into Yreka. Turning on his headlights, he flipped on the windshield wipers to the low setting as a fine mist covered the glass. A flash of light filled the sky, then the thunder rumbled. These storms played havoc with the forest and put many fire fighters on alert. A bolt of lightning could start a fire in the high mountains, which could develop into an inferno and devastate everything in its path as it roared through. No one in the area enjoyed these types of thunder storms, and they always kept a wary eye on the nearby hills.

He turned the corner toward the Parker place and as he approached the property he noticed a shadowy figure scurry from under the carport and disappear behind the house. Instead of stopping, Hawkman drove past the house, circled the block, then turned into the alley at the far end.

Coming to a halt near the mound of blankets still piled by the fence, he climbed out of his vehicle. He prepared himself for a confrontation and strolled cautiously toward the makeshift abode.

"Frank, wake up. It's time to talk again."

About that time Detective William's unmarked vehicle entered the alley and drew up next to Hawkman's 4X4. The mist had turned into a light rain as Williams walked up to the mound and pulled away the covers.

"Come on, Frank, I need to talk to you. I don't want to get soaked, so let's go down to the station."

The old fellow looked up at the men wide-eyed. "Why are you taking me in?"

"I'm not arresting you. I just want to get someplace dry," Williams said, pulling the collar up on his coat. "Hurry up. Let's go."

The old fellow climbed out of his bedding, tenderly folded his prize blanket, slipped it into the plastic bag, and slapped on his ratty hat. He grabbed his walking stick resting against the fence and limped toward the car, grumbling. "A fellow can't even get a decent night's rest anymore."

Hawkman followed the detective's car to the station. The three men made a dash for the door as the rain developed into a downpour. Once inside, Hawkman removed his hat, shook off the moisture, then placed it back on his head. He trailed behind the two men as they made their way to Williams' office. The detective had Frank take the chair in front of his desk. Hawkman grabbed an extra seat that rested against the wall and placed it in the middle of the room, so he could see both men's faces.

Frank placed the plastic bag on the floor and jostled his cane against the desk until it held firmly. Once settled into the chair, he thumbed toward Hawkman. "If this one eyed guy ain't a cop, what's he doing followin' you around?"

"He's helping me out," Williams stated, taking off his coat and flipping off the droplets of water before placing it over the back of his chair. He sat down, fished a recorder from the drawer and plunked it down on the desk. "Hope you don't mind if I record this conversation. Writing cramps my hand."

Frank squirmed in his seat and licked his lips as he stared at the small machine. "Not sure I like it one bit."

"Don't worry, nothing's going to be used against you. I just need information. Say your name first."

"Frank."

"You have a last name?"

"Smith."

"Okay, we'll go with that for now."

"How long have you been bedding down in that particular alley?"

Frank shrugged. "A long time. I don't give no one any trouble."

"I didn't say you did. I just ask, how long?"

"Close to a year."

"Did you make friends with the Parkers?"

Running his fingers over the edge of the desk, Frank glanced at Hawkman with narrowed eyes, then shifted his gaze to the detective. "Only with the missus. She's a generous and good woman."

"Did you know Burke Parker?"

Frank shook his head.

"The recorder doesn't work well on silence. It needs a voice to record."

"I never met the man."

"Did you know what he looked like?"

Frank stared at the detective, his eyes turning a strange color.

Williams cleared his throat and shot a look at Hawkman, then back at the vagabond. "You all right, Frank?"

The old man raked his hand over his long beard as he stared into space. "Yeah."

"Tell me about Burke Parker."

"He was a mean son-of-a-bitch. One night, I saw him hit Ms. Lilly several times. She kept whimpering and begging him to stop."

"Where were you when you saw this happening?"

"Checking the porch, where she usually left me something to eat."

"Did she do this every night?"

"Almost. She always left it on the far corner. I was never to bother the food on the steps. That was for her old man. And he'd get mighty mad if it wasn't there. Sometimes I'd hide in the carport and watch him drive up in his car. He'd stagger up the sidewalk and growl like a dog when he spotted the bag. Then, he'd snatch it up and usually he'd leave." His eyes narrowed. "But one night Lilly didn't get home until late and she didn't have anything out there for him."

"What happened?"

"Parker pounded on the front door until she opened it a few inches and held the food bag out the crack. He knocked it out of her hand, and screamed at her for not having it ready, then he tried to grab her. I could tell he scared Lilly and she tried to push the door shut." He shook his head and rubbed his mouth with his hand. "But she didn't have the strength and he forced it open. When he dashed inside, I could see him through the windows chasing her through the house. Finally, he caught her by the hair. She screamed." Frank sucked in a breath and clenched his fist.

"Go on," Williams coached.

"He hauled back his arm and slugged her as if he were fightin' a man. Everything got mighty quiet. It scared me. I thought he'd killed her. But it wasn't long before he ran out the front door, grabbed his bag of food off the porch, jumped in his car and drove away." He lifted his head and stared into space. "I hated that bastard."

"Why didn't you call the police?"

He abruptly guffawed. "How? I'm a street person. I don't carry no cell phone."

"What if he'd killed her?"

Frank held up his hand. "I ain't through yet. Even an old derelict like me knows better than to mess up any finger prints or evidence the police might need to get that son-of-a-bitch. So, I went around to the back door and found it unlocked. I opened it a few inches and called her name several times. I could hear her groaning, so I stepped inside. She lay on the floor in the living room, her face covered in blood." He sniffed and wiped the back of his hand across his nose. "I've been in many a fight in my life, but never hit a woman. I couldn't believe this man could do such a horrible thing."

"So, what'd you do?"

"I didn't want to move her, so I grabbed a towel off the kitchen cabinet and wet it, then washed her face with cold water. She finally opened her eyes, and glanced around scared to death, but didn't say a word. Too afraid to talk, I guess" He chuckled. "I'd be afeared too, if I woke up to a mangy old man hovering over me. But then she recognized me, grabbed my arm and cried like a baby." He shook his head. "Sliced through me like a knife. I asked if she wanted an ambulance or the police and she said no. So I helped her to the bathroom, then got some ice out of her freezer and made an ice pack with a plastic bag I found in the kitchen. She came out and slumped down at the kitchen table. Took the bag from me and held it to her face. That's the way I left her."

"When did all this happen?"

The old fellow scratched his beard and glanced toward the ceiling. "Hmm, must have been seven or eight months ago. Maybe longer, I really can't remember."

"Did Mr. Parker come back again?"

Frank frowned. "Every night. But she made sure his food and booze were out on the steps as soon as she got home, then she'd lock herself inside. But another night, he yelled and pounded on the wall until she opened the door. He pulled her outside on the porch, screaming she was a whore and he tried to slap her around a bit. I couldn't stand it any longer and banged him on the head with my cane from behind."

"What'd he do?"

Frank snickered and slapped a hand on the desk. "I'm a lot bigger man than Burke Parker and I look pretty mean. He almost fell off the porch trying to get away, but kept yelling, 'Wild man, wild man, somebody call the police'. He run to his car and disappeared down the street."

"Did Lilly say anything?"

"She thanked me, then said to wait a few minutes and she'd get me something to eat. I told her not to worry, just go take care of her wounds. But she insisted and within a few minutes brought out several pieces of fried chicken in a bag. Such a kind lady. Thinks more of others than herself."

"Frank, Lilly and her daughter have disappeared. Did you see anything unusual at the house yesterday?"

He looked at the detective with a puzzled expression, then

pointed at Hawkman. "He says she's a suspect. You're wrong. Lilly wouldn't hurt a fly."

"I'm asking if you saw anyone around the house yesterday?"

"Only the big Indian fellow. But he's a good man. Maybe he took Lilly and her daughter on a vacation."

"Did you see them leave together?"

Frank let out a groan. "Why do you want to find Lilly?."

Williams leaned back in his chair. "Unfortunately, Mr. Casey was right when he told you Lilly and her daughter are wanted for murder."

Frank jumped out of his chair shaking his head and pounding his fist on the desk. "No! No! Lilly didn't poison Burke Parker."

CHAPTER FORTY-FIVE

Frank grabbed his cane and wheeled it above his head. Hawkman leapt to his feet and grabbed him around the neck, knocking off the man's grimy hat. Williams, anticipating a hit, dropped to the floor, rolled out of reach, then came to his feet with his gun aimed at the vagabond's heart.

"Take it easy, Frank." Hawkman said, yanking away the stick. The smell of greasy hair and dirty clothes swirled around his nose. "There's no reason for you to act this way."

Trying to pull Hawkman's arm from around his neck, he wheezed. "He acts like my Lilly killed that horrible man."

Hawkman tightened his grip. "We're only trying to get at the truth. Are you willing to sit down and talk? Or do you want us to call in the officers and take you to a cell."

Frank waved his hands in the air. "No, I'll talk."

Hawkman felt the tension leaving Frank's body and released his hold, then pushed him down into the chair. "No more shenanigans."

The detective sat back down and replaced his gun in the shoulder holster. At that moment, the phone rang. "Yeah," Williams said in an agitated voice. He stiffened and glanced at Hawkman as he listened. "Have him stay with them. I'll get back to you later." He then turned his attention to Frank. "Who told you Burke Parker was poisoned?"

"You did?"

"No, I never said a word about how Parker died."

He pointed at Hawkman. "He must have said something."

Hawkman shook his head. "You want to tell us about it, Frank?"

The old man bowed his head and his lips quivered. "The last time I saw that horrible man hit Lilly, I vowed he wouldn't do it again. I'd nosed around the house a couple of times, sort of straightening things up for the missus. She shore didn't have time to do any work outside. I used to be a gardener years ago and noticed an old bottle of paraquat in the carport cabinet. I knew the stuff was deadly. One night when I noticed Lilly had left food for her husband on the step, I just doctored it up a bit with the poison. And gave his booze a squirt or two. Figured that'd fix him up good."

❧

Maduk raced inside the hospital and straight to the information desk. After he explained his father had been brought into emergency, the nurse on duty nodded.

"Oh, yes," she said. "He's being attended to at this moment." She pointed down the hall. "The people who brought him here are in the first waiting room."

Madux hurried to the door and stepped inside. Lilly glanced up, let go of Maryann's hand and dashed into his arms with tears in her eyes.

"Oh Madux, I fear your father has had a heart attack."

He enfolded her in his arms and hugged her close. "He's a tough old guy, he'll be fine." He then stepped over to the officer. "You can go, I'll handle the situation now. Thank you very much."

"Uh, I'm sorry sir, but my instructions are not to leave these two women."

Madux frowned. "Why?"

He shrugged. "I've just been told to not let them out of my sight."

"I don't understand. Have they done something wrong?"

"Those are my orders."

"It seems a bit unusual, but I guess you have to do what your superiors tell you." In a sense, this relieved Maduk's mind. Obviously, there wasn't a warrant out for their arrest, or the officer would have already taken them in. He took Lilly by the elbow and ushered her to the corner of the room with Maryann in tow.

"What happened with Father?"

Lilly wiped the tears from her eyes with a tissue. "Early this morning, he cried out in pain. Maryann and I rushed to his side. He held his chest and said he felt like it had a fire inside. His coloring turned ashen and he seemed to have trouble breathing. I knew we needed to get him to a doctor immediately."

Maryann sighed. "We didn't know what to do, so I ran out to that old truck, discovered the keys inside and switched it on. The engine turned over and I figured if the gas gauge was correct, we had enough fuel to get into town. But we didn't get far before it conked out on us near the new house. I didn't know what we were going to do, as we hadn't passed or seen a car on the road, and houses are miles apart."

"So how'd you get here?" Madux asked.

She glanced toward the officer. "I spotted an automobile parked up the road and not knowing if it was even occupied, I waved frantically. The car soon pulled out onto the road and came toward us. When a uniformed cop stepped out, it scared me. I didn't know what to expect."

"Do you think he knew who you were?"

Maryann clenched her hands together. "I'm not sure. He helped us get Happy out of the truck and into his vehicle. On the way, he called into headquarters and described the situation, then eyed us pretty suspiciously. Then he slammed a red light on top and turned on his siren, I didn't know where we might end up."

Maduk put his arms around both women and gave them a squeeze. "You did the right thing. We'll work it out."

The officer's phone beeped and he stepped into the hallway, but watched the trio through the glass window as he talked. Soon, he poked his head inside.

"I've been relieved of my orders. I hope the old fellow's okay. Detective Williams says he'll be here shortly."

Just as the officer strolled out of sight, the doctor entered the waiting room. "I'm looking for the relatives of Happy Madukarahat."

Maduk stepped forward with Lilly and Maryann stood behind. "He's my father."

The doctor smiled. "I hope I pronounced your name right."

"You did fine. Is he okay?"

"Yes. I know you feared he'd had a heart attack, but we've done several tests and his heart is strong. After a bit of questioning, I've come to the conclusion he ate too much rabbit stew and suffered a good case of gastroesophageal reflux, a form of indigestion. We'll keep an eye on him for a few hours, but I'm pretty sure you'll be able to take him home by evening. He's already responding well to medication."

Maduk smiled. "That's good news. Thank you, doctor."

"Check back about six tonight."

Lilly breathed a sigh of relief and tucked her hand into the curve of Madux's arm. "Thank goodness. He sure gave us a scare."

He patted her arm, clamped his jaw tight, and stared into space.

"What's the matter?" Lilly asked.

"I'm not sure what to do. Do we wait here for Detective Williams or do I get you and Maryann out of here?"

Lilly gazed up at the big man. "Madux, I don't want to run the rest of my life."

He looked into her face. "Tell me Lilly, did you kill Burke?"

She shook her head. "No." Then she glanced at her daughter. "But I'm not going to let them take her away. She has a full life ahead."

Maryann jerked her head around. "Mother, I didn't poison Burke. I thought you did. That's why I wanted to save every bit of evidence of what that horrible man had done to you. He deserved to die and I didn't blame you at all."

Madux frowned. "I don't understand. The lab test showed his food and drink had paraquat in it. You two were the only ones giving him food, plus both your fingerprints were on the food containers. I took the paraquat bottle I found in the carport, wiped it clean and buried it." He led the women to the chairs lining the wall. "Something has happened. The officer left and the detective wants to see us. Let's take the chance he has good news and wait here."

Within a few minutes, Detective Williams and Hawkman entered the waiting room.

"Is your father okay?" Williams asked.

"Yes, he's fine," Madux said, studying the detective's expression. "Why did you want to see us?"

Williams pulled a chair from the wall and sat down facing the trio. Hawkman did the same.

"As you know, the three of you were the prime suspects in the murder of Burke Parker."

Madux nodded.

"Hawkman convinced me to question a homeless man living in the alley behind your house."

Lilly gasped and stared at the detective. "Frank!"

"Yes. He'd seen Burke beat you several times and decided the man didn't deserve to live. Appears Frank took you on as family and vowed to protect you. He knew you left food on the porch for him and Burke. One night after he found the paraquat in your carport, he seasoned Burke's portion."

Maryann put her hands over her face. "Oh my God!"

Hawkman sat forward, leaning his elbows on his thighs. "I'd searched the carport and figured something had been taken out of the cabinet recently, but didn't know what until I accidentally found the square box with a bottle of paraquat buried in the field behind Madux's house. After the lab reported that Lilly and Maryann's prints were on the food and drink containers, we came to the conclusion the three of you had plotted to get rid of Parker. If it hadn't been for Sam telling me about the homeless man living in that alley, we'd have never questioned him and the three of you would be behind bars for murder."

Williams put out his hand. "Madukarahat, I admire you for protecting the ones you love, but from now don't fool with evidence. It could get you into serious trouble for obstruction of justice."

Lilly wiped the tears from her eyes. "I can't believe Frank would do such a thing. He was such a nice man."

Hawkman stood and slipped his thumbs into the front pockets of his jeans. "We caught him in a slip of the tongue, but I think he would have come forward once he saw that you were going to be put in jail for a murder he committed. He couldn't have stood the idea of you suffering anymore. You were good to him Lilly. Maybe the only one in town who seemed concerned. To him, you were family."

THE END